LETHBRIDGE-STEWART

THE LAUGHING GNOME
LUCY WILSON &
THE BLEDOE CADETS

TIM GAMBRELL

CANDY JAR BOOKS · CARDIFF
2019

Range Editor: Andy Frankham-Allen
Editor: Shaun Russell
Editorial: Keren Williams
Licensed by Hannah Haisman
Cover Art by Steve Beckett

Printed and bound in the UK by
CPI Anthony Rowe, Chippenham, Wiltshire

ISBN: 978-1-912535-44-6

Published by
Candy Jar Books
Mackintosh House
136 Newport Road, Cardiff, CF24 1DJ
www.candyjarbooks.co.uk

PREVIOUSLY...

SIR ALISTAIR LETHBRIDGE-STEWART IS NO LONGER IN
the black, and yet it is dark. He can see a blur of light,
almost as if his eyes are closed. And he hears voices, the
sound of people hugging.

'I was so worried when Fi rang.'

It is a voice he knows well. His wife, Doris. Dear
Doris, who he has known on and off since 1965. Over
thirty years before they married. Possibly the slowest
burning romance in history!

Alistair attempts to open his eyes, but he cannot. He
is home – in *the* home, in fact. Finally, after months of
travelling his own timeline, jumping from body to body,
he is home. 2011. Or is it 2012 now? Have months passed
on Earth too?

He dismisses his rambling thoughts, and focuses.

The important thing is, he's back home. Back in his
own ageing form. And he can't move.

Panic begins to set in.

'What happened to you?' Doris asks.

The voice that answers is also familiar to him. Dame
Anne Bishop. If she has returned too, then it follows that
her husband, Bill Bishop, must have returned as well.
Finally, all three of them are home!

Alistair tries to talk. But still he cannot move. Has his
body finally quit? Has he returned to find his body dead?
Being in the bodies of strangers was bad enough, but to

1

be trapped in his own body, unable to move, to interact with those around him...?

It would be a literal living hell.

'Shouldn't he be back too?' Bill's voice breaks in on Alistair's fears.

He hears people approaching. Feels a hand grab hold of his. It is his wife; even blind he can tell it's her hand in his. Small, soft skin... Delicate yet strong. Doris in a nutshell.

'Anne, what exactly has been going on?'

'We were cast through time,' Anne explains. 'By that thing.' Clearly referring to the calcified Gnome. 'It was just meant to be Alistair, not Bill and I, but we got caught in his wake. Wherever he went, we followed.'

'It never ends, does it, dear?' The new voice belongs to Fiona Campbell, his ex-wife.

Well, his two wives together! Would wonders never cease?

'No,' Doris agrees. 'And he would insist on throwing himself back into the fray when the UN offered him that job. But would we have him any other way?'

'Well, at least you knew what you were walking into, Doris.'

Alistair hears himself chuckle in his own head. Decades of resentment; hard to just brush away. But still, he has to admit he is pleasantly surprised at how civil the two women are being towards each other.

'The real question is,' Doris says, 'if you two were following him, and you're both back, then where's Alistair?'

I'm here! he tries to shout, but still no words form on his immobile lips.

What the blazes has gone wrong?

The light blurs, changes, and he finds himself... elsewhere.

A figure forms before him. Human, or at least

humanoid. It's features blur constantly, as if they are there, but Alistair's mind is unable to focus on them. He has seen this creature before. Eleven years ago.

The Accord.

On their previous encounter, the quantum life form had stolen various versions of Alistair in an attempt to fix the discontinuity of Earth's timeline. It had succeeded, more or less.

'What is the problem this time?' Alistair asks, glad his voice is working again. And, more importantly, that it is *his* voice, and not some stranger's.

'We have met twice before, but this time there is no threat to the quantum realm. This time I am... *doing a favour*, I believe the phrase is.'

'A favour? For who?'

'A name I cannot speak, but you know him.'

Like the last time they met, the Doctor's name was unable to be spoken aloud.

'And what favour is this?'

'He cannot cross his own timeline; his path was locked when he learned of your death.'

'My...?' Alistair would swallow if he were able. But he has no real form. This is just another astral projection of him. He knows his death is near; from the moment he agreed to go into the nursing home, he knew. And he has accepted it. But to hear it mentioned so casually... 'I keep a glass of brandy for him, just in case he turns up. If anybody can find a way, it'll be him.'

'I've been asked to present you with a parting gift. A chance to view your life from the outside, to see the decisions you made, those you didn't, to... gain perspective.'

Well, Alistair agrees that he certainly has gained that over the last few months. Saw things he didn't previously understand, relived moments he once regretted... Even managed to spend some time with his eldest son when he was a child. And had one final day with his own father, Gordon.

'I'll be sure to thank him when I see him,' Alistair says. 'But why can I not move? I was returned to my body, but...'

'You were only returned to 2011 so that your hitch-hikers could return. I did not intend to take them, too, but soon realised they were meant to travel with you. Their actions were a part of established Earth history.'

'You...? You are the Gnome?'

The Accord seems to nod. 'The Gnome is an interface, created by...'

Yes, Alistair thinks, *yes, who else would make such a macabre thing as a gift and think it appropriate?* 'So, you're saying he left it in the graveyard?'

'Correct.'

'And he couldn't simply have said hello?'

'As soon as he learned of your death, he became locked to your timeline. He could not...'

Alistair waves it away. 'Yes, laws of time and all that balderdash. You know, I'm pretty sure he makes all that up when it's convenient for him.'

The Accord seems to consider. 'There are no *laws*, but there are limitations to corporeal existence on the quantum plane. He is bound by such limitations.'

'Very well. So, this interface...?'

'It allows me to influence the corporeal plane, to tune into your delta waves. And thus, I was able to send your essence through time. One last gift to you.'

'I see. And now? What's next? Now, as you said, you've returned Anne and Bill home, you intend to cast me back into the past again, I take it?'

'A look into what's to come.'

'The future?'

'2018. To *secure your legacy.*'

Alistair thinks of his grandchildren, Obasi, Kadiatu,

4

Conall, Gordon... If anybody is to secure his legacy, it will be them.

'I am ready.'

The Accord vanishes in the blink of an eye, and Alistair finds himself tumbling, once again, into the black...

CHAPTER ONE
Who Can I Be Now?

AT FIRST SIR ALISTAIR WAS UNSURE WHERE HE WAS – who he was. But then he saw the woman waiting at the school gates. A face he hadn't seen in a very long time, and certainly not looking so young. It was his mother. Which meant...

He glanced down at the small body he was in. The duffel coat, the woollen mittens hanging from the sleeves by a piece of string... the short legs. His own body, as a child. How old? Judging by the school, he was back in Bledoe, so around eight... If the weather was any indicator then it was probably late April, maybe early May. Not 2018 like the Accord had said.

A thought occurred to him. If it was April or May 1937, then not only was he back in Bledoe, but his brother was alive. James. The brother that had once been stolen from his memory. That put a skip into his step; except it didn't, he couldn't. He tried again. Same result.

Something was wrong. Or different, anyway. Not only had the astral jump not taken him to the period he'd expected, but he had no influence or control over his younger body. Little Alistair continued towards the school gate, a smile plastered on his face. Sir Alistair could do nothing but observe. He was simply a passenger in the body of his childhood self.

The sensations he felt were real enough, though. Sheer joy swept through him as his mother gathered him in her arms and kissed his forehead.

'Mum!' Young Alistair grumbled, as he twisted out of her clutches.

Sir Alistair wanted to laugh at his child-self. One day he'd regret losing such closeness.

'Come on, you, let's get back home for tea.' They started off homewards along the narrow path.

Sir Alistair had returned to Bledoe several times as a man, but his memories of it during his childhood were vague, seen through the murky mists of time. It hadn't changed much from the way it had been when he'd last visited. Of course, through the eyes of a child, and a short child at that (he would experience a growth spurt during his late teens, fortunately), the village was huge.

The old roads in Bledoe had narrow footpaths – those that actually had footpaths. There was rarely much traffic and young Alistair was something of an expert at walking along the pavement's granite kerbstones.

It was strange to read the thoughts of his child-self. When he was astral projected into the body of Neil Martinez in 1993, he had learned to access the thoughts of his host, a trick he had used on every jump since, but the thoughts of his chid-self... That was a *very* different kettle of fish.

'What about James?' Young Alistair asked, his arms outstretched like a tightrope walker.

'He's old enough to walk home with his friends, you know that.'

'Wish I was. Will Dad be with us for the bank holiday?'

'Not this time, Ali, sorry.'

Ali. Sir Alistair chuckled inside at the name. He hadn't been called it in such a long time.

Ali effected a sudden pirouette turn to face his mum. 'Can we go to the seaside?'

'I'll think about it. Maybe on Monday.'

He swivelled back and continued along his perilous

perch. 'All right. Can we make cakes though?'

'You'll have to see farmer Dury tomorrow for some eggs.'

'Or his hens.'

'Don't be smart, young man,' she chided him, clipping his ear good-humouredly, causing him to lose his balance and step down into the gutter. 'Come on,' she continued, tugging him back onto the pavement. 'Let's just walk sensibly.'

'We had the police in today, from Liskeard. Customs and exercise –'

Excise, Sir Alistair corrected his young self automatically, before remembering he couldn't be heard.

'Special assembly. There was a sergeant and a constable. They didn't have guns like they do in America.'

'I'm glad to hear it!'

'They told us to keep our eyes open, especially during the bank holiday – for smugglers.'

'Is that for a school project, then?'

'No, they said there was a lot of "conter-band" goods coming in from the coast and we had to be their eyes and ears.' He looked up at his mother. 'What's "conter-band", Mum?'

Inside, Sir Alistair laughed at his child-self and was instantly reminded of Conall as a kid. He hadn't realised how much like him his grandson had been.

His mother stopped. 'Contraband, Ali. Illegal goods. This is all a bit serious for school. Are you sure it wasn't a play with actors?'

She didn't get an answer.

'I reckon it'll be a good assignment for the Bledoe Cadets, and then they'll have to let me join because it was my idea.'

Sir Alistair had heard many stories of barely remembered times when he'd done his utmost to become a member of his brother's gang. Despite the lad's best

8

effort, Ali would never succeed. Not until it was much too late.

The fulsome aroma of baking bread greeted Sir Alistair as Ali and his mother entered Redrose Cottage. Sir Alistair had rather hoped for a tour of his childhood home, but he was thwarted by his young self's over-excitement. Sat at the bottom of the stairs by the front door, still in his coat and shoes, little Ali was waiting for James to return from school. The resultant apprehension this brought to Sir Alistair was considerable. He was nervous enough at the prospect of seeing his brother. But just sitting there and waiting for him to burst through the door? That wasn't his style at all.

And burst in is exactly what James did. Little Ali stood up immediately to accost him and got the swinging front door in his face for his troubles.

'What you doing hiding back there, Ali-stare?' James yelled, unsympathetically, as Ali found himself grabbed by the arm and yanked back to his feet again.

Raymond Phillips was there too, peering over James' shoulder with a smirk on his face. Little Ali focused on his brother at last, allowing Sir Alistair to do so too. The late spring sunshine shone through the open doorway, granting Gordon James Lethbridge-Stewart a saintly golden halo, marred only by the somewhat pitiful grin on his face.

Sir Alistair took in all the detail of that face; the contours, the colours, the way the hair fell across his forehead in its after-school unkemptness. James' face. Blanked from his memory for so many years. Hazy at best, even after the Doctor had accidentally broken the Intelligence's spell in 1983. It was more than vaguely familiar to him – of course it was – because it was very similar to the face that had looked back at him from the mirror throughout his life. Brothers, indeed. And yet, as if the moment was briefly frozen in time, Sir Alistair could see mapped onto James' face the visage of General James Gore. The eyes, the turn of the mouth. What was playful and innocent in young James, would signify very different things in his adult alter-ego.

The moment seemed to last forever, and yet it was gone in the blink of an eye. With the front door closed, their mother appeared from the kitchen flinging a tea towel over her shoulder and, like the flick of a switch, the hallway was a maelstrom of noise and activity.

'I didn't mean to hurt him, Mum!' James said.

Raymond backed him up. 'He was stood right behind the door as we opened it.'

Little Ali was not in the least bit bothered about the bump to his head, though. He was tugging on James' arm and desperately trying to get his brother's attention, while their mother fussed about Ali's forehead looking for damage.

'Never mind. Ali, leave him alone, he couldn't help it. I'll rub some butter on it, that'll help bring out the bruise.'

'What bruise? Mum. No, James, listen to me, I need to tell you about the smugglers!' But no one was listening to Ali.

Sir Alistair wished for a voice right then. How he wanted to bellow an order. Instead the overlapping voices continued, and little Ali was dragged into the kitchen, himself dragging James along behind. An unexpected 'ow!' from a prod to his forehead showed that there was in fact a 'hurt', to which butter was applied with all skill and speed. While this was happening, James and Raymond disappeared.

Having escaped the clutches of their mother, Ali wanted to find James again. He checked the living room first. Nothing. Upstairs, then. Sir Alistair wryly observed that he was getting the tour he'd hoped for, but at a much greater speed than he'd have preferred. There were hushed voices coming from James' bedroom. Sir Alistair watched as his younger self raised a knuckle to the door, then decided to just barge in unannounced.

'James, Raymond, you've got to listen —'

'Go away,' James said, cutting him short with obvious irritation.

'But I've got a mission for the Bledoe Cadets!'

Sir Alistair shared the anxiety of his younger self. At a nod from James, the two older boys stood up, grabbed a few things and headed to the doorway. Ali remained there, trying to stand his ground. James gave a tiresome eye roll.

'Out of the way, Ali-stare.'

'But its smugglers. The police need help. I thought —'

James again halted little Ali in his tracks. 'Well you can't, so there.' He barged past, Raymond following closely behind.

'Can't what?' Ali challenged. 'You don't even know what I was gonna say!'

Sir Alistair felt his own bile rising on behalf of his younger self. Memories of such injustices were still affecting after all these years.

James' voice filtered up from the hallway beneath. 'We know what you were going to say, Ali, because you've said it so many times before. You come up with a plan for the Cadets to do something which somehow also involves you, because —'

Ali hared down the stairs after his brother, who halted him at the bottom with a prod to the chest.

'Because,' James continued, 'you still think you can join the Bledoe Cadets even though you've been told time and again that you're too young. Little boy.'

Sir Alistair gave an involuntary 'ouch'. That final dig was unnecessary.

'We've got it all in hand, anyway,' Raymond said.

11

'The police spoke to us too.' He pointed to his wristwatch. 'We should go.'

James nodded and opened the front door. 'We're just off out to meet with the lads, Mum.'

Their mother peered out from the kitchen. 'Don't you be late back for tea, mind. You too, Raymond Phillips. I don't want your poor mum coming around here again looking for you.'

Raymond's acquiescence was bulldozed by a cunning move from Ali.

'Can I go with them, Mum?'

Sir Alistair knew this was Ali's final chance. If their mother said so, James would have to take him along.

'No dear,' she said, checking her hair in the hallway mirror. 'We're going to pop some of that bread I've just baked over to Mrs Hardy. You can come along and play with Christopher.'

Christopher Hardy. One of his best friends from school and a name Sir Alistair hadn't heard in such a long time. As he felt himself awash with nostalgia, the front door slammed behind him and James' and Raymond's boisterous laughter disappeared into the distance.

James may have won that particular battle, but Alistair knew his younger self's resilience. This wouldn't be the end of it, he was sure.

In a small community like Bledoe word got around very quickly, and even those without children were soon discussing the smugglers as if the police had come and spoken to them all in person.

Tempers were certainly raised in the public bar at *The Rose & Crown* that evening, and landlord Jonathan Barns deftly monitored the ebb and flow of grumbles as they drifted through the smoky fug. He had concerns himself, of course – his boy, Henry, was there at the school and was wont to go shoving his nose into all sorts of things with his friends. Particularly if there was, what they termed, a *mystery* to investigate. Jonathan rearranged a couple of bottles under the counter as Sam Dury's throaty tones reached him from the fireside snug.

'Contraband? Where from, ahh? The coast? All the way up 'ere?' Sam settled himself deep into his usual chair with a dismissive 'yeeeeeeeaaaa'.

Jonathan couldn't help but smile at this as he pulled Willie Blackmore a tankard and himself a cheeky half bitter. Leaving a couple of coins on the bar, Willie hobbled over to the snug, half on and half off his crutches, and eased himself into his usual spot opposite Sam.

'If it's come Bledoe way, then they've already missed it, I'll tell 'em that fer nothin'.' Blackmore often delivered these pearls of wisdom as if they were the answer to everything. 'Leave well alone, I say.' He wagged a cautionary finger.

Jonathan considered the crate of cognac in the back, but said nothing.

Alf Gloyne, the blacksmith, finished encouraging the fire and stood upright, swaying slightly. He stretched, stiffly, before sniffing and wiping his sooty nose on his grubby sleeve.

'Growing concerns about foreign goods coming in, they told our boy up at his school.' The sheen of his blacksmith's grime glistened in the heat as the fire perked up. 'Very pacific, they were.' He sat with Sam and Willie, downed his drink and delivered a hearty burp. 'That one never touched the sides.'

'Do any of 'em?' Jonathan muttered with a wry smile. Then he called out to the blacksmith. ''Ere, Alf, when's your bath night due?'

Alf grinned. 'I'll take a dip come summer-time, maybe.'

'Along wi' my sheep, no doubt!' Old Sam said, to general laughter.

Jonathan opened a drawer in the sideboard by the door. 'You four gents want the crib board tonight?'

But the fourth member of the group, Ben Hoyle, was keen to continue discussing the police. 'Underhanded,' he said, scowling. 'Out of order.' And he stamped his fist, causing his own drink to slosh over the side of the glass. 'Trying to get at us through our kids, of all things.'

Alf nodded. 'Sounds like they'm wanting something better to do with their time up Liskeard, if y'ask me.'

Willie rolled his eyes and supped briefly at his tankard. He appeared to be about to respond to Alf when he stopped and looked at Jonathan. 'Hey, landlord?'

Jonathan ventured nearer, grinning. 'Is that you under that frothy moustache, Willie Blackmore?'

'Tis an' all. I ordered a pint o' bitter, not a pint o'head!' This was greeted with more general laughter.

'You heard about the police leaning on our kids, I s'pose?' Alf asked, handing his glass to Jonathan and nodding for a re-fill.

'My Henry said, yes. Near the coast I could understand, but way up here?' Jonathan wiped the table of the slight spillage with the cloth tucked under his belt, smiling slyly. 'Maybe they took a wrong turning out of Liskeard this morning, poor coppers.'

'Reckon more likely they suspect we're involved, somehow,' Ken Thompson said, leaning across from his seat at the next table. 'You know, village folk. They can look all they like, they'll find no smuggled goods at my shop.' Ken tapped the side of his nose and winked. 'A few unmarked tins maybe, but nothing foreign.'

'They'll find nothing smuggled here either,' Jonathan confirmed.

'No,' Willie grumbled. 'Nothing to be found here but froth!'

It was the next morning. Sir Alistair woke in his boyhood

bed for the first time in some sixty-six years. He had to laugh at the incongruity of it all, being a passenger in the body of his eight-year-old self. Little Ali had slept well. Sir Alistair wasn't sure if he'd slept, *per se*, but the night had passed and left him feeling refreshed, ready to face whatever the day might throw his way.

Saturday, May 1st, 1937. It held no particular significance as far as he could recall. But it was a whole day for him in Bledoe, and he had two clues to chase: the smugglers and the Bledoe Cadets. Common sense was telling him that by following up on these hints, he would find the reason behind the Accord sending him there and not straight to 2018. That was his intention, of course, but then he remembered that he wasn't actually in command of the body he occupied. He smiled to himself; he had nothing to worry about. The thoughts of his host shone like beacons as the boy dressed. They showed him that his and little Ali's plans were very much aligned.

Both Ali and James were breakfasting like they didn't expect to eat again that week. Bacon sandwiches, porridge, toast and marmalade. Mother was always eager for them to eat a hearty breakfast. But the rate they were going, Sir Alistair half expected one of them to explode. How he'd loved those old weekend breakfasts in Bledoe. They'd changed, of course, when the war came. Rationing – even out there in the country.

They ate quickly and in silence. When James finished and left the table, Ali was quickly at his heels.

'I know what you're planning,' he said, trailing his brother through the living room and out to the hallway by the front door.

James didn't even look at him. 'No, you don't.'

'I know where you're going, anyway. Your secret meeting place. Puckator Farm.'

James didn't rise to the provocation. He silently grabbed his coat before sitting at the bottom of the stairs to tie his boots. Sir Alistair could feel the desperation growing inside his younger self.

'Let me come with you. Please?' He elongated the final word and leaned in to James' face. James shifted his head to one side. Ali followed. 'Come on, James.'

This time James bit. 'No, Ali, clear off out of it would you?'

Ali ducked, easily avoiding James' half-hearted swipe as he got up. Ali trailed the older boy back towards the kitchen.

'But smugglers! It's exciting!'

'No way,' James said, suddenly stopping and facing Ali with a raised finger.

'But it's my idea!' Ali wailed, before James had time to speak. 'Not fair.'

'It's not your idea, actually. We already came up with a plan after school yesterday, when small boys were visiting friends with their mummies.' James grinned smugly, and Ali glared back at him crossly.

'But it's the bank holiday. Mum!' Ali yelled. 'Tell him.'

'You want to make that cake, then, Alistair?' called their mother from the kitchen. There was a lot of noise, like she was emptying one of the cupboards.

'No, I want to join the Bledoe Cadets!'

'What?' There were more clangs and clatters.

'He said yes, Mum!' James yelled.

'Hey!'

'Good boy,' their mother called back. 'Grab a sixpence off the mantelpiece and go see Farmer Dury then, get half a dozen eggs.'

Ali scowled as James smiled at him victoriously and pinched his cheek.

'Better run along.' James called into the kitchen, 'I'm off too, Mum! Back again for tea!'

Sir Alistair watched his elder brother run through the door, and it swung shut behind him. He could feel his child-self's frustration. No, more than that; rejection. He barely remembered his childhood these days; it was all so long ago for him, and he was surprised to see how horrible James was to him. He thought of Conall and Nicky as boys – were they so spiteful to each other? He didn't think so, but how could he tell? They always behaved when they were with him.

Ali stomped into the living room, and Sir Alistair had no choice but to go with him.

Even though it was late spring, the disused barn at Puckator Farm was a chilly meeting place. That morning the walls rattled in the breeze, while the Bledoe Cadets huddled around a small fire in one of the more solid sections. Henry Barns lit a fire in the rusting remains of an old oil drum, and the others joined him, squatting around it like a totem.

Due to its dilapidated state, the disused barn was both exposed *and* sheltered, allowing it to encompass all of the most extreme conditions Mother Nature could offer. From the Cadets' perspective, though, this meant that no one else was likely to use it, and they could always rely on it as a base of operations. They had secret signs, which only the regular members knew; it was a sort of communication system, using the odds and ends of farm junk that had been discarded at the barn. This way they could inform any stragglers about what was going on and where. For major operations or manoeuvres, coded notes would often be found posted inside one of the discarded barrels along the right-hand wall. Different barrels for different days of the week, naturally. Virtually everything that could be moved or adapted within that barn held some secret significance to them.

The ranks of the Cadets were swelled that day by the bank holiday. In addition to the regular core of James, Henry and Raymond, around the fire today squatted three additional boys: Tuck Shop, Smiffy and Nobby. At the height of summer, the Cadets would once again rise to a grand total of eight, what with Jason Starling and Edwin Stone joining them. But this bank holiday, those two lads were away visiting relatives.

Terry 'Tuck Shop' Thompson's pockets swelled with sweet things either given or stolen from his parents' shop. Smiffy was the nickname of Raymond Gloyne, the blacksmith's son (two Raymonds was too confusing). He was a little older than the others, and would soon be leaving school to be apprenticed by his father – although everyone knew he'd much rather be playing football instead.

The biggest surprise, though, was posh boy Graeme 'Nobby' Clarke. Nobby was away at boarding school usually. He deigned to mix with them from time to time when he was home, and although his plummy tones regularly riled Henry and Smiffy, James only ever objected to his institutionalised snobbery. James' father had fondly told him that Nobby looked like what some in the RAF called a 'boffin'. James liked this idea and it became his chief reason for tolerating Nobby – that and the expensive gadgets he would occasionally show off, courtesy of his wealthy father.

James looked at the huddled group of unlikely comrades. Not necessarily all friends; there were often tensions between Smiffy and Nobby, for a start. But that was just a question of man-management.

'So, are we going to help the police, or what?' James asked.

'It's what your little brother thinks we should do,' said Raymond, with a smirk.

'Yeah, well, never mind him.'

Henry Barns looked up. 'I thought it was all agreed? You seemed pretty set on it when you came over to mine yesterday.'

'Fine,' James said. 'Let's make a plan.'

Smiffy immediately held up his hands. 'Woah, hold on – it's Cup Final day. I'm not spending it trying to find smuggled goods in handbags and prams. I came out to play football with you lot, and grab a liquorice shoelace from Tuck Shop, 'ere.'

Smiffy prodded Tuck Shop in the ribs. The smaller boy groaned and produced a handful of assorted sweets for everyone.

'I can't imagine anyone agreeing to let *you* anywhere near their prams and handbags.' This was Nobby Clarke, a vision in tweed with a supercilious smirk on his spectacled face.

James checked to see where his attentions would be needed first: calming Smiffy down or reining Nobby in. Neither, as it turned out. Nobby looked surprised as Smiffy merely threw him a sweet.

'Just for you, Nobbo,' the blacksmith's son said with a grin. Nobby turned the large round sweet over in his fingertips. 'Gob stopper.'

There was much laughter, and even Nobby appeared to accept that he'd got his just desserts on that occasion.

'Come on then, boys,' James yelled and clapped his hands. 'What's it to be? Hunting smugglers or playing football? We've got all weekend, after all.'

Henry and Raymond both stood up simultaneously and stretched their legs.

'I think you've just answered your own question there, James,' Henry said. Raymond nodded in accord. 'And we can listen to the Cup Final on the wireless at mine if you want, too.'

Smiffy nodded his approval. They all knew his father didn't have a wireless.

'Fine,' James agreed. 'But this morning, then, how can we help about these smugglers? If the police are focusing on us here, then Bledoe must be a key point on the route

19

inland from the coast. Right? So, where are the best places to hide stuff around here?'

Nobby stood and stretched also. 'Draynes Wood?'

'Long way,' said Henry.

'Pengriffen Fougou?' Smiffy suggested in mock-sepulchral tones.

'I'm not looking up there!' Raymond burst out.

Henry shook his head. 'Too far again, surely?'

James looked at Henry and grinned. 'Who are you, Henry Barns, the distance police?'

Henry stood his ground and argued that if someone was lugging loot for miles across Bodmin Moor, there was a big risk of being spotted.

Tuck Shop sucked up the end of his liquorice lace. 'Also, how's it all getting in?'

'Nice one.' James snapped his fingers and pointed around the group. 'How indeed?'

'River or road, I reckon,' said Smiffy.

'Because there's *so many* other options,' Nobby muttered.

'Wanna smack?'

'Leave it, you two,' James warned. 'The river's tricky, cos it's upstream. Anyone seen any gypsies about lately? My mum reckons it's them.'

Raymond smiled. 'Your mum blames everything on gypsies.'

James knew this was true of most of their parents. 'I reckon we start with the roads in and out of Bledoe. This morning we'll try monitoring all traffic in and out of the village. Anything suspicious, we follow it and see where it ends up. Agreed?'

There were general nods and consents around the group.

'And I can photograph vehicles with my new Leica camera.'

'Thank you, Nobby,' James said, trying to distract the

posh boy from the eye rolls of the others. He was being helpful, after all – even if it was couched within a boast.

'I haven't got a bike, remember?' Smiffy pointed out. 'But I'll do my best.'

'We're the Bledoe Cadets, that's as much as any of us can do,' James said, and every one of them agreed. Except Nobby, of course.

CHAPTER TWO
Join the Gang

SIR ALISTAIR HAD SPENT A VERY PLEASANT MORNING with his mother. They'd made cakes, a pie and baked some rolls to take to church the following morning for Pastor Stone. He'd enjoyed it a lot more than his younger self had done. Poor little Ali had moaned and complained his way through much of it. When freedom finally came, after lunch ('Lunch? Where's he putting it all?' Sir Alistair had wondered) Ali set off on his bike to try to find out what the Bledoe Cadets were up to.

Ali took him on an inadvertent tour, until he found what he was looking for.

Smiffy was patrolling the junction to the old lane up to Higher Tremarcoombe and, as soon as he spotted the older boy, little Ali zoned in on him. But before he could pry into what Smiffy was up to, the blacksmith's son tried to flag down a fast approaching car. It was Nobby's father, Doctor Clarke, in his Riley Nine Merlin. Ali would know the car anywhere and Sir Alistair, with something of a *penchant* for classic cars, shared his younger self's adoration of the vehicle. Nobby's father clearly had no intention of stopping, though. Sir Alistair was certain the car even sped up as he tried, uselessly, to yell out a warning from within his younger self's body.

Smiffy was lithe and wiry. He easily dived out of the way. Doctor Clarke reacted as if he'd only seen the boy at the last minute. He swerved the car to avoid hitting

Smiffy, but the swerve took the car straight through a large muddy puddle left by the recent rain. Smiffy, soaked by the torrent, looked up at Ali as if he expected the boy to kick him while he was down. Ali dismounted and helped Smiffy to his feet while the car sped off into the distance.

'I'm all right,' Smiffy said. 'But that's the second time that's happened today. I'm not doing this anymore.'

He asked Ali for a ride home. It was a struggle, with the extra weight behind, but Ali was thrilled to be able to help in some way.

Sir Alistair was carried along with them and, in his passive way, he thought about Smiffy and the man he grew up to be. This virile youth was a far cry from the obsessive introvert he became in later life.

They pulled up outside the blacksmith's yard. Smiffy thanked Ali and dashed straight inside. There didn't appear to be anyone else home, and Sir Alistair recalled something about Smiffy's father spending a lot of time in *The Rose & Crown*. That was where Smiffy said he was heading himself once he changed his clothes.

Cup Final day, of course. Little Ali wasn't much into football. Sir Alistair was more of a rugger man himself. But the FA Cup Final was one of those special events that seemed to draw everyone in. Ali planned to wait for Smiffy to re-emerge, but James, Raymond and Henry could be heard heading his way, so he quickly slipped down a side street out of view.

One thing little Ali was sure of, though: if the Bledoe Cadets were going to listen to the Cup Final together, they'd go for a kick around after. And their favourite place for a kick around was over at Redgate Smithy, the stone circle close to Draynes Wood. He had the length of a football match to get up there first and pick his hiding place.

*

Jemima Fleming's legs powered against the pedals as she cycled along the lanes. Her parents didn't like her straying so far from home, but the girls had decided they'd go and spy on some boys that day. At first all they'd found had been little Alistair Lethbridge-Stewart at a distance, but they ignored him. Jemima had her sights set on Ali's brother, James. He was a couple of years older than her, but that didn't bother her at all. Jemima's best friends, Janet Hoyle and Nancy Pardew, rode alongside her. She was convinced that Nancy was soft on Raymond Phillips; she certainly giggled a lot if she sat near him in church. Janet would only ever pull faces and say that boys smell, but she still wanted to see what they were up to that afternoon.

The Bledoe Cadets had finally been spotted heading off towards the moors with a football. That meant they'd be going to the ancient stone circle; the girls knew that much. According to Jemima's dad, Redgate Smithy was 'a bit like that Stonehenge but nowhere near as impressive'.

Jemima eased to a halt by a five-bar gate, the other two girls skidding slightly in the churned-up mud. This was a tell-tale sign that cattle had recently passed this way. The muddy trail led further on up the lane.

Farmer Blackmore's milking herd, no doubt. Some of the nearby moorland was used for grazing.

The Cadets wouldn't be happy about being followed or spied on. Jemima, at least, tried to affect an air of nonchalance, so if they were challenged, she could say that the girls were just out for a bike ride and it was a free country.

As they approached the stone circle, they could see the boys playing football. Nancy started to giggle.

'Boys stink!' Janet yelled out.

The footballers paused briefly and hurled some comments back their way about 'little girls' and 'getting lost'. The girls rode past and parked up on the far side of the circle.

Ali watched the Bledoe Cadets from his vantage point behind one of the large standing stones on the far side of the circle. Sir Alistair, for his part, could feel the swelling pride of his younger self. It may have been getting late in the afternoon already, but Ali had guessed right about what the Cadets were going to do. The advantage was all his.

Ali found himself interested less in the football and more by the antics of Nobby Clarke, who was doing his own thing near the flat stone in the middle of the circle, the stone they all called 'the Altar'. As he watched Clarke scuttle about, he was distracted further by movement behind and above the eccentric public-school boy. Three girls on their bikes.

Ali had left his bike concealed under the wall back at the roadside entrance as he'd waited for Farmer Blackmore's cows to pass through. It could be a tough ride on a bicycle over the moors.

He was surprised when he made out who the girls were. *So*, he thought, *I'm not the only one out spying on the Bledoe Cadets today...*

Jemima looked at Janet and Nancy and indicated that they should head across to where the boys were playing football.

'Why bother? They'll just shout at us,' Janet grumbled.

'Please yourself.' Jemima headed off to stand by one of the goalposts.

She watched Tuck Shop sucking on his gobstopper, then recoiled from the stone goalpost as the hefty brown football smacked against it and rebounded back out into play, accompanied by a blast of 'ooooohhh' from the players and a slow round of applause from Tuck Shop.

The sarsen, thoroughly embedded in the moorland, didn't move at all under the onslaught.

Ali watched the girls park their bikes.

Good Lord! Sir Alistair thought. Only now did he recognise Jemima Fleming as the lead girl. Another wave of nostalgia washed over him.

Little Ali was not surprised to find Nancy Pardew and Janet Hoyle following in Jemima's wake. They were in the year above him at school and used that fact to look down on him at every occasion. He watched as Jemima left her friends and headed over towards the footballers. Nancy, he saw, pointed to Nobby by the altar stone. As the two girls headed over towards Nobby, Ali's curiosity was raised further, and he started to make his way nearer there too. They were up to something.

Jemima turned and looked back for her friends. It took her some time to locate them at first. Then she noticed that the posh boy, the one the Cadets called Nobby, was kneeling before Janet and Nancy, just next to the stone roughly in the middle of the circle. Intrigued, she decided to join them.

Nobby was talking, but he stopped briefly when Jemima's shadow fell over him. He looked up in response.

'Another one? What now?'

'You lost something?' Jemima asked.

'Slightly less vacuous than your friends here, I suppose.' Jemima wasn't sure what he meant, but it sounded like a compliment, so she smiled at him, and he continued, 'No. I'm collecting specimens.'

She squatted down next to him and pointed to the camera hanging around his neck. 'I like your camera.'

'And so you should, young lady. It's a Leica IIIa; probably the best compact camera money can buy.'

She was genuinely impressed, despite the pomposity,

and asked what he was photographing.

'My aim is to understand the flora and fauna of this area in the late spring period,' Nobby explained, clearly enjoying her attention.

Jemima knew how easily she could make a boy feel good; all it took was a smile and acting like they were the most important person in the world.

'I'm planning a seasonal comparison and review, with pressed live samples and accompanying photographs of them in their natural live habitat. I shall be presenting it all to the school's horticultural society before my father arranges with the Head for me to have a display in the school's entrance foyer next term. Would you like to help?'

Jemima shrugged.

'I'll take that as a yes. What about your chums?' Janet and Nancy both nodded and gave a little giggle. 'Pop this on the stone with the others and follow me. And try not to get in my light.'

He handed Jemima another small glass specimen jar, with a waxed lid, filled with cuttings of a shrub and a few – presumably slowly suffocating – insects. She passed it to Nancy, who added it to the 'display'.

Ali stood with his back to a standing stone. He was gradually making his way around the circle to a better vantage point. But he had to take it slowly, make sure he didn't get picked up in their peripheral vision.

Decent set of camouflage gear wouldn't go amiss, thought Sir Alistair. The football match and the others had slipped into the background now.

A clicking and ratchetting noise caught his ears. It was fresh and lively, like it was coming from just the other side of the stone. Little Ali froze. There it was again, then the clinking of glass. Ali remembered one of his parents' warnings about going up on the moors; how sound travelled in curious ways there, which caused people to get lost easily. He was certain there'd been no one anywhere near this stone when he'd dashed to it.

Sir Alistair was enjoying the thrill of his young self's nervousness. He tried to think encouraging thoughts, as if that might make a difference somehow.

Ali took a deep breath and peered slowly around the edge of the stone. No one. Nothing. Except Nobby and the girls in the middle. The noise came again, and this time Ali saw that Nobby was using a camera. Photographing the girls? No, the ground, the plants and Jemima's open palm, holding out something that made the other two girls squirm. Then it was placed in a jam jar, by the looks of things, and left on top of the altar stone.

He watched them for a while, waiting for his best opportunity to dash over to the next stone. There wasn't much of a gap to the next one. Ali thought briefly how he'd never noticed such a small gap between the stones before, then let it pass. Interesting words were filtering his way from the centre.

Jemima turned back to Nobby again, having dropped the caterpillar into its prison. She found him holding out his rucksack to her.

'You can help yourself to the sample jars, then I can get on more quickly,' he said.

She grabbed the rucksack and passed it straight to Janet, behind her. Jemima watched with thinly veiled amusement as Nobby *hmmed* and *aahed*, and myopically scanned the ground nearby for other interesting specimens.

Janet was staring into the rucksack. 'Here, does this mean we've joined the Bledoe Cadets?'

Nobby stared past Jemima, presumably checking to see if Janet was being serious or not. Jemima could see that she was.

'Yes,' he replied. 'See James afterwards for your

membership cards and a booklet of codewords for secret operations.'

'Eh?'

'And there's half a crown joining fee to pay.'

'Half a crown?' Nancy sounded appalled. 'I only get thruppence a week.'

Nobby shrugged and returned to his task. Jemima was fully aware that the boy was joking. Janet and Nancy were always a little slower on the uptake. She'd put them right later.

'*Lumbricus terrestris.*'

Jemima thought how much more pompous Nobby sounded when he was talking foreign.

'Looks like a worm,' she said.

'It is a worm. That's its Latin name.'

He clicked his fingers. Janet held open the bag, Jemima selected a jam jar and passed it to Nobby. He dropped the worm inside and passed it back along the production line to have it sealed and added to the collection on the stone.

'Ooh – quick, another jar.' Nobby held up another wriggling form between finger and thumb. 'Come on, Slow Worm.'

'Slow worm yourself. We don't have to help,' Jemima said as she produced another jar. She saw Nobby roll his eyes and decided that was enough. 'I thought this was gonna be interesting, but I'm not standing around while you just show off. Come on, girls,' she said to Janet and Nancy. 'Let's go do something else.'

'Hey, look at this!' Nobby called, suddenly.

'What? You found a snake, now?'

'Dried blood.'

The three girls peered closer. Just outside the shadow of the central stone, some of the larger plant leaves were spattered a rusty reddish-brown colour.

'Could it have been the Beast of Lanyon Moor?'

Nancy suggested.

Nobby blew a disparaging raspberry. 'That old tale. It's going to leave more than a little spray of blood over a few leaves when it eats Farmer Blackmore's cows, now, isn't it? Anyway, what would it be doing all the way down here?'

Jemima was bothered by the blood. 'Come on then, Professor, where do you think that blood came from?'

Nobby smiled. 'Legend has it that pagans used to make sacrifices in temples like this stone circle, to appease their gods.'

He doesn't know, she thought.

'And this stone here was the sacrificial altar. Perhaps it's still being done now, from time to time?'

A cloud passed overhead, momentarily putting the moors into shade. The wind suddenly picked up.

Janet came to stand by Jemima. 'You mean for killing people?'

A sudden cry made them all jump and look to one of the nearby stones.

Ali watched the others, intrigued by what they were up to. Sir Alistair found himself rather bemused by his child-self. Such curiosity would one day lead him to the Fifth Operational Corps, UNIT and beyond.

The girls looked like they were about to leave Nobby, and Ali was torn as to whether he should stay put or move on to the next stone as planned.

The tufts of tall grass around Ali's feet fluttered and flailed in the breeze as the clouds suddenly darkened the moors. Sir Alistair remembered his parents telling him how quickly the moors could turn from a bright, happy place to somewhere ominous and discomfiting. A warning all the children had heard. His parents weren't wrong; he'd seen it happen during many visits to Cornwall in the years since.

The girls appeared to have a change of heart. They'd re-joined Nobby in a huddle on the ground. This was Ali's chance. He dashed over to the next stone, but when he got there and grabbed it, it made him recoil. There was something wrong.

He reached out a tentative hand and touched the stone again. He'd been right. It felt different – not like stone at all. Warm, or at least not cold, and the surface gave slightly when pressed. He looked down to where it met the ground and discovered that it rested on a wooden plinth. Sir Alistair noticed the hatch on the side of the 'rock' before Ali did.

The boy knelt down. The next thing Ali knew, a hand had locked on to the scruff of his duffle coat and hauled him around to the inside of the circle. Only now did it occur to him that he'd instinctively yelped when he'd backed away from the strange stone.

He was now faced with an angry-looking Jemima Fleming, demanding he account for himself. She was slightly taller than he was, but he did his best to look at her eye-to-eye.

'What are you girls doing here?' Ali said, refusing to answer Jemima. 'You're not Bledoe Cadets.'

'Yes, we are,' Janet called out from where she and Nancy stood with Nobby. 'He said so, cos we helped.'

Ali watched Jemima roll her eyes and Sir Alistair chuckled inside at the children's need to belong to the Cadets. He supposed it was like wanting to serve in the most prestigious regiment of the British Armed Forces.

Ali roughly yanked his coat from Jemima's grip and turned to Nobby. *That's my boy*, Sir Alistair thought, feeling oddly proud of himself.

'There's something not right about this stone,' he told the older boy, deliberately ignoring Jemima. 'Feels soft and weird. Come and see.'

Nobby looked intrigued and dashed over. He reached

out a hand and touched the stone. As Ali had done, he withdrew his hand immediately, then reached out to it again.

'By Jove!' he whispered. 'This isn't a stone at all. It's a fake.'

Nancy called out from where the girls had left their bicycles. 'There's another one here that feels strange.'

The delight on Nobby's face was palpable. 'Two fake stones at least. Right, I've got a job for you lot. I think a comprehensive test is in order.'

'Oh,' Ali said with a groan. 'I'm no good at that.'

'Clearly you aren't,' Nobby said unkindly. 'I didn't say comprehen*sion*, I said comprehen*sive*.'

Sir Alistair frowned inside, and willed his child-self to knock that smug tone out of Nobby. He wondered how the rest of the Cadets suffered the boy. Maybe they didn't; maybe that's why he wasn't playing football with them. Sir Alistair barely recalled Nobby; he remembered the rest of the Cadets, but not Nobby. Sure, he'd heard the name mentioned, but...

'Two pairs,' Nobby continued. 'I'll stay here and keep track. I want you and you,' he pointed to Nancy and Janet, 'to go around the circle anticlockwise from here. Then you and you,' he indicated Ali and Jemima, 'can do the other half of the circle clockwise. That way you'll meet opposite, at six o'clock from here, and we'll know we won't have missed any of the stones.'

'What time is it now?' Nancy asked.

'Never mind,' Nobby said, exasperated. 'Doesn't matter. Just touch each stone in turn and call out if you find any more fakes.'

The fake stones were far more conspicuous when the children knew what they were looking for. The structures may have looked fine from far away, but closer scrutiny revealed that they were tatty, weather-worn and even going soft in places. Also, Ali realised a little too late that he could have saved everyone some time and effort. Earlier, he'd thought how short a distance it had been when running between two of the stones. Now, having found the three fakes, it was clear that they'd been positioned within the widest gaps between the existing stones.

Ali was just processing this information when a thump and a scream right next to him caused him to jump in alarm. He turned to find Jemima bent double, about to collapse on the ground. Smiffy's heavy leather football was bouncing away from the poor girl and the rest of the Bledoe Cadets were running over to them through their makeshift goalmouth.

James ran straight to Ali and accosted him, but he didn't get any further than a snarled *what are you doing here?* before it was obvious that Jemima was in need of help.

'Girls!' said James, as if he was cursing.

Henry ran straight to Jemima and was doing his best to offer her some assistance, but she gave him short shrift. Sir Alistair noted, with the fondness of old age, how Jemima's pained gaze immediately fell to James, but his brother either didn't notice or didn't care.

Smiffy retrieved his football and Ali expected to see him apologise to Jemima, but instead the blacksmith's son started to harangue Raymond, who was loitering sullenly nearby. It was Raymond who had fired off the powerful shot from close range. As if Ali needed any further proof of this, Nancy and Janet appeared and began to hassle Raymond, like a couple of fireworks going off in his face.

'What's the matter with you?'

'What did you do that for? Boot the ball straight at Jemima?'

'You did that deliberately, we saw you.'

33

'Yeah, we did. Bet you haven't even said sorry.'

'Why aren't you helping her? You afraid?'

'I was right, Nancy. Boys do smell.'

The lad relented and wandered over to join Henry in trying to assist Jemima, but she told him to shove off too, still trying to catch James' eye, Sir Alistair wryly observed. Jemima only gave that up when Janet and Nancy started fussing over her instead.

Sir Alistair recalled very well how heavy those old brown leather footballs could be. Doubtless Jemima would have some nasty bruised ribs as a result. He also realised how none of the boys, and particularly Raymond as the one responsible or James as the boy in charge, had said sorry to Jemima. The general view seemed to be that it was an accident (Sir Alistair agreed with this) but that it was also Jemima's fault for being somewhere she oughtn't have been for it to have happened at all, which meant no apology was necessary. He felt ashamed that, as a young boy, he was a part of this situation and by doing nothing to change it he was also condoning such treatment of not just a girl, but anyone.

Sir Alistair couldn't help but feel that this was one instance where rose-tinted spectacles had painted a different view in his memory of the period, such as it was.

'James!' Nobby yelled, capturing both Sir Alistair's and Ali's attention, as he slowly wandered over to the Lethbridge-Stewart boys. 'You might want to call the troop to order, we've made some discoveries.'

But James was clearly more concerned about the influx of interlopers. Ignoring the girls for the moment, James grabbed Ali's duffel coat hood and held him up like a freshly-caught fish.

'My brother's not allowed to join in, Nobby, you should know that. He's too young.'

You are only eleven, you little toe-rag, give your brother a... Sir Alistair let out a sigh. Was it any wonder his child-self was so put out when Jemima, only a year above him, was allowed to join the Cadets later in the year? Sir Alistair wished he could speak out, challenge James on behalf of his child-self.

'He wasn't joining in, James,' Nobby said. 'He was helping out.'

James released Ali, who then saw the look of derision on his brother's face as he stared at Nobby. Sir Alistair recognised that look. He'd seen the same on the adult version of James he had once known. He'd always assumed that had his brother lived and grown into a man, he'd be totally different from General James Gore. But it was clear that the seeds of that man were present in his brother now.

'And the girls?' James demanded. 'You know what Mr Fleming's like, he'll be around complaining to our parents.'

'He won't get to see mine. I'll tell the housekeeper not to let him in.'

'You are such a pompous twit sometimes, Clarke.'

'Yes. Yes, I bally well am. And proud of it too.' Nobby was not backing down. He had two school years on James, but Ali's brother was still able to confront him face-to-face, much to Sir Alistair's delight. He'd met his fair share of officers like Nobby in the Forces, and always enjoyed seeing them taken down a peg or two. 'These little non-members here helped us establish that three of these standing stones are fakes.'

James' expression changed immediately. 'Fakes?' he asked, all belligerence gone. 'How'd you mean?'

'Come on, little Ali. Come and show your oh-so-very big brother what we've found.'

As Ali joined them, Sir Alistair noticed James' clench his hand into a fist, clearly about to smack Nobby about his turned head. Was his brother really just a bully, or was this some front when around the Cadets? With the vague memories he had, Sir Alistair didn't remember him being so mean and angry all the time. *Those rose-tinted spectacles again*, he thought.

'Have you got your penknife on you, James?' Ali asked.

James produced the tool and handed it to him without a word, but then with such an expression on his face, words weren't needed. With the blade open, Ali started to dig away at the surface of the standing stone.

'Hey, my blade — !'

'Fine!' Nobby snapped. 'You do it then!'

He yanked the knife from Ali's hand and thrust it clumsily back at James.

'Strange,' James said, as he continued the work. 'Feels like the material they make egg boxes from.'

'*Papier maché.*'

Ali's eyebrow went up at Nobby's odd pronunciation, and inside Sir Alistair chuckled. Not a term the Bledoe Cadets were familiar with.

'There's something underneath. Chicken wire, I think, and a wooden frame.' James turned and stared at Ali, wide-eyed. 'It's totally hollow!'

Good to see you don't know everything, James, Sir Alistair thought, old resentments bubbling to the surface.

Ali nudged his brother. 'There's also that one.' He pointed to the stone he'd originally hidden behind. 'And another over there that Janet and Nancy found. You see where the gaps between the stones are much smaller elsewhere? The fakes have been slotted in between the existing stones.'

James looked at Ali, impressed. 'Flipping heck,' he muttered, before turning to the others. 'Oi, you lot, fall in over here.'

Raymond and Henry jogged over, while Smiffy planted the football among the bicycles and brought up the rear. Ali watched Janet and Nancy help Jemima over to them too. They all stood in a rough line. James stuttered as he saw the three girls. He cast a confused glance at Nobby.

'I'll explain later,' Nobby said.

'Yes,' James said, sharply. 'You will. Fall in!'

Nobby pushed his glasses further up his nose, sighed and obliged.

More insubordination, Sir Alistair observed.

James indicated that Ali should stand beside the fake stone. Sir Alistair smiled inside as a sense of pride filled his child-self. That was more like it; the sense of wanting his brother's acceptance was one Sir Alistair recalled. Much better than the reality of James the bully.

Before James could speak again, Henry piped up. 'What's he doing, your little brother? And what're these girls doing here? Are you letting them join?'

James glared at Henry, then asked Jemima if she was all right.

A flush painted Jemima's cheeks when James spoke to her directly, but nobody else seemed to notice. Sir Alistair, of course, recognised it for what it was. She had always fancied James. A pity it was destined to never go anywhere, but still, at least she would end up happily married to Henry with two children one day.

Jemima nodded.

'Right then,' James said, once he'd sorted his gang out. 'Now, look at this. Al found it.'

Ali hummed with pride as his brother singled him out.

'It's a stone,' Henry murmured. 'We're in a stone circle. What does he expect?'

'No, Henry,' said James. 'It's a fake!'

'Fake?'

'This and two more,' Ali said. 'We found three.'

Raymond nodded thoughtfully. 'Okay, then who would go to all that effort to build three fake stones in

Redgate Smithy?'

'What were we talking about this morning?' James reminded the Cadets.

Henry found his voice again. 'You reckon it's the smugglers?'

'But they're not very good fakes, when you look at them properly,' Nobby said.

'I dunno, they fooled all of us up here for long enough,' James said. 'You too, Clarke!'

Nobby looked away haughtily.

'They don't need to be perfect,' said Ali. 'Hardly anyone comes over here and who's going to tell what's real or not from a distance?'

'Good call, Al.'

Ali glowed inside, and Sir Alistair felt it. This was the James he distantly remembered.

'Unless they blow over,' said Jemima. 'They're not made of much, and it gets windy up here. Are they sunk into the ground like the proper stones are?'

'Didn't look like it,' James said. 'No.'

Nobby Clarke adjusted his glasses and began to toy with his camera once again. 'Presumably,' he mumbled, 'they're full of smuggled goods, to keep them upright.' Then he looked up at the rest of the group, with that challenging, haughty expression on his face. 'I'd imagine that's their purpose, wouldn't you?'

Sir Alistair was reminded of a plethora of conceited Ministry men who doubtless started off as boys like Nobby, but it was largely lost on little Ali who happily indicated the hatch on the other side of the stone, in response.

It took up the lower third of the structure. He tried to force his fingertips around the edge.

Sir Alistair wondered what was inside. He knew he should remember these events, but they were lost in the foggy part of his brain.

'Here, let me.' James crouched down beside his brother and wielded his penknife again.

Ali was quietly chuffed to note that all of the Cadets, plus the girls, had followed and were standing around in an eager huddle.

'Oi, let the dog see the rabbit,' James said curtly over his shoulder. The huddle backed off a bit.

After some manipulation, James found a catch and the door hinged downwards at the base.

'Bingo,' Raymond whispered.

The inside was filled with wooden crates. James tugged one free and used the corkscrew on his penknife to lever off the nailed down lid. Bottles. James pulled one out and Smiffy grabbed it from him, holding the label up to the light.

'What does it say, blacksmith?' Nobby asked.

Smiffy gave Nobby a sharp look. Once again Sir Alistair wished somebody would tear a strip off Nobby. Smiffy could barely read, and, as time would reveal, it wasn't his fault. Sir Alistair had seen first-hand how cruel people could be towards children and adults with dyslexia. His grandson, Nick, suffered with that condition, and Sir Alistair had done nothing but encourage him to find a way to live with it. People could be so cruel – children and adults alike. A tough lesson, one Smiffy would spend a lifetime learning.

Smiffy handed the bottle back to James. 'It's foreign, whatever it is,' he said.

'Brandy,' Henry said. 'Look, it says cog-nac. Dad has brandy in the pub that has cog-nac on the label.'

'French,' Nobby said. '*Cognac*, you ignoramus.'

A look passed between James, Henry and Smiffy. Smiffy stepped forward. Sir Alistair felt his child-self's fear. The boy didn't like confrontation. He hated to admit it, but his child-self was soft. Too much of a thinker. Which, Sir Alistair reflected, was wonderfully ironic given his ultimate career path.

'Sick of your voice,' Smiffy said. 'Heading for a smack, you are.'

Sir Alistair smiled inside. *Go on, son, teach him a lesson.*

But James reined Smiffy in.

Raymond, meanwhile, was eager to look further. There were two more crates to open. The first contained more cognac, the second was very heavy and contained damp soil. As Raymond tugged it free, the stone tipped over into the circle with a dull crump. Janet and Nancy gave a startled yelp and Jemima laughed.

'That answers that question, then,' said Nobby. 'The bottom crate is ballast for stability.'

Henry and Smiffy lifted the 'stone' upright again, while Raymond slid the soil-filled crate back into position. They checked for damage, but since it had only landed on grass it was fine. James addressed the group.

'What shall we do with this lot, then?'

'Take it to the police,' Raymond suggested.

'You want to lug this lot back home?' Henry asked, clearly not being of the same mind. 'Go ahead.'

James replaced the other two crates. 'We'll put them back and tell the police where they are. That's as much as we need do.'

'Let's check the other stones first, though, yeah?' Raymond asked, almost dancing with excitement.

The group moved around to the next fake stone, the one behind which Ali had originally hidden. Janet and Nancy stood around at the back of the group, trying to look involved but not really very interested, while Jemima joined the rest of the gang. James found the catch with his penknife and the hatch clicked open. Again, there were two wooden crates along with a heavy ballast crate at the bottom – which they left in the stone this time.

James cracked open these crates to reveal dried, cured meats in one and chocolate in the other. There were yells of delight from everyone and squeals from the girls; even the otherwise aloof Nobby was interested. They all reached in for handfuls of spoils, which for some of them – such as Smiffy – was better than Christmas.

Having gorged themselves on the unexpected bounty, they all lay back on the slightly damp grass and heaved very satisfied sighs. Ali basked in the warmth of being part of his brother's gang. At least for now.

'Hey, Tuck Shop,' Henry said. 'Bet you wish you hadn't filled up on sneaky pocket sweets earlier, eh?' There was no answer. 'Tuck Shop?'

James sat up, and Sir Alistair felt the mood of the gang instantly change. Come to think of it, he now realised that he hadn't seen Terry Thompson fall in with the others earlier.

'He's not here,' Ali said.

James called out for Terry, and soon the others were joining in.

'He's probably fallen asleep by the goal, after all that exertion,' Nobby said, dismissively.

'Hey!' Tuck Shop called, as if on cue.

Little Ali, the Cadets and the girls all looked up.

Tuck Shop could be seen running towards them from the goalmouth, waving his hands in the air. Behind Terry, pointing their way and starting to pick up the pace, were two men, one tall and thin, the other short and fat.

'Look out!' Tuck Shop yelled, wheezing and struggling for breath as he ran. 'The smugglers are here!'

CHAPTER THREE
Dancing With the Big Boys

SMUGGLERS? SURELY THIS IS THE KIND OF THING THAT would *get lodged in one's memory?* Sir Alistair, not for the first time in his life, raged against the effectiveness of the Great Intelligence's plan to remove James, and thus a large chunk of his childhood, from his mind. Over sixty years on and still the damage lingered. As he watched through the eyes of his younger self, he imagined it wouldn't have been any less disconcerting had he found an old cine film of his childhood in a dusty loft.

James shot to his feet. 'Smugglers? Quick, everyone! Split up! Hide!'

Ali didn't know whether to run or not. He hid behind the nearest stone, hoping James would tell him what to do. He realised this was one of the fakes and with mild panic he sprinted across to the next stone instead. As he did so he noticed Janet and Nancy on their bicycles, pedalling away as fast as they could. No sign of Jemima, though; she had to still be around the circle. He watched Janet and Nancy, wishing he'd ridden his bike all the way up there too. But then this was what he wanted, wasn't it? Adventure with James and the Bledoe Cadets.

Judging by their shouting, the smugglers didn't appear to be paying the retreating girls any heed.

Ali had to find James. That was his priority, apart from not getting caught. Sir Alistair was loving the thrill of the adventure and he desperately wished he could assist the boy somehow, but he remained a passenger in his younger self, passive and disconnected.

Jemima was with Raymond. Ali could see their feet behind the next stone along. It was one of the larger stones. This was good. It gave him some reassurance that he wasn't alone. He ventured to peer around the stone into the circle, to see what the smugglers had been shouting about. Ali saw both smugglers picking themselves up off the ground while Nobby and Tuck Shop made their way off on their bikes, heading the same way as the girls. It looked like Nobby had even found the time to gather his samples off the altar stone too.

Not so loyal as one would expect. Leaving their mates to fend for themselves! Sir Alistair continued to watch, indignant and impotent. Then, as an afterthought, he considered that they might raise the alarm. But were they the type?

'Collier!' the skinny smuggler barked, as he got up and wiped his hands on his trousers. 'Check the goods.'

'Hang on!' the short, fat one yelled back, resting against the altar. 'Lemme get my breath back first, eh, Snirtle?'

'Check the goods now. Or I'll set the dogs on you!'

The Alistairs watched as Collier heaved himself off the stone and staggered towards the nearest of the fake stones; the one that the boys had cut into. Collier had only taken three paces before he was stopped by a football, thudding into his large belly. He immediately doubled over with a cry and collapsed to the ground.

Ali heard chuckling, and Smiffy appeared, running behind him around the outside of the circle to retrieve his football. He tried to take the other smuggler down too, but this time the advantage of surprise was lost. Instead, Smiffy dribbled the ball into the circle before hoofing it at the smuggler called Snirtle from close range. Snirtle was agile, though, and arched his spindly body to avoid the oncoming missile.

Smiffy cursed and continued past his intended target in pursuit of the ball. Snirtle turned and hared after the boy.

James yelled after his friend, warning him that the man was on his tail. Ali was overjoyed; he now knew that his older brother was still thereabouts and watching the action also.

Smiffy was on fire. He'd taken a leaf out of Raymond's book and felled the tubby smuggler easily. But the gangly one was a tougher opponent. Smiffy chased down the ball and brought it under control, but before he knew what was happening, he found himself clattering untidily to the ground. Snirtle had slid in and tackled him from behind, taking the ball cleanly from Smiffy's feet. The boy was back on his feet again quickly, but not quickly enough and, as he watched, Snirtle punted the football away across the moorland towards the lanes. Smiffy watched it go. He was about to give chase again, but Snirtle was jumping, waving and gesturing towards the lanes; obviously signalling to someone.

James and the others needed to know there were going to be more smugglers joining the fray. Smiffy left his ball (he could look for it later) and ran back towards his friends. He saw that the fat smuggler – Collier, was it? – was trying to get back to his feet. Smiffy sprinted harder and ran up and over the back of the man on his way, forcing him back into the ground with a squeal, face-first. Smiffy gave a whoop of joy as he did so, then rounded the tall stone where James and Henry were hiding.

Ali had taken advantage of the distracted smugglers to join Raymond and Jemima. He could see James and Henry behind the next stone, and he was about to join his brother when James indicated that he should stay put. He felt Raymond's restraining hand on his shoulder, as if to emphasise the point. A short while later, Smiffy joined James and Henry, and Ali watched the three of them confer.

'There's more of them, gotta be,' Smiffy said, pointing the way he'd come. 'You see? Signalling down to the road.'

James looked worried. 'Somehow we have to alert the police.'

Ali looked up at Raymond. 'Maybe Nobby or Tuck Shop will report it?'

Raymond shook his head. 'You don't know them very well, do you? Nobby only thinks of himself. Tuck Shop's terrified of his own shadow. He'll be quivering under his bed by now with a bag of boiled sweets.'

Sir Alistair realised he'd been right first time about the boys who fled. How he wished he could tear a strip off the pair of them.

'What about your two friends?' Ali asked Jemima.

He noticed that Raymond gripped her more firmly. This was no surprise to Sir Alistair, who knew full well how much Jemima would want to be with James.

'Don't count on it,' the girl replied.

Henry caused Ali, Raymond and Jemima to suddenly look their way.

'We'll go, then.' He slapped Smiffy on the shoulder. 'The post office can put a call through.'

'Good. Be fast, and stay safe, okay?' James looked at everyone hiding behind the two stones. 'The rest of us'll try to keep the smugglers occupied here for as long as possible. '

Ali watched the intense concern and belief on James' face, as he entrusted his two friends with the mission. Sir Alistair admired his brother, knowing full well that his young-self did too.

They were about to make a dash for it when Henry paused. 'Hang on, we'll be heading straight towards the smugglers if there's more coming this way.'

James looked momentarily panicked. 'You'll have to circle around wide and low.'

Smiffy wasn't convinced. 'That's gonna take us ages, James. We should just try our luck.'

'And what if they're armed?'

Smiffy and Henry both blanched.

Sir Alistair had an idea, but he couldn't share it. *Come on, Ali, tell them*, he urged his child-self. Immediately Ali waved across to James, and signified going over a hump with his hand.

James' eyes sparkled. 'Yes! You don't have to go back to Bledoe, just somewhere with a telephone. Go over the humps and up to Higher Tremarcoombe. It can't be any further away.'

Well done, Sir Alistair thought, and was amused to feel his child-self's surprise at the idea. Evidently having no clue where it had come from. *Well, maybe I do have some influence after all*, Sir Alistair considered.

Henry tapped his coat pocket. 'They don't have a post office, and I don't have a ha'penny.'

'We're on our way,' Smiffy said, shoving Henry out of hiding and towards the bicycles, while reminding him he didn't need money to telephone the police; the operator would connect them for free.

This time both Smiffy and Henry trampled over the fat smuggler, who was once again trying to pick himself up off the muddy ground. The man looked up after the boys, his face caked in fresh mud, spat out a clod and swore loudly.

Ali watched as Henry rode off, his tyres occasionally spinning in the mud. Smiffy followed speedily on foot as they left through the side of the circle and headed up the slight slope to the prow. Then, at the top, he jumped on behind Henry and rode pillion as they headed off towards Higher Tremarcoombe.

The children diverted their attention back to the smugglers. Snirtle had returned to the circle. He ran over to his pudgy companion, hauling him up off the ground ungraciously and virtually hurling him over to the nearest fake stone.

'What is the matter with you? Letting yourself get beaten up by a couple of schoolkids.'

Sir Alistair watched on intently as Fatty delved into the hatch and reported to Skinny that the goods were safe and secure. The next fake stone was the one nearest to where Ali, Raymond and Jemima were currently hiding. They had to move.

Ali resented Raymond's hand in the small of his back, shoving him along to join James, but now was not the time to be squabbling.

'It's just us left, now,' James said.

Raymond looked very concerned. 'What are we gonna do?'

'We need to keep these fellows here, somehow, until the police come.'

'That could be hours!' Raymond was appalled.

'I know,' James said gruffly. 'We'll just have to do what we can.'

Sir Alistair watched Jemima's face, her eyes locked on James. How nobody noticed her virtual worship was beyond him. It was little wonder she'd never really got over his death.

'Look out!'

At James' alarm, Ali and the others looked up, but Collier was being lazy. He took the shortest route between the final two fake stones, which thankfully meant he bypassed their hiding place. He just wasn't very happy with what he found there.

'Snirtle, this lot's been eaten! Ruddy kids! I'll wring

their ruddy necks.'

'Catch us if you can!' James called, and grabbed Jemima's hand.

'There they are. Get 'em!' Snirtle yelled when he saw the two of them emerge.

Accompanied by Jemima's delighted squeals, James and Jemima dashed in and out of the stones, trying to entice the smugglers to chase them.

Sir Alistair welled up with admiration for his brother, before he realised that the feeling belonged to his child-self, not him.

Collier waddled off in pursuit.

Ali looked at Raymond. He had the urge to follow James and Jemima, to get both smugglers running around. But Raymond held up a hand in caution.

'Listen,' he said. 'Can you hear it, Al? There, in the distance?'

They felt it through the ground as much as heard it on the air. The rhythmic, heavy pounding of animal feet. Snarling and panting. Visions of hellish monsters filled Sir Alistair's mind, the fear of a young child.

The fear in Raymond's eyes mirrored Ali's.

'Dogs,' Raymond said, his voice dry and cracked. 'Now we really are in trouble.'

Normally Sir Alistair would disagree, but he was trapped in the body of a boy who was only eight years old. If the dogs attacked, there was nothing he could do.

'We have to get away,' Ali said.

'Yes, I know, but to where?'

And that, Sir Alistair realised, was a very good question.

Both boys turned to run and got in each other's way. Suddenly one of the dogs was there, snarling, poised to jump. Sir Alistair tried desperately to influence his younger self again, but everything went black.

*

James knew he was taking a huge risk. Going uphill on a bicycle, Henry and Smiffy had a heck of a trek to Higher Tremarcoombe, and that was before the police could even be contacted. Then the police had to get to them from Liskeard. The more he thought about it, the worse the idea seemed to him. Unless these smugglers were particularly dumb, there was no way he and Jemima could keep them occupied, chasing around the stone circle and playing hide and seek until the police showed up – if they even did!

James was impressed with Jemima. For a girl she was pretty bolshy. Didn't muck about or run away. Unlike some of the others. Damn Nobby and Tuck Shop for scarpering like that.

And what about Ali? Even his little brother, youngest of the bunch, hadn't run off. Instead, he'd stayed with them and hid behind the stones. He'd be safe enough with Raymond, unlike James if his mum found out. She'd kill him for letting Ali get caught up in all of this. Not like it was his fault. He hadn't told Ali to follow them!

James and Jemima continued to zig-zag in and out between each of the perimeter stones, in an obvious and predictable fashion, trying to elicit a response.

'Oh no!' Jemima said. 'James, look!'

James turned. He'd overlooked his and Raymond's bicycles, which had been left at the side of the circle. Collier wasn't running after them anymore; he'd picked up Raymond's bike instead and was coming after them on that.

Suddenly this seemed a lot less fair.

'We need to get to my bike,' James said, baring his teeth.

Jemima looked up at him, her eyes wide with... something. James wasn't sure what.

'I'll distract him,' she said. 'Help you get away.'

'I'm not running away.' James was horrified at the idea. As if he'd leave his brother and Raymond behind.

'I know. You're brave, James.'

'Yeah, I am. Okay,' he said, 'this is what we'll do.'

Raymond was swimming in the sea; Sunday school outing to St Ives, probably. Had to reach the surface, needed to breathe, but which way was it? No, he realised, he wasn't swimming, he was drowning! Raymond had never been great in the water. So, what was he doing there now? He reached out his hands, clawing at the water which was stopping him from breathing and —

Came-to, dragging deep, desperate breaths and wiping the cold water from his face. He sat up and found himself still within the stone circle on the moors, on the central stone. The tall, skinny smuggler stood before him, screwing the lid back on a canteen, presumably having just splashed Raymond in the face to bring him around.

His head was pounding, and his ears were ringing. Seemingly as an afterthought, the smuggler offered Raymond the canteen.

'Drink, boy?'

Raymond took it without speaking, swigging from it deeply as another figure – another of the smugglers – entered the circle with one of the dogs yapping and panting at his heels. A second dog came across to greet its chum from where it'd been sniffing at the base of one of the standing stones.

'Growler was haring off across the moors like a thing possessed,' the new figure said. 'Nae damage though, I managed to call him back.'

'I told you to be careful,' Snirtle spat. 'God knows it could have reached the village, or people wandering out on the moors.' He indicated the dogs. 'Having these things snarling around is bad enough, McLeish. You should keep 'em on a Mc-leash.'

50

'You're no funny, Longshanks. But...' McLeish paused to sniff. 'What's that smell?'

'My shoes,' Snirtle grumbled. 'Bloody lad here threw up all over 'em.'

McLeish gave a loose, phlegmy laugh which descended quickly into a hacking cough. Eventually he was able to speak again.

'Och, that's just typical, eh, Snirts?' He was strongly accented, with a distracting lisp.

Raymond focused in on the newcomer and saw that the man's teeth were as ragged and as poorly spread as the stones in the circle around them. Raymond recalled more through the fuzz of his headache.

The dogs had appeared and chased him and Al. The boys had panicked blindly. He'd turned and run smack into the standing stone they'd just been hiding behind, like a clumsy oaf, before quickly shinning up the side of it. Balanced on the top, he'd assumed he was beyond the reach of the dog's scrabbling paws and snapping jaws. But he'd not factored in Snirtle, who was as tall as the stone. Raymond realised just too late, as his ankle was grasped by the gurning smuggler and he found himself falling, out of control, onto the ground at the base of the stone.

Shouts brought Raymond back to the now. The new smuggler, the Scottish one, was jeering at something, but Snirtle appeared to be unhappy.

'Don't just stand there, McTeeth!' Snirtle yelled. 'Get and help 'im.'

'Ach, McLeish.' There was an audible weariness to the correction, suggesting this happened far too often to be pally banter. 'Tae hell wi' you, Longshanks.'

McLeish turned, scowling, and ran off to Raymond's left. A few minutes later he returned, dragging James by the wrist, who was complaining bitterly. The tubby one, Collier, puffed and wheezed behind on Raymond's bicycle.

James was deposited next to Raymond.

'You all right?' James asked, once McLeish and Snirtle turned on Collier.

Raymond shook his head gently; no point in pretending things weren't as bad as they were.

'Where's Jemima?'

'Got away. On my bike. I thought one of their dogs was after her, but that guy called it back. Hopefully she'll call the police when she reaches home.' James looked around, his eyes growing wide. 'More importantly... Where's Alistair?'

A pit opened in Raymond's stomach. He had no idea.

CHAPTER FOUR
What's Really Happening?

THE THREE SMUGGLERS STOOD BEFORE RAYMOND AND James. Raymond noted with concern the way Snirtle, in the centre, toyed suggestively with a flick-knife. Collier and McLeish flanking him. Collier was ruddy and muddy-faced, looking miserable and still panting, even now. Not a healthy man. McLeish would have been risible under different circumstances; he was solid-looking, but as he stood there with lank hair, a snaggle-toothed overbite and protruding eyes, Raymond couldn't help imagining him as a character out of one of his comics. No wonder they called him McTeeth. The Scot produced a packet of cigarettes from his jacket and lit up, before offering them to his compatriots. Collier took one without hesitation. Snirtle, on the other hand, was less than impressed.

'What the hell are you doing? That's merchandise!'

McLeish pointed his cigarette at Snirtle aggressively. 'Get tae—'

But in a flash Snirtle had his knife at McLeish's throat. 'Go on!' he spat.

They stayed like this for some moments, each waiting to see what the other would do. Snirtle could slit McLeish's throat with a flick of his wrist.

'Come on, lads, eh?' Collier forced a chuckle. 'Joke's a joke. Snirtle? Jock? No need to fall out over a smoke.'

Raymond glanced at James and indicated that they

should try to sneak away, but James shook his head. He meant so that they could look for Al, but he didn't want to say anything in case the lad was still free.

'That's not what he said when he was helping himself!' James called out, provocatively. 'I heard him. "I'm taking my cut now," he said.'

'What?' Snirtle said through gritted teeth.

'Lad's a wee radge!'

'And the fat one, he said he's looking forward to going back to prison, cos he doesn't have to exercise there.'

Despite everything, Raymond had to try hard not to smile.

Snirtle lowered his knife and stepped away, a nasty smile playing on his lips.

'I knew that already. And I see what you're trying to do, boy. Very clever. Set us against one another so you can run away. Fortunately, I've got brains, not like these two clowns.'

'What are you going to do with us, then?' James sounded angry now.

Snirtle slowly turned his flick knife over in his hand. 'Yeah,' he said. 'What *are* we gonna do with you two, eh? Friends all run off and left you here. I wonder what would persuade them to keep their mouths shut?'

'Let us go,' Raymond said, his mouth suddenly dry. 'We'll find them and tell them to keep quiet. We will too. We won't come here and play anymore.'

The three men laughed hard at this.

'He's got such a trusting face, too,' Collier said, his voice dripping with sarcasm.

'I think we can keep your friends quiet,' Snirtle said with a grin. 'We've a contact or two down in the village, happy to do a little something for a little reward.'

Raymond looked at James. Neither could believe there'd be anybody like that in Bledoe.

Snirtle continued. 'D'you know what used to happen

here, years and years ago?'

'No, we weren't around then,' James said, maintaining some defiance.

'Sacrifices,' Snirtle said. 'Human sacrifices to pagan gods. Just where you're sat now, in fact.'

Neither boy moved. If the smugglers had expected them to react, they were disappointed. They were the Bledoe Cadets. They didn't scare easily. Or least that's what they always told themselves.

Snirtle continued, unabashed. 'They say that some of those old pagans still worship here to this day.'

'Not ones that bother to count the stones, though, clearly,' James mumbled.

'I think a few sacrifices could be explained away as pagan freaks up to no good, keep old bluebottle looking in the wrong direction.'

Raymond felt the bottom drop out of his stomach again. 'You're not−?'

'Yeah, that's right,' Snirtle said, nodding and holding up his blade. 'I'm thinking we just slit your throats where you are.'

It was at times like this when Raymond realised how well he and James knew each other. Without a single word they both spun around on their bottoms and off the other side of the stone, sprinting away as quickly as they could.

Raymond heard Snirtle bark, 'After 'em!' Then there was a whistling, like the local farmers calling their sheepdogs. Raymond hoped to goodness he could keep his footing, but to outrun those slavering dogs? His heart sank a little.

But as they left the stone circle, something appeared in front of them, chugging out clouds of exhaust as it made its way over from the direction of Bledoe.

It was a tractor, driven by old Farmer Dury, with Smiffy and Henry clinging on to the sides. Police whistles could be heard from behind the vehicle and a number of policemen suddenly jumped down from a trailer. They blew their whistles again and brandished their truncheons.

Raymond very nearly sobbed with joy.

Henry knew they'd been very fortunate, all things considered. He and Smiffy had a breath-draining struggle up the steep moorland into Higher Tremarcoombe, essentially egging each other on when they might have given up. It could all have gone horribly wrong, but it didn't, and they reached the village in record time. An added bonus was that the village telephone box was just next to the public toilets, and they both needed a pee after their journey.

The police had said they were already aware of something going on down at Redgate Smithy, and that officers were already on their way. This confused Henry at first and he started to question the duty sergeant to make sure they weren't at cross purposes. Once reassured, the sergeant then instructed the boys to return home and leave it all in police hands. The boys guessed there was little else they could do after that, so they started the long ride home to Bledoe.

They'd not cycled far when they encountered old Mr Dury, chugging along the lanes in his tractor, pumping out clouds of dirty fumes which the boys tried, and failed, to avoid. Mr Dury stopped, having fortunately spotted the boys when they paused at the side of the road, coughing the diesel from their lungs. The old farmer called back to them, offering them a lift. It seemed sensible to be upwind of the tractor's exhaust, so Henry lay his bicycle in the tractor's empty trailer and joined Smiffy. Each clung on to either side of the cabin, thanking the farmer politely.

'I've told you lads before, no standing on ceremony;

none of this *Mr Dury* rubbish, call me Old Sam; everyone else does!'

They all had a soft spot for the farmer, who was full of wild tales. He also made the best sausage sandwiches this side of the Tamar, or so he claimed. He was on his way back to Bledoe after making a few deliveries thereabouts and was amazed to hear what the Cadets had been up to.

'You lot don't half get up to some larks,' he said, shaking his head. 'My Franklin and Jack were the same at your age, though. Bit old for all that malarkey now, of course.'

Smiffy impressed on him how much he'd like to get back and help the others, if not the police. With all the youthful exuberance he could muster, Old Sam yelled in the affirmative and stepped up his speed. Henry grinned at Smiffy, energised by the farmer's enthusiasm, and they bounced and trundled along, leaving ever-growing clouds of diesel fumes in their wake.

About half way back to Bledoe, the moors to the left of the road flattened out for a stretch, and Old Sam pulled over all of a sudden. The boys clung on for dear life as the tractor made its way over the shattered remains of a section of dry-stone wall damaged by an accident some months back. Henry silently apologised to the memory of the drunken driver who'd ploughed into the wall and died that night, and gave thanks that no one had yet rebuilt it, allowing them easier access out on to the moorland.

Smiffy, who always had a keen eye, pointed ahead. There were some dark figures making their way across the land, and a smaller figure on a bicycle. A girl.

And that was when they found the police and Jemima Fleming. The police had parked up by the van the smugglers had left in a passing point on the lane. They were making their way up by foot as quickly as they could, with a map and a compass. They'd intercepted Jemima riding James' bicycle back the other way.

Henry felt Jemima glare at him as she was hoisted up onto the trailer with James' bike.

'This thing makes a hell of a racket, Mr Dury,' said the policeman in charge. 'They'll know we're coming long before we get there, I reckon.'

'You leave it to me,' Old Sam replied, tapping the side of his nose. 'Wind is with us today, and the moors hide many a secret. I'll slow down when we get nearer; they won't hear us until we're almost upon 'em, you mark my words.'

The policeman nodded and motioned for the small squad to mount the trailer. They headed off again, with Henry feeling like he was riding a cavalry charge to rescue the others.

Jemima must have already told the police all she knew. Henry caught snatches from the policeman briefing the constables in the trailer. Three smugglers, two dogs, and three local boys remaining in danger.

Some fun Cup Final kick around this turned out to be, Henry thought.

As they approached the stone circle, Henry could see the group of figures within and James and Raymond running towards them, hell for leather. One of the smugglers was pursuing the boys, along with —

'The dogs!' Henry yelled back at the policemen in the trailer behind. 'They're chasing my friends!'

The policemen clamped their whistles to their mouths and stood up, clambering over the side as the tractor neared the circle and slowed to a halt. Henry and Smiffy jumped from the sides of the cab and prepared to help James and Raymond mount the trailer before the dogs got them. There was a sudden cry and the fat smuggler fell to the ground, while the tall skinny one raged and looked about.

Henry noticed Old Sam reach for something by the side of his seat and hand it to the policeman in charge. As James and Raymond reached the tractor, two shots rang out, each followed by a whimper, and both dogs tumbled to the ground. Before a sense of relief could hit any of them, raw emotion erupted from the third smuggler, whom Henry hadn't seen before.

He stared at the dogs as they lay still on the ground. Then he howled with despair and recklessly ran at the policemen.

It was an oddly compelling sight. Henry noted the figure's wild, protruding eyes and dreadful teeth. There was an obsessive ferocity about him as he ran at the policeman holding the gun, screaming something incomprehensible. The policeman quite calmly stood his ground. He upended the rifle at the last minute and smashed the stock into the smuggler's face, felling him immediately.

At a motion from the policeman, the four Bledoe Cadets swiftly mounted the tractor's trailer to safety.

Given a new vantage point, Henry could see that most of the police had spread out around the perimeter of the stone circle. As he watched, they started to close in on the other two smugglers. The fat one was slowly getting to his feet and had already raised his hands in surrender. The tall thin one looked poised and defiant, but Henry couldn't see how he had any chance of escape. He edged nearer to the central stone as the police closed in on him, brandishing their truncheons. He, in turn, pulled out a flick-knife.

The police held back slightly, allowing the smuggler to leap on to the stone and then launch himself feet-first at one of them. He took the policeman down, then Henry saw his plan. The smuggler was aiming for the remaining bicycle. It was Raymond's. But the police had anticipated this, and Henry could see two of them hiding behind the stones nearest the discarded bike. As the skinny smuggler reached his goal, they appeared and jumped him.

Desperation was clearly fuelling the smuggler, though. He threw his attackers off, then held them at bay with his knife, while he worked the bicycle into an upright position with his free hand. But two of the policemen had wisely moved outside the circle, and as the skinny figure mounted his escape vehicle they dashed forward. He turned and made a panicky jab at one with his blade, while the other's truncheon connected with his exposed wrist.

The crack and snap of the bone was audible from the tractor. It turned Raymond's stomach, even without the accompanying scream of pain.

A sharp blow to the back of Snirtle's head stemmed the swearing and abuse that followed, and the smuggler was carried limply over to the tractor to join his two comrades, who had both been cuffed.

Jemima huddled nearer to the boys – particularly James – to keep away from the smugglers, even though they were now completely harmless, with only wheezing Collier conscious. The policeman in charge leaned on the side of the trailer.

'They wouldn't have got very far if they'd run. Their van had two flat tyres. Anyway, you boys all right?'

James suddenly jumped to the ground. 'My brother! He's still out here, somewhere. I can't leave him!'

'Your brother, eh?'

Raymond quickly followed James. 'Yeah, we... lost him.'

'What's his name?'

'Alistair,' James said. 'Ali for short.'

The policeman nodded. 'Okay, lad.' He turned to two nearby constables. 'Spread out and see what you can find.'

'Worth checking the old smithy.'

The policeman frowned. James elaborated.

'Tumbledown cottage not too far away. He may have run there to hide from the dogs.'

'Thank you.'

'What about Golitha Falls?' Raymond suggested.

James' face drained of colour as he considered it. 'No, Ali isn't stupid enough to run that way. It's too dangerous. With his legs he'd easily fall in.'

The policeman gave James what he must have thought was a reassuring smile. 'Easy to get lost up here. We'll have a good look around. In the meantime, I think it best if you—'

'Do you want us to show you where the smuggled goods are, sir?' Raymond offered.

Henry, Smiffy and Jemima jumped down and joined them. If there was one thing the Bledoe Cadets were good at doing, it was making sure they stayed involved. Before the policeman had time to answer, the Cadets and Jemima were already heading off towards the artificial stones. Better than being carted off back to Bledoe.

Smiffy rapped his knuckles against the fake stone.

'Ridiculous!' the policeman said. 'Why didn't anyone notice?'

The boys shrugged. Jemima pushed her way in between the boys and shrugged also.

'To be honest, sir,' James said, 'people don't come here much, unless the weather's really nice, so who's going to spot the difference from afar?'

A couple of constables were summoned, and they quickly removed the smuggled goods.

'Is there a reward, sir?' Henry asked.

The policeman stopped one of the constables as he walked past. He opened the lid of the wooden chest. It happened to be the one containing all the empty chocolate wrappers. The policeman peered at the boys archly, then closed the lid and sent the constable on his way.

'Looks to me like you lot have had your reward already.'

They all looked away sheepishly.

'What about my brother?' asked James, sounding a bit more desperate now.

'Yes, he might have been attacked by one of those dogs,' Raymond said. Then he looked at James and saw that his friend had gone as white as a sheet. 'Sorry,' he added.

The policeman clamped a reassuring hand on James' and Raymond's shoulders. 'Now, now,' he said. 'Hark at you lot, eh? Let's try calling out for him first. He might be waiting on a reassuring voice.'

They all called Ali's name in various directions. After a couple of shouts, they paused, waiting to see if there was any reply. Yes, there was a muffled response, but they couldn't tell from which direction.

They looked at each other, confused. Then Raymond noticed one of the artificial stones was wobbling slightly; the one the police had yet to empty.

The four boys rushed across and released the catch on the hinged flap. Revealed inside were Ali's shins and feet; he was stuck!

James' relief was immense; he virtually hugged the fake stone.

The policeman used his truncheon to break through the *papier maché* covering higher up and Ali's smiling, tear-stained face appeared through the exposed chicken wire.

'Clever hiding place, eh?' he said.

Sir Alistair had not enjoyed that experience. After the dog had attacked and everything had gone dark for him, it took some time for Sir Alistair to realise the move his young-self had brilliantly made. But he was now doubly helpless, stuck, impotent, inside the mind of a child who was also now trapped inside the fake stone and equally unable to affect or influence what was going on outside!

A hellish time then commenced, during which both Alistairs could hear aspects of what was going on outside through the relatively flimsy structure. The sounds painted awful pictures in their minds, especially when the gunshots fired and later the dreadful agonised scream. While his young-self whimpered and wept, the old soldier tried his damnedest to calm him with reassuring thoughts. He wasn't sure if the message got through – he'd largely been ineffectual in that body thus far – but something had helped little Ali hold his nerve until they finally heard the Bledoe Cadets calling his name. And then, the relief!

Ali had held James for what felt like such a long time. And James had held him, too. Ali half heard a comment from Henry, to which James spat an angry response, and then there was nothing else. By now the police had cleared the smuggled goods away onto the tractor. Little Ali sat on the altar stone, gazing over at Bledoe.

The policeman returned. 'We're done. You young'uns want a lift back down to Bledoe?'

'No thank you, sir,' said Ali, immediately, and Sir Alistair instinctively knew that this was his influence.

He had a niggling feeling about Redgate. The odds of this lark with the smugglers not being connected to him being sent to 1937… It deserved further exploration.

Smiffy reappeared, having retrieved his football at last. James looked at the other boys and agreed with Ali. They'd make their way home later. There was still some daylight to enjoy.

'How about you, miss?'

Jemima. Ali had forgotten about her. She shook her head.

'You're not one of us!' said Henry, pointing an

accusatory finger Jemima's way.

'It's a free country, isn't it?' she yelled back.

Ali watched the policeman smile and head back to the tractor for his lift.

Smiffy called after him. 'Here, mister, you not taking the fake stones with you?'

The policeman paused and turned to them. 'No, you can keep them for hide and seek. And by the way, we'll be around to speak to you all tomorrow. Witness statements, all right? Make sure you're home in the afternoon.'

They all sat on the altar stone and watched as the tractor turned and pulled away with its police load.

'Well,' said James quietly. 'That was a mad Cup Final afternoon.'

'I dunno,' said Smiffy. 'I won!'

Ali smiled.

'Is it always like this, with you boys?' Jemima asked.

Raymond nodded. 'Sometimes.'

'Thanks for your help today, Jemima.' This was James.

Jemima was visibly flustered. She managed to squeeze out a 'thank you' before bowing her head to hide her obvious embarrassment.

'You too, Alistair. Good team effort. You're still too young to join, though.'

Sir Alistair sighed. Always with the little age digs.

Henry spoke up. 'You know, I've just thought. My bike's still on Farmer Dury's trailer.'

There were smiles, and James nodded.

'Yeah,' he said. 'Mine too.'

Although the sky was clear, and the late afternoon sunlight was still strong, Sir Alistair had a sudden sensation that the light had got brighter. Ali turned and pointed.

'James, look!'

Sir Alistair saw them too. Two new figures now stood within Redgate Smithy, apparently examining the fake stones. James glanced at the others.

'Steady, let's not surprise them.'

'They weren't there just now,' said Henry.

The Bledoe Cadets, Ali and Jemima included, slipped off the altar stone and steadily approached the new arrivals. As they got nearer, they could hear part of the conversation and paused.

'Look at this,' said the boy. A lad who looked like he was in his teens, and completely hairless. There was something familiar about him, Sir Alistair realised, as if maybe he'd seen a picture of the boy before.

He forced his child-self to advance further towards the two young people, leaving the others behind. Their mode of dress was not typical of 1937. Indeed, it looked much like the young people of his time; the kind of clothing he'd expect to see his younger grandchildren wear.

'Easier to leave them up here and let them rot, I guess,' said the girl. She looked familiar, too, with her light brown skin and big hair. As for her voice... It was older, but he was sure he'd heard it before. 'It's not National Trust or anything.' She squatted down to check the fake stone. 'Ewww. Yep, no goods here, just the ballast.'

'No brandy or chocolates for us then,' the boy said.

'Too late, mate,' James said, coming up behind Ali and placing a hand on his shoulder. 'Coppers cleared all that out.'

The boy turned to look at them, and a look of surprised recognition shot across his face. For a moment, Sir Alistair had the strangest sensation that he was standing in two places at once. He was there, looking through the eyes of his child-self, and he was also *there*, in the body of that bald kid looking at himself as a young

65

boy.

His mind flashed back to 1983 and 1977. *Blinovitch Limitation Effect.* Ali's hand moved out as if to touch the bald boy. *No,* Sir Alistair thought, *not again.*

The girl stood, and the moment passed. Now Sir Alistair knew why the girl seemed familiar. He'd seen her before, exactly as she looked now. For many years he'd had a photograph of her on his mantlepiece; indeed, even now it sat on the mantlepiece in his room at the nursing home. The girl, the bald boy, and his child-self standing there with James.

It was only in recent years that Sir Alistair had realised who the girl in the picture was. The picture had been given to him years ago, by Ray, but as with so many events in Bledoe, he had just assumed it was another memory he'd never recall. But then, as she grew, it became clear that the photograph was the start of a mystery, and now, finally, in 1937, he was going to solve it.

The girl looking at him and the Bledoe Cadets was his granddaughter, Lucy Wilson.

Sir Alistair wanted to say something, but even if he could manage to get the words out of his child-self's mouth, he felt the all-too-familiar pull.

And off he went, once again, into the black...

CHAPTER FIVE
Strangers When We Meet

SIR ALISTAIR CAME-TO, TO FIND THE BALD TEENAGE BOY
from Redgate Smithy looking at him closely. He jerked
his head backwards and the bald boy did the same.

It took him a moment to realise what was happening.

He was looking in a mirror.

He *was* the bald boy.

He stared more closely. No eyebrows, not even a hint
of the bumfluff that plagued teenage boys. He looked
down at his arms. No hair there, either. He really did
have no visible hair at all. Alopecia, he assumed. And,
he realised, flexing the boy's hand, he was once more in
a body where he had control. Was this 2018 at last? It
seemed reasonable. Well, as reasonable as anything else
in his life. And if he was in the body of the teenage friend
of Lucy... Then, it followed he would soon be seeing
Lucy.

He thought of his six-year-old granddaughter... now
a teenager herself. Or almost at least, if he got his sums
right. He couldn't help but smile at the thought.

'Come on, Hobo,' said a well-spoken Welsh voice
from the open front door.

Not Bledoe, then.

He looked around. He was in a hallway and there was
a hefty camping rucksack at his feet.

'I'll be right there, dear,' Alistair said automatically,
and loaded the rucksack onto his back.

The woman laughed as he left the house. 'What are you talking like that for? That's not how they speak in Cornwall, you know, if you're trying to sound like a local.'

He nodded and smiled, then stood to one side as she closed and locked the front door. So, he was still in Cornwall, then. With a woman from... Bridgend, that was the accent. Or was it Porthcawl? He made a few quick assumptions and figured she was likely his mother. Or Hobo's mother, rather.

Hobo. The name just popped into his head. Funny kind of name. A nickname? Or a codename...? Alistair smiled at the memory, and touched his new face, feeling the young muscles work themselves beneath his hand.

Alistair followed Hobo's mother. There was a vibration in his trouser pocket. Mobile phone, no doubt. They all had them in his present, so it followed they would have them seven years in the future. His mind was starting to wander. He had to concentrate hard on his surroundings to find his focus again. What was that ahead? The sea!

The white-tipped grey mass contrasted starkly against the clear blue of the sky until they both joined at the hazy horizon. As his confusion subsided, the lapping waves were all he could hear, and the fulsome aroma of dried seaweed filled his nostrils. He was reminded of childhood day trips to Polperro or St Austell. He'd never done very well at holidays and breaks as an adult. Something always seemed to get in the way – work, mainly. His brief reverie was broken by the car park sign at the end of the road:

Short stay

Arhosiad byr

Ahh, Alistair thought. He seemed to recall there was some pressure to have bi-lingual signage in Cornwall. But the next sign made him think again.

Bridgend

Oh! Wales.

He chuckled and gave himself a pat on the back for recognising Hobo's mother's accent. She was taking a call on her mobile phone, giving Alistair the freedom to gather more information as they walked.

Near the seafront he saw another sign, referencing Ogmore-by-Sea, or *Aberogwr*. Not a place he'd heard of, but evidently near Bridgend and Porthcawl, two places he did know.

So, Hobo was from Ogmore-by-Sea and was, presumably, going to visit Cornwall. That made sense, after all that was where Alistair had seen him a short while ago. Only the Cornwall of 1937, not 2018. Clearly the two time periods were connected, and something, or someone was going to take Hobo, and Lucy, back in time.

Well, he had little option but to allow events to play themselves out naturally, but it was a very odd feeling already knowing where you were going to end up. Not for the first time, Alistair's thoughts flew to the Doctor. He could only marvel at how well the old chap managed to maintain a clear line of sight with so much adjacent knowledge to muddy the waters.

Hobo's mother stopped near the sea wall. She was imparting some very specific information rather animatedly to her caller. Alistair got the feeling it was something to do with her job, possibly the police; he recognised some of the technical language she threw in from time to time. He doubted she should have been having the conversation in the open like that, but in fairness they'd seen no one else around, aside from a couple of passing cars.

The prospect of other people gave Alistair the sudden fear that he'd be expected to mimic the accent. He never was particularly good at accents, although he could manage a decent Spanish and French when pushed, but Welsh... Well, he always sounded more Swedish.

He only noticed that Hobo's mother had finished her call when he felt her hand on the back of his head, guiding him forward once again.

'Come on then, dreamer. Said I'd have you around there for ten o'clock, didn't I? Get a shift on.'

Alistair decided this was a good chance to give the accent a go.

'Sorry, Mam,' he said, remembering the standard Welsh terminology for mother. 'You was chopsing on the phone.'

Hobo's mother glared at him, and he realised too late that instead of just using the accent he'd actually put on a voice. And possibly been a little bit rude.

She wagged her finger at him, sternly. 'Don't you take the mick out of me, George Kostinen. I've put people away for the night for less than that.'

'Sorry,' he muttered, in his normal voice, and sauntered off like a stereotypical disheartened teen.

George Kostinen. Well, a better name than Hobo, that much is certain.

They continued in silence further around the bay and a little higher up inland.

Hobo's mother tapped his shoulder. 'Where do you think you're headed?' she asked, breaking the silence.

'Erm...' He looked around. Houses, small driveways. Cars.

She placed her hands on his upper arms and looked him in the eye. 'Are you all right? You've seemed very out of it since we left the house.'

'I'm okay, Mam, honest.' There. Bang. He'd nailed the accent that time without even thinking about it.

'Come on then, go and knock on the door.'

He walked up the path of the house outside which they'd stopped. Alistair raised his hand to press the doorbell, feeling an odd sense of trepidation, certain he knew whose house this would be.

He was proven right when it was opened by a mixed-race girl with a halo of wild, tight curls and a winning smile.

'Hi,' Lucy said, through her grin. She looked past him and greeted Hobo's mother. 'Hi, Meg!'

'Oi! Mrs Kostinen, to you!' came a familiar voice from inside the house. Lucy's mother and Alistair's daughter-in-law, Tamara.

Alistair was vaguely aware that Meg Kostinen was chuckling to his left. But his main focus was on his granddaughter. His heart welled. He'd barely had a chance to regard Lucy properly in 1937, but now he was able to take her full measure. When he'd last seen her, she was only six, and now here she was... well, either twelve or thirteen, depending on when in 2018 it was. Very nearly a young adult. And she was living in Wales...

Wonder why they moved? Did something happen between Albert and Tamara? Being in the future... Too many questions.

He couldn't help himself. He rushed forward and enfolded Lucy in his arms, warmly, before leaning back and cupping her face in his large hands.

'Oh, my sweet girl.'

'Hey, hey!' She batted his hands back and then, almost as a second thought, shoved him gently in the chest. 'Calm your boots there, Romeo, a simple *hi* is usually enough between mates.' She looked aside to Meg, questioningly. 'And what's with the plummy accent?'

Alistair felt the burn as his cheeks reddened. He'd dropped the accent again. He needed to concentrate.

'He's been doing silly voices ever since we left the house, Lucy,' Meg said. Then she whispered in his ear, 'Bring her flowers next time, eh?' She ruffled his shoulders. 'To be honest, Lucy, he's mostly been distracted this morning by this asteroid business.'

Alistair's ears suddenly perked up. *Asteroid business?* This was more like it, certainly more his line of interest than smugglers in 1937. Although, he reflected, the odds of both not being connected...

'Honestly, if it was going to collide with us they'd have evacuated us all to the moon months ago,' Meg said.

Alistair looked at her just to make sure. Yes, she was joking.

Lucy raised her arms in mock alarm. 'You should see all the conspiracy stuff about it on social media. It's a clickbait frenzy.'

'I guess we'll find out on Tuesday night, then, when it arrives,' Meg said, closing with a 'dun dun duhhhn', much to Lucy's amusement.

Alistair remembered the vibrating in his pocket. He pulled out Hobo's mobile phone and checked the screen. It was a smartphone. He'd had a special UNIT smartphone while he'd been posted in Peru, and Con had given him an iPhone in 2011, too, so he knew his way around the apps and screens, even if this model appeared to be a massive advancement on what he'd used before.

Alistair searched Hobo's mind for the log-in code. The phone's wallpaper showed a happy family of four: Hobo, his mother, and... Names sprung to his mind; Sacha Kostinen, Hobo's dad, and Gavin Kostinen, Hobo's younger brother. He quickly accessed the internet and searched on Google.

Mayday for May Day! The screen claimed. *Asteroid set for 'near miss' flight past Earth!* The clarity of the screen amazed him. Scaremongering or not, he'd have to make sure he read up on that properly as soon as he could.

A woman breezed through the doorway, and Alistair looked up from the phone. He almost went to hug her too, as was usual when he saw her. But he held back just in time.

Tamara Wilson, his daughter-in-law of twenty-one years – well, almost twenty-eight years now, he supposed. He peered behind her, wondering if his son was home too. Seeing Lucy almost seven years hence was strange enough, as was seeing Tamara, but to see Albert too? And what about Con, Nicky…?

Alistair wasn't sure how the Doctor managed to cope with all those journeys into the future…

Tamara kissed Meg on the cheek. 'Time for a quick cuppa?'

'Just the one, my love.'

'Lucy? You and Hobo get this stuff in the car, eh?' Tamara suggested. 'We'll be back out in a mo.'

Meg followed Tamara into the house.

'Is your dad around?' Alistair asked Lucy.

'Is he ever? He's gone to London, work stuff. Also popping in to see Aunty Pam probably.'

Alistair almost smiled at the way Lucy said that name. Pamela Wilson, Albert's sister, had never be the most reliable person in the world. Good to see that seven years on she was still so highly regarded.

From further in the house, Tamara cautioned Lucy for being cheeky.

'I know, I know,' Lucy said. 'Did you wanna ask for my hand in marriage or something?'

Alistair cringed further. This was unbearable. Up to now, on his jumps through time, he'd mostly been around strangers and old work colleagues, or, on a few occasions, in the past with his family. But interacting with future versions of his own family? He wasn't sure he was prepared for this. Being around James had been difficult enough, but at least then he had only been an observer…

'It's okay, I'm only teasing,' Lucy said. 'Just hold back on the too-much-strange, yeah?'

He nodded, and Tamara appeared again, this time with a satnav and cable. She was talking to Meg about

Albert.

'He'll be back later, then he has some important accounts to sort out, so he needs to work in isolation for a few days. So, this is an opportune trip,' she finished, looking at Lucy pointedly.

Lucy continued the story. 'Work were going to put him up in a hotel, but Mum and I said we'd have a few days away instead, for a change, and he can work from here, surrounded by homely comforts. Sure he'll be glad to be free of Aunty Pam, too!' She grabbed a couple of the bags from the hallway to take to Tamara's car.

'Lucy, don't be so mean about your aunt,' Tamara said, but Alistair could tell her heart wasn't in it.

Lucy rolled her eyes and turned from her mother to Alistair. 'I told you all this before, I'm sure. Honestly, you don't listen to a word I say, sometimes.'

Alistair shrugged what he hoped was a causal apology.

'Come on.' Lucy walked past him. 'Bring your bag and grab one of these others.'

Alistair nodded energetically. He was a little disappointed that Albert wasn't around, but relieved too. Things had never quite been right between them, not since Tibet. And much like Kate, Albert had blamed him. So, even if his son had been there right now, what could Alistair really say to him? He didn't care. It would have just been nice to see Albert, to see how his son was in the future.

The boot was full, so Alistair shoved Hobo's backpack into the rear seat well, then gave Meg a slightly awkward hug as she returned from inside the house. She kissed him on the forehead; a tear glistened in her eye.

'How about when we get back?' he asked, vaguely. Assuming he was still around then, maybe he could somehow talk to Albert...

'Sometime Monday afternoon I expect,' Tamara said,

while fiddling with her satnav, clearly misunderstanding Alistair's meaning. 'We can keep him till the evening and give him tea if you'll be working, Meg?'

Hobo's mother smiled. 'I'll be home with Gavin during the day. Got the six to midnight shift to cover each evening, though.'

'Hope it's quiet for you.'

She nodded to Tamara and then, with a little wave to Alistair, she walked away. He watched her go, reminded of the times his mother had sent him packing on school trips. 'Bye, Mam,' he called. She turned back and waved once more.

'She's missing you already.' Lucy had appeared at his shoulder.

A call from the car. 'Right, ready?'

Alistair and Lucy looked at each other. She nodded at him and he found himself nodding back instinctively. But no, he wasn't ready; he didn't know anywhere near enough about what was going on.

The drive to Cornwall would take several hours, at least, and if he was clever about it, Alistair hoped he could fill in a lot of the gaps on the way without arousing his granddaughter's suspicions.

'Any last-minute toilet requirements?' Tamara added. 'If so, go now or forever hold your—'

'Oh, Mum, do you have to be so embarrassing?' Lucy locked the front door and joined Alistair by the car. He was smiling from ear to ear. 'She only says these things to show off in front of you, you know that? I take it you didn't need to go?'

Alistair shook his head. A trip with Lucy. They'd been on trips before, of course, but he'd always been the old grandfather, her the little girl he'd bounce on his knees and tell stories to. But not this time. This time they were, more or less, on equal footing.

'All right then, smiler, get in the car. What's making

75

you so cheerful, anyway?'

'Just thinking,' he told Lucy. 'This is going to be fun.'

Sometime later, Alistair and Lucy emerged from the services, their first stop since entering England via the Severn Bridge, to find Tamara was waiting for them at the car, finishing yet another coffee, which she justified as 'one for the road'.

For the second leg of the journey, Lucy sat in the back with Hobo. Because – according to her blunt terminology – Hobo was being less weird. (He banked that as a success.) Tamara grumbled that it made her feel like a taxi driver, but she seemed to lose herself in the driving once she started singing along loudly to someone called Ariana Grande on the stereo.

Alistair had assumed that he and Lucy would talk and plan discreetly in the back, but Lucy went straight onto her iPad again, just as she had done since leaving Ogmore-by-sea.

Alistair assessed the situation and decided he'd have a rummage through Hobo's rucksack, to see if he could find out a little more about the boy he was supposed to be. The tent and sleeping bag were strapped to the bottom of the pack. Deodorant and a water bottle in the side pockets. Inside, he found a single change of clothes (hoodie, jeans, underwear) and the obligatory wash bag. There was a packet of Barley Sugars, which he offered around (no takers). Paracetamol, plasters, antiseptic wipes, a worn mug featuring a faded image of the Tower of London, banana, peanuts and raisins, some small change, a Yale-type key on a chain, a book of advanced puzzles and brain teasers, and an unread paperback: *The Search for Mister Lloyd*, by Griff Rowland.

Hmm, Alistair thought. *Intelligent, practical and enjoys puzzles.*

'You okay?' Lucy asked. 'Left something behind?'

'No, just checking.' He gave what he hoped was a reassuring smile.

She nodded and returned to her iPad. Alistair was about to speak again when he recalled Hobo's phone in his pocket. He felt it was a bit intrusive, looking at someone else's private phone, but he wanted to check out that asteroid news item he'd seen earlier.

He pulled out the phone. He noticed a few things he'd not clocked earlier, such as the date: Saturday May 5th. So, just under six and a half years since he left 2011. He quickly worked out that this made it May Bank Holiday weekend, and roughly eighty-one years since he was transported from Redgate Smithy. May Day would be Monday 7th.

He tapped the news app. The page now had three major headlines:

Trump Knew of Payments
Months Before He Denied Them.

Trump? Alistair read on a little and was shocked to learn that oaf Donald Trump had been elected to President of United States of America. He read on further and couldn't believe the man was *still* in office. *How things change so easily in less than seven years,* he wondered. What could possibly have happened in the intervening years to allow that? He'd known less oafish and self-serving civil servants.

Theresa May encouraged to pursue
"no compromise" Brexit after UKIP voters
flocked to Tories in local elections.

Brexit? What a ridiculous word! He dreaded to think who thought up that catchy buzzword. Nothing he loathed more than buzzwords to explain what was, almost certainly, a vastly complicated issue.

He pressed on the third headline, the one he'd been looking for.

Mayday for May Day! Asteroid still set for "near miss" flight past Earth.

Lucy must have been watching him discreetly. 'You realise that's just clickbait to alarm people, don't you?' He read on, regardless.

> The asteroid up to 100m in width, is due to skim past the Earth on May bank holiday Monday.
>
> Asteroid NJ 1936 will pass by at less than one-fifth the distance between the Earth and the Moon. The huge flying rock was first spotted in 1936 on its last approach by Professor Nigel Jacks at the Norman Lockyer Observatory. He thought it was going to collide with the Earth and cause some local panic, claiming it would be the end of the world. It was later revealed to have what is known as an 'elliptical orbit' around the sun, which means it travels further away before swinging back in closer. NASA's Catalina Sky Survey facility in Arizona has recently been mapping the asteroid's path further on its 81-year journey.
>
> However, while the pass is relatively close in astronomical terms, it's nowhere near close enough to be a threat.
>
> "Asteroids of this size approach this

close to Earth maybe once or twice a year," said Fran Kitley, manager of Nasa's Center for Near-Earth Object Studies. "There's no danger."

NJ 1936 will skim past us at a distance of 70,000km (43,500 miles), which is roughly twice as far as the belt of satellites which orbit Earth in geostationary orbit.

A government spokesperson said that there was no danger to mobile phone and GPS signals either.

See also: Phil & Holly *This Morning*: Should NASA have tried to land a deep space probe on the asteroid to save on fuel?

Love Island asteroid chat: Brandon & Kellee OMG! *THAT* moment: Kellee 'I just love *Armageddon*,' Brandon 'Yeah baby? I'm more into *Deep Impact*!'

Related Topics
Asteroids | NASA
| Halley's Comet | Love Island
Share this story
Facebook | Twitter | Instagram | WhatsApp

1936... Clearly the asteroid was the link. He didn't believe in coincidences at the best of times, and especially not when he was deliberately sent somewhere. In some ways, Alistair reflected, it wasn't that much different to some of his old missions, and it wouldn't be the first time a near-miss asteroid caused him trouble.

'Clickbait, Hobo, told you.' Lucy's nudge on his arm threw his concentration and he almost spat an invective. 'If there was anything serious in that asteroid story we'd be right on it, yeah? Lethbridge-Stewart stuff.'

'Lethbridge-Stewart stuff?' he asked, without thinking.

Lucy gave him a look. 'Yeah, you know it's never far away.' She nudged him again. 'Look, why not check this out.' She tapped a little icon on the phone called Google Earth. An aerial image appeared on the screen. 'See, this is what I want to base my assignment on, with lots of cool pics and local gossip. Grace's mum is one of the wardens.'

He was looking at the stone circle near Redgate Smithy, from above. It had wardens now? Ahh, there was a Cornish Heritage sign hovering over the image. Of course, all places like that must be protected sites these days.

That at least explained something of why Lucy and Hobo were in the stone circle. Not why they were in the past, of course, but clearly in 2018 they must have reached Redgate Smithy. Or *would do*, that is.

'What d'you think?' Lucy asked.

Alistair sighed and gave up. There would be time to ponder on these things later. He looked at Lucy, a little vacantly this time.

She gave him an enormous pout. 'You're useless today, Hobo. Honestly, it's like no one's home.'

That's a bit rich, he thought, *since she's spent most of the journey so far buried in her iPad.*

'Does. This. Sound. Like. A. Good. History. Assignment?' Lucy asked, stressing every word like Hobo was slow.

'Lucy! Be nice!' said Tamara from the front.

'Yes,' Alistair said with a grin. 'It sounds great.' The name Lucy had mentioned finally caught up with him. 'By the way, who's Grace?'

Lucy's mouth dropped open slightly, and she was clearly about to release another tirade at him, but she glanced at her mum's back and appeared to relent.

'Grace Pemberton? My old school friend? We're camping in her back garden, yeah? Her family and grandad's go back, like, forever.'

Alistair forced himself not to smile. *We certainly do.* He knew Grace, or at least who's child she was. Daughter of Daniel and Helen, and granddaughter of David Pemberton. Apt, he supposed, that he should be going to visit a Pemberton, since it was at the funeral of Grace's great grandmother where he'd first found the Gnome.

Almost as if it was all planned, he thought, *and it probably was.*

Lucy scrolled along on the image on Hobo's phone. 'She lives over here in Liskeard, so not far. But you know this. Mate, what happened? Didn't you sleep last night?'

Alistair smiled. 'Too excited, like, wasn't I?'

Lucy narrowed her eyes, then another idea appeared to grab her, and they opened and gleamed with mischievousness.

'Grace's mum looks after lots of heritage sites around Cornwall. I'm hoping she'll have some bloodthirsty stories about human sacrifices up there by moonlight!'

'I hope not!' Tamara said. 'I've already told you, my girl, I don't want you going to that stone circle if stuff like that goes on.'

Lucy laughed, and Alistair found himself joining in.

'We're talking years ago, Mum! Pagan times, not these days.'

'Well, just you watch it, anyway.'

Lucy rolled her eyes dramatically, and Alistair chuckled again. He'd always loved Lucy's expressive energy.

'So,' he said. 'How do you know Grace? Just cause your grandad's family and hers...'

'Come on. *Seriously?*'

'Positive.' Alistair was gambling somewhat, but he felt it was a risk worth taking. It was great that their families kept in touch after he was gone, but he was curious to know why Lucy and Grace were such great friends. He fumbled around in his memories for another friend Lucy used to tell him about when she visited. 'You usually just talk about Ayesha from your London lot.'

Lucy looked at him. 'My London lot?' She shook her head. 'God, you're weird today. Now, pay attention this time. Grace and I were friends back in London. She left in Year Five when her parents split up.'

Alistair didn't need to struggle for a reaction. He didn't know Daniel and Helen very well, only met them once and that was at Joan's funeral, but out of fealty to Old Spence, he felt bad that his friend's grandson was no longer married.

'Her dad—'

'The rat,' Tamara said, interrupting Lucy.

'Her dad stayed in London with his new girlfriend,' Lucy continued. 'Her mum went to Cornwall and Grace went with her.'

'Why Liskeard?'

'She got this job with Cornish Heritage. But Grace said her mum had got a few job offers and specifically picked this one, and picked Liskeard to live, cos she'd always liked the stories she heard about the area.'

Stories, Alistair thought, *that no doubt started between me and Old Spence. It's like the Gnome has taken me full circle.*

It was around four o'clock when Tamara's car finally pulled up on Castle Street, Liskeard, just along from the Pembertons' ground floor flat. The thick blanket of cloud overhead was prompting the afternoon to draw in early, making it feel a lot later than it was. By the time the three of them had clambered out of the car and stretched, Grace and Helen were waiting for them.

Bless those girls, thought Alistair, as they hugged madly and squealed with delight. He held back by the

82

car, watching the others with a raised hairless eyebrow. Well, a partially raised one, since Hobo didn't appear to be able to raise a single eyebrow very well.

On the promise of freshly percolated coffee and a good gossip, Helen led Tamara inside. Alistair noted, however, the bottle of wine subtly poking out from the top of Tamara's large handbag as they crossed the threshold. He gave a wry smile, thinking how much like her father she was.

Lucy finally noticed that Hobo waited by the car. She beckoned him over.

'Hobo Kostinen, meet Grace Pemberton.'

Alistair looked at Grace, and tried to imagine her six years younger – she *had* been there at the funeral in 2011. Long before Daniel and Helen had parted ways. Grace shared plenty of style choices with Lucy: torn, tight jeans, cartoon slogan t-shirt, pea-green hoodie and customised Converse boots. But there was something in the slant of the brow and the curve of the mouth that confirmed she was definitely the great granddaughter of Old Spence. Good to know.

Grace grinned. 'You've got alopecia? How cool. And you're like proper Welsh?'

Well, Alistair thought, *more Scots than Welsh at the moment.* But he settled for a, 'I'm as Welsh as I come, I am.'

'Complete with Valleys accent today,' Lucy said, and playfully punched him on the shoulder.

'Hashtag USP overload,' Grace said.

'USP?'

'Unique. Selling. Point.' Grace spelled it out for them. 'It's what marks you out from the crowd as an individual.'

'For bullying?' Alistair asked, toning the Welsh accent as best he could.

'Nuh-uh, Geek Chic. Up town is full of indie boutiques.' Grace made quotation marks with her fingers.

'*Nerd* is the new "cool". I've just got the one USP myself; I'm Geezer Grace round here, guv'nor, all Cockney-loike, apparently.' She grabbed imaginary braces, stuck out her elbows and waggled them around. 'Everyone else is all *"get orf my laaaaand!".'*

Grace and Lucy laughed. Alistair forced himself to join in.

He was too old for such nonsense.

The rest of the day passed pretty merrily. Tamara and Helen picked up whatever friendship they'd had years ago over a couple of bottles of wine and the barbecue. Lucy and Grace clearly enjoyed not having to chat over messenger, although he didn't understand why they felt the need to say 'hash-tag' so often.

Alistair was still basking in the joy of being in Lucy's company, but when the girls Facetimed Ayesha, he decided that it was more girlie chat than he could stomach. He left them to it and set to putting up the tents instead; a bad move as it turned out as that was Lucy's favourite job. But, as Tamara pointed out to her, she couldn't be everywhere at once.

Thanks to the cloud cover, the night wasn't too cold. The Ogmore contingent were all eager to turn in, though, after the long journey. *Longer for some*, thought Alistair when he realised he'd not slept for about twenty hours real time, or eighty-one years linear time.

As he lay in his tent, waiting for sleep to take him, he could hear Lucy and Grace giggling in their tent next door, and in the background a few shrieks of laughter from Tamara and Helen inside. Tomorrow they were off to Redgate Smithy.

And, he hoped, some answers...

CHAPTER SIX
The Width of a Circle

IT WAS MID-MORNING THE FOLLOWING DAY. CHURCH bells could be heard in the distance. Sunday, of course. Alistair buckled his seatbelt. He sat in the front of Helen's tatty Cornish Heritage four-by-four, and placed his rucksack by his feet. The girls were on the backseat and Grace was not happy.

'You said you didn't have to work today, Mum.'

'I said I hoped I wouldn't, that's all.'

'But you were going to show Lucy the stone circle. That's the whole point of her visiting.' Grace raised her hands in a show of despair.

Helen pulled away, talking all the while. Alistair was never a happy passenger while the driver was trying to concentrate on several things at once, although doubtless it was something he'd repeatedly done himself in active service.

'I don't need a day off to do that,' continued Helen. 'I'll drop you there on my way to Land's End.'

'Land's End? What the hell's Lucy's mum supposed to do all that time?'

'You watch your language, young lady. And Tamara's fine. She knows the situation. She's going to pop into town, probably give herself some retail therapy. Not often she gets time off, either, you know.'

Grace turned to Lucy. 'Sorry, I thought we had this all planned.'

'It's fine,' Lucy replied. 'Mum'll be in her element. And she has been working a lot since the New Year.'

'Yes,' Helen agreed. 'Call her when you need picking up. Not sure what time I'll be back.'

Everyone settled into an awkward silence for the remainder of the journey.

Alistair was surprised to find that Redgate now had its own postcode. Also, part of the moorland approach to the stone circle had been converted into a shingle track, allowing vehicular access up to a drop off point only a hundred metres or so from the stone circle. No more breathless yomps across the moors from the old Higher Tremarcoombe road.

2018 was a few years after he'd last been to the area, but it wasn't *that* long. He was still surprised by how much new development there'd been, though, alongside plenty that he recognised as familiar. In places the old roads had been replaced to accommodate the residential developments and business properties that had sprung up nearby.

The car pulled up at the bottom of the shingle track and they climbed out. Helen lowered her window.

'You can walk the rest of the way, do you good.'

Grace was fuming. 'Mum! You were supposed to show Lucy around.'

'I'm only a glorified caretaker, Gracie, you know that. I don't know any more about this place than it tells you on the information board over there. There might be a bit more on the website. Maybe check later when you're home? Stay safe and dry now. Hope you get what you need. Byeee.' And with a slight wheelspin, Helen was off.

Grace watched her go. Alistair looked at Lucy and the two of them grimaced.

'Grace, it's fine, really,' said Lucy. 'We'll check out the info board like she said, take some pics, then if there's anything else I need we'll do some digging around online later.'

'Just kind of feel I'm letting you down, that's all. Long way to come from Wales, especially if you could have done it all online.'

'That's what everyone else will be doing,' Lucy confirmed. 'Whereas I'll have actual photos of me actually with the stone circle. Come on, snap me now with it in the background.' She handed Grace her phone. Grace checked the screen, then took a few steps back. 'What's wrong?'

Grace grinned. 'Your hair's too big. I can't get any of the stones in shot unless I'm back here!'

Lucy and Grace shared a laugh. Alistair looked back towards Bledoe. Whatever they did here today, he'd make sure Tamara picked them up from Bledoe, so he could have a look around the old place again. *One last time?* He snorted grimly at the thought. He hadn't been to Bledoe for some time, not since around 2005. Which was now almost thirteen years ago...

He knew he had to see if any of his old friends were still alive, still there. Find out how they were. And he wanted to show Lucy where he had been born. All the trips he'd taken with Lucy while she was growing up, all the stories he'd told her, and not once had he ever taken her to Bledoe.

'Coming then, Hobo?'

Alistair turned to find Lucy and Grace had already set off. As he headed up the track after them, he felt the cool moorland wind play over his exposed skin. Alistair supposed Hobo must be used to it, and he supposed that he would be, too, after a while.

He practically walked into Lucy, who had stopped suddenly. She was leaning over a large, laminated tourist information board. He noticed a logo at the bottom of it, and a website, plus some sponsorship information and something about a local bed and breakfast. There'd been a large building not far away from the circle on the Google Maps image, and now it made sense; someone must have finally done up the old tumbledown Redgate Smithy and turned it into a B&B.

That's another slice of yesterday gone, he thought.

'Check this out, Hobo,' called Lucy, and he stepped in next to her.

'*The name Redgate Smithy,*' he read, '*has become synonymous with the megalithic stone circle on Bodmin Moor, which now forms part of the grounds of the hotel.*' Alistair inwardly groaned. He disliked the modern tendency to refer to B&Bs as hotels. He read on.

'*The stone circle is protected under heritage and dates from c.2500BC. The site originally consisted of twenty upright and ten cross-beam stones, with a woven or thatched roof. Only remnants of nine upright stones now remain. These large stones, known as sarsens, originate from Wiltshire. They would have been very difficult and costly to transport. Cornwall is abundant in granite. The use of imported stone here indicates that the structure held special status. Local myths have long linked the circle with pagan worship – the altar stone in the centre of the circle is thought to be one of the cross-beam stones that fell and was later incorrectly positioned by Victorian antiquarians. However, it is just as likely that Redgate Smithy acted as a local council chamber or market place. See also Stonehenge in Salisbury and Avebury in Wiltshire.*'

'Sarsens?' Lucy wondered aloud. 'Don't they make vinegar?' She was clearly chuffed with her pun and chuckled away to herself as she photographed the text and the small lithograph which showed the circle in the mid-Nineteenth Century. 'See if I can find this image online later,' she added before turning suddenly to Alistair and Grace and addressing them as 'team'.

Alistair and Grace glanced at each other.

'We know what we're doing, yeah? Pics of all the stones, measurements across the circle and in between the stones, compass points. You both got compass apps on your phones?'

Alistair found himself nodding although he didn't know for sure.

'And then later we'll concoct some wild theories about what the place was used for, before I just re-word the tourist info. Okay?'

Again, Alistair found himself picked up and carried along by the sheer enthusiasm and *joie de vive* of his granddaughter. He nodded and grinned. The three of them continued up the short stretch and into the stone circle.

Alistair laughed at the NO BALL GAMES signs that had been planted at regular intervals outside the perimeter of the circle. And at the front and back of each standing stone was a sign warning people not to LEAN ON, PUSH OR INTERFERE WITH THE STONES.

Not in my day, he thought, and suddenly felt very old.

As they worked, he stole glances down towards Bledoe. The village continued to grow, that was clear enough, but it still remained a village. New housing estates had sprung up where previously there had been farm land or huddles of tumbledown cottages. Muddy tracks and rough stony lanes had been widened, lengthened and made solid; like tarmac fingers splayed out on a grass-coloured cloth. He felt a tinge of regret.

Progress, eh? What will the old rural community be like in another hundred years?

Useless speculation, he told himself.

'Hobo!'

The name caught him by surprise. He tried to focus on where the voice was coming from.

'You okay?' It was Lucy calling.

Alistair walked as quickly as he could to join the girls.

'What d'you make of this?' Grace indicated a faint

mottling on the stone, like a shadow but not quite where the light played.

Alistair approached and peered closer. As he did so the marks faded.

'Curious,' he said, then stepped back a few paces. The patterns again became visible. He repeated the action a few times, with the same results.

'Hobo,' said Lucy, as if talking to a disturbed relative. 'Are you trying to confuse the stone, or something? Cos, you know, it's just a stone and all that.'

'It's the mottling effect. It disappears if you get too close. But it's not the sunlight as far as I can tell.' He sucked his teeth thoughtfully. 'It's like the shadow of a memory on the surface of the stone.'

'Oh, very deep,' Lucy scoffed. 'I'm stealing that!' She quickly scribbled the words on her notepad.

Grace was now copying his curious routine. 'I see what you mean.'

Alistair nodded. 'I'd swear it's not the natural colouration of the stone, though.'

'You sure?' Lucy pointed to the next stone further around the circle. 'It's here too, but slightly different.'

They all turned roughly on the spot and picked out the faint rippling on each of the stones, like a wave.

'Bam! That's my story, then. And a mystery to solve. Nail this, nail a top mark.'

'How the hell are you going to tell what caused that though?' Grace asked, a level of dismay evident in her tone. 'These stones have been here for thousands of years!'

'We'll ask some locals, check online.' Lucy began taking pictures with her phone, but the mottling effect was not coming out clearly on the images; same with the iPad. With a grumble of frustration at technology letting her down, and saying they should have remained clear of it after all, Lucy produced her notepad again and started sketching the pattern on the stones with a pencil instead.

'Hey, speaking of high-tech,' Grace said, 'are you guys planning to watch that asteroid pass by tomorrow night? They've got cameras up on some satellites; they're showing a live feed online. Should be pretty cool.'

Alistair looked up, intrigued.

'We'll probably have it on in the background,' Lucy confirmed. 'Hobo's been obsessing about it, so no doubt he'll be glued to his PC.'

Alistair ignored Lucy's obvious attempt to wind Hobo up. 'What time is it due to pass?' he asked.

'Around 11pm, I think,' Grace said.

'We won't see very much,' Lucy scoffed. 'It'll still be miles away. Unless they've got a camera with a super zoom, or the asteroid suddenly changes course and comes straight at us.'

'Or releases little alien invaders,' Grace suggested.

The girls laughed. Lucy glanced his way and Alistair forced himself to join in. Muttering about how cool it would be, Lucy continued with her sketches.

Alistair's smile quickly dropped. It was unwise to joke about such things, in his experience.

Alistair strolled over towards the altar stone. As he approached it, the sole of his shoe scuffed the top of another, much smaller, stone embedded in the ground. He looked more closely, expecting it to be a chunk of sarsen, chipped off from the altar stone or weathered away. But when he parted the longish grass, he found a hard, black stone breaking through the soil. Its flinty edges glistened, as if impregnated with quartz; very different from the rest of the circle, and different again from the area's native granite.

Crouched there, Alistair ran his fingertips along the edges of the stone. Physical contact brought an immediate clamour to his ears, the sounds of people chanting. He snatched his hand away and stood up into darkness.

Had he travelled again? Lucy and Grace were nowhere to be seen. The stone circle around him was lit by flaming torches. Indistinct, hooded figures swarmed around him in an insane dance, confusing him.

He staggered onto the altar stone, recoiling, trying to protect his face from the flickering flames. A large goat-faced mask loomed towards him; some sort of coven leader. A word screamed inside his head from somewhere: *Traveller*. But it wasn't the masked figure speaking. Alistair instinctively knew that was a man. He brandished a ceremonial knife, holding it aloft. Alistair felt helpless, a passive victim. The blade glistened in the light of the flames, then he watched as it came slicing down towards him. He flinched and yelled, in anticipation of the cold steel piercing his body.

But at the point of contact, the scene was shockingly cleansed by a bright orange fireball erupting all around. Spared from being sacrificed, Alistair instead writhed in agony as his clothes and flesh bubbled and burned…

…and he came-to, seated on the ground at the perimeter of the stone circle. He still wore his backpack and he was leaning against one the sarsens, very much in disregard of the warning signs.

He checked himself over: no fire damage. No apparent injuries at all, just some grass stains on his elbows and knees from rolling on the ground.

'Look at the state of your hoodie,' said Lucy as she squatted next to him and grabbed his hand. 'What happened, Hobo? You've been a bit odd since yesterday, but… That was full-on, all-out nuts.'

He stared back at her; confusion and concern were writ large in her young eyes. He knew at that moment that he had to end the pretence. It wasn't fair on any of them; Hobo included. Lucy had to know the truth, and, after all the stories he had told her, Alistair believed she could handle it. But only her. He glanced from side to side.

'Where's Grace?'

'She's gone to that hotel place. To get help. No mobile phone signal here, can you believe it?'

Alistair was relieved. 'Lucy. I've got something important to tell you. But, first, I need you to tell me what you and Grace saw.'

His granddaughter nodded and seated herself on the ground next to him.

'Grace didn't really see anything, for a start.'

That's a relief, he thought.

'She was checking out the other side of the stones for more of that mottling. There's none, by the way; it's all on the inside of the circle.'

Alistair smiled and nodded. 'And you?'

'I was sketching the stones. There was a kind of flash on my periphery and there you were, writhing in agony over that altar stone. I pulled you off and dragged you here.'

'I see. Thank you.'

'Were you struck by lightning or something?'

He shook his head. 'I had a vision. No, not just a vision, it was more real than that. There were... rituals, a ceremony. Then the circle was consumed by a fireball. And I was burning to death.'

Lucy didn't scoff, she just looked deeply concerned.

Yes, he thought, *I'm making the right decision.*

'But, how?'

'I think it's this place,' he told her. 'I think it's sending me messages from my past.'

'Like a race memory? Psychic stuff?'

He placed a hand on her shoulder. 'Who do you see before you, Lucy?'

'Hobo, of course.'

'Lucy, something strange happened yesterday. I can't explain it. This is Hobo's body, but inside I'm actually—'

'Grandad?' She whispered the name as if only half hoping it could be true.

He nodded. 'You never cease to amaze me.'

'Never cease to amaze myself, after all I've been through since moving to Ogmore.' Lucy grinned. 'But I'm a Lethbridge-Stewart, so...'

'You are indeed.' Alistair tapped the end of her nose. 'Hello, Lucyloo.'

They both smiled and uttered simultaneous sighs of relief.

'That explains your behaviour at my front door, then, and your various random accents ever since.'

'Oh,' he grumbled, disheartened. 'I thought I'd been doing quite well.'

Lucy laughed. She paused, looked at him and laughed again, before giving him an enormous hug.

'But how is this possible? You... Grandad, you passed away. Years ago.'

He could see how much this had affected Lucy; it was something she'd never fully overcome.

'Lucy. It's okay. No one lives forever.'

She nodded and tried to smile away the tears that had welled in her eyes. 'I've missed you. So much.' She gave a big sniff. 'How long are you here for?'

'I don't know. Until I've fulfilled my purpose, I suppose, whatever that is. It's not like a social visit. I've been sent here, you see, by... Well, by a gnome.'

'A gnome?'

'Yes. Long story. But I believe I'm here to solve a mystery... With you.'

Lucy nodded. 'Lethbridge-Stewarts unite.' She grinned again. 'Oh, Hobo's gonna be so annoyed he's missed this.'

'Yes, I can't tell you how much of this he'll be aware of or remember once I'm gone.' Alistair stood and flexed. 'I don't think we should tell Grace.'

'Or Mum.' Lucy stood too. 'Yeah, no way. As far as everyone else is concerned, you're still Hobo Kostinen. Lethbridge-Stewart stuff – it stays between us. Well, Hobo and me.'

'Now before we go any further, young lady, just what is this *Lethbridge-Stewart stuff* you keep hinting at, eh?'

Lucy grinned and stood a little more rigid, looking proud. 'Aliens, Grandad. Since I moved to Ogmore and teamed up with Hobo, we've been fighting aliens and protecting the Earth from all sorts. Like you used to do.'

'But—' He felt worry and pride, both at the same time, and was reminded of a promise he'd made to Lucy's other grandfather in 1990. Could it be that Anne was still alive in 2018, watching over his family as she said she would on the event of his passing?

'It's okay,' Lucy explained. 'We have help, if we need it. From your friend, Dame Anne Bishop.'

Alistair smiled. 'Good,' he said, nodding slowly. In the back of Hobo's memories he could just make out something. The Great Intelligence, Clowns, trouble at Monknash, and… The Billy Bandril Show? He blinked.

'What is it?' Lucy asked.

'Just a… It's a little harder this time, but I've learned to access the memories of the host bodies on my travels. I can kind of see some of Hobo's…' He smiled, and patted her hand. 'Just, please, go careful in the future.'

'We do. Besides, Dame Anne gave me a special ring, in case things get really hairy.'

She showed him the ring, which she kept on a chain around her neck. Alistair recognised it; Anne had two of them, both from her father. A family heirloom, containing a Kontron crystal… He narrowed his eyes, a thought coming to his mind. Anne wouldn't have passed one on, unless she had known...

'And Hobo...?' he asked, while his mind pondered other possibilities.

Lucy grinned. 'He's kind of like my scientific advisor.'

Alistair laughed. 'An apt nickname then.'

Grace reached the hotel to find the place in some consternation, and all the telephones in use. She looked about the reception area, desperately. There was a huddle of people near the entrance to the bar and a member of staff at the front desk on the telephone. An elderly lady – a resident, presumably – approached Grace.

'Can I help you, dear?'

'Yes. Up at the stone circle, one of my friends has had some kind of fit.'

'Like him, then.' The lady pointed into the middle of the huddle.

The group parted slightly. A couple of staff were lifting a very frail, elderly man off the floor and into one of the comfy lounge chairs. Another resident was fanning him with a small wad of tourist leaflets, while an old colonel-type came back from the bar with what he called 'a constitutional'.

Grace was fascinated by the old man's face, which bore evidence of heavy scarring or abuse in years gone by, particularly the nose which was bent badly to one side, as if it had been broken and never re-set properly. The elderly female resident continued to chatter away to her in the background. Grace only half listened.

'About to play Bridge, we was. Then it was like he'd put his fingers in a socket. Went all rigid, fell to the floor and started having these palpitations. Never said he was epileptic, but what else could it be? Ambulance'll arrive soon, no doubt. Want us to send it round for your friend after they're done here?'

Grace gave an involuntary shiver as the old man's

dazed eyes seemed to hone in on her. His wrinkled brow creased further, and his tongue played along the edge of his teeth. Grace had been to the hotel many times before, when her mum had to pop by on official business for the stone circle. She'd never felt this uncomfortable there though. She wanted to turn and run, but her feet wouldn't move.

'No.'

The plummy, nasal voice sounded as ancient as the stones on the moors. It filled the room with its sombre rumble and Grace took a moment to realise that it had come from the old man. He was now shaking his head slowly and sitting further back in the chair.

The colonel-type thought the 'no' was for the proffered drink and endeavoured to argue in support of its medicinal qualities.

The staff thought the 'no' was for the ambulance they'd called and agreed to ignore the old man because they knew best.

Grace knew the 'no' was aimed at her.

The old man spoke again. 'But you are connected. We sense...' He paused. 'Come to us, the Traveller must understand... Must commune with you.'

'He's raving,' said one of the staff, calling across to the reception desk. 'When's that ambulance getting here?'

The old man spasmed in the chair suddenly, stretching out until his back arched. Grace wondered how such a frail old frame could cope. He let out an agonising wail, which he tried to contain through gritted teeth. Four staff members each took a limb, as if they were prepared to restrain him, but he sank back into the chair. Almost *through* the chair, Grace thought, his body was so thin.

'Active,' he muttered. 'Do not. Too soon. Too soon. Misaligned. We are... too weak.' His head fell forward, and he appeared to lose consciousness.

There was clearly a concern that he may have died, but staff immediately felt a pulse and asked the crowd to disperse while they waited for the ambulance. Without the old man's gaze distracting her, Grace found she could move again. She turned back to the entrance.

'Well, love?' It was the old lady again.

Grace looked confused and the lady repeated the offer to send the ambulance around to the stone circle afterwards.

'Oh, yes. Thank you,' she said, with half a smile, before running off as fast as she could.

Alistair and Lucy were examining the area around the altar stone.

'Something here must have caused it,' Alistair reasoned. 'I've seen some odd things in my time, but nothing that can't be traced to a root cause.'

'Could the altar stone be a psychic conductor?'

Before Alistair could respond, Lucy stepped in closer to the recumbent sarsen. He saw her rise up slightly as she stepped onto the same buried rock he had previously stepped on. Her whole body went rigid, arced with electric blue light momentarily, which then seemed to almost throw her onto the altar stone, as one would be thrown by a strong electrical current.

'Lucy!'

In a flash he was with her, holding her tight in his arms. Her eyeballs had disappeared up inside her head. Her face had lost its healthy hue, giving her a sickening death-mask. Alistair had never felt so helpless. With a massive gasp, as though she'd been drowning, Lucy lurched back into consciousness and buried her head in Alistair's chest.

Oh, the relief! Alistair gave Lucy a few minutes before he risked speaking.

'How are you feeling?'

'A little hollow. And there's a kind of metallic taste in my mouth.'

He nodded. 'Iron. Haemoglobin.'

'Am I bleeding?' She opened her mouth.

'Not that I can see, but that's how I felt when I came-to. Must be residue from the... whatever it is.'

'Are you okay now?'

He chuckled and patted her cheek. 'That's what I should be asking you, Lucyloo. But yes, I feel fine now, thank you.'

'Good.' Lucy sat up. 'Chances are I probably will be in a few minutes then, as well. And, Grandad...?'

'Yes?'

'I know it's you inside there, but it's still Hobo on the outside. Do you mind keeping the affectionate pats to a minimum? Just feels a bit... wrong, you know?'

'Sorry,' he said. 'Of course.'

They both took a long swig of water from the bottles in their backpacks. Alistair looked at the ground from their vantage point on the altar stone. He could see the edge of the black rock poking out of the ground.

'I don't like this, Lucy. I don't like it at all. Before I came here to 2018, I was transferred into myself as a young boy in 1937.'

'To solve another mystery?'

'Not really. It felt like a stepping stone on my way here. We were playing up here, at Redgate Smithy. Me, my brother James, his friends. This place was being used by local smugglers, to store goods inside fake stones.'

'Did you find them out and call the police?'

'We did, yes. But you'll never guess what happened next.'

Lucy narrowed her eyes. 'People only say that when they want to tell you something themselves and hope that you'll be impressed. Go on.'

'You and I turned up.'

'In 1937? Okay, I *am* impressed.'

'Well, you and Hobo's body, with me inside, as we are now. I was briefly in two bodies at once.'

'At the same time? Oh.' Lucy's face fell. 'That could be dangerous. The Blimamitch Liberation Effect.'

'*Blinovitch Limitation* Effect.'

Lucy laughed. 'That makes more sense.' She shrugged. 'I was only a kid when you told me about it.'

'I'm surprised you remember.' Alistair went to pat her, but stopped himself in time. 'Anyway, I was wondering how we got there at first, but now I know.' He nodded at the ring on the chain.

'Nice one. Are you suggesting we go there immediately?'

'No, no. We need to understand *why* before we go back there. For me, that all happened yesterday, so my memories of this stone circle from back then are, basically, immediate experience in my head.'

'You're gonna tell me that black rock wasn't there in 1937, aren't you?'

Alistair nodded again. 'And I'm certain that it caused those psychic attacks we both experienced.'

'What d'you reckon it is? Alien artefact?'

Alistair jumped down near the rock, but not touching it. The ground around it didn't feel strange in any way.

'Hey!' Lucy called.

Alistair held up a cautionary hand. 'I'll be careful.' He crouched near it. 'Looks just like an ordinary rock to me.' He waved his hands around just above the rock. There was a definite tingle to the air, a faint blue glow. 'See that?'

Lucy groaned and looked up at the sky. 'This was supposed to be an ordinary history project,' she grumbled. 'And already I've got a best friend possessed by my late grandfather, unexplained markings on ancient standing stones, glowing rocks and psychic visions of a hellish past. I won't be able to hand this in; Mrs White will think I've spent the whole weekend watching the Horror channel!'

'Life as a Lethbridge-Stewart, eh?'

'Nobody would believe me. Like when I performed that Stand-Up about you a couple of months ago.'

Alistair raised his eyebrows. 'Stand-Up?' He waved it away. 'It doesn't matter, you can tell me all about it later. Now, I take it you saw the same as me in your vision?'

'Pretty much what you described, yeah. It was only very fleeting, but it was enough.'

'I got to you as quickly as I could.'

'Yeah, you were writhing around for quite a bit before Grace and I could get to you, sorry.'

Mention of Grace's name reminded them that she was supposed to be around somewhere. Almost on cue they heard her calling from the direction of the B&B.

Alistair and Lucy glanced at each other, mouthed 'Hobo' and nodded. That special bond they always had when Lucy was small, it was very much still there, and it thrilled Alistair to the core.

Alistair gave a casual wave as Grace approached him and Lucy.

'Hey,' said Grace. 'You're okay then? That's a relief. I couldn't get help.'

'Not sure what came over me, to be honest,' he said. 'Maybe low blood sugar?'

Grace came right up to them both, stepping on the black rock as she did so. A warning died on Alistair's lips as nothing happened. He and Lucy looked at each other and frowned.

'We going to find somewhere to have our lunch, then?' Grace asked when they didn't move. 'Not allowed to eat here. Mum would kill me.'

'You got all you wanted from here?' Alistair asked Lucy. She nodded. He turned to head off. 'Right. Let's go to Bledoe, see if we can get some of that local gossip you wanted, Lucy.'

'Oh yeah,' she replied. 'Nice one, *Hobo*.'

He glanced back. Maybe he'd overdone it then. He put on his Welsh accent again, and affected a more youthful walk. 'We'll eat there. It's not far,' he said with a grin. 'I know a few shortcuts.' A beat, then he added, 'Saw them on Google maps.'

From behind one of the sarsens to the children's rear, a pair of ancient eyes above a crooked nose watched as they left the stone circle. The old man nodded.

'Yes,' he said. 'Yes... They are the ones! How strange...'

'Come along now, sir.' A large hand rested on his shoulder and the old man turned to find two paramedics and a female member of staff standing close behind him.

'Are you talking to us?' he asked.

'To you, sir, yes. Mr...?'

The old man thought.

The paramedic waited for a moment, before turning to the staff member and asking the man's name. She answered with a shrug.

'We are... the Traveller,' the old man said, at last.

'Fine, come on then, Michael Palin. You don't half move for an old boy, I'll give you that, but we were called out and we need to check you over.'

The paramedics grabbed the old man's arms. The Traveller felt incensed. How dare they?

'Do not touch us.'

'Come on, sir, best not to struggle.'

The old man was gripped by rage, and his hands began to glow with a blue light...

CHAPTER SEVEN
I'll Take You There

ALISTAIR LED THE GIRLS INTO BLEDOE ALONG FORE
Street, past the sports ground. There was a Sunday league
football match being played. After his recent experiences
in 1937, Alistair couldn't help but wonder what Smiffy
Gloyne would have made of it. He realised he'd
automatically assumed that Smiffy, being older than him,
would be dead already; not necessarily the case. He
paused and scanned the small crowd cheering the players
and jeering at the referee. Plenty of grey and snowy white
heads among them, and perhaps some old friends. In fact,
he was sure he spotted Ray's wife, Ethil, watching from
the comfort of a fold-away chair.

Alistair briefly considered taking a detour via
Redrose Cottage, for Lucy's benefit. But if they did, he'd
have to explain why to Grace as well, and he didn't want
to start getting bogged down in strategic lies and excuse
scenarios. Easier just to avoid the situation from the start.
He reminded himself that Lucy would see his childhood
home at some point anyway. The photo from Ray Phillips
that he had in his room showed Lucy and Hobo outside
Redrose Cottage, after all. He glanced at Lucy, who had
been walking slightly behind him with Grace. They both
had their heads buried in their smartphones, now that
full network coverage had returned.

Lucy looked up. 'Are we there yet?'

'Not quite,' Alistair replied. 'Just thought I'd see who

was playing.' Hobo's phone vibrated in his pocket. He'd remembered enough to know how to silence the thing at least. It was probably Hobo's mother checking up on him again. He'd selectively responded to three enquiries after his wellbeing since they'd arrived yesterday already. He pulled the phone out and checked the screen. There was a text from Lucy!

Alistair was about to point out that he was standing right by her when he realised that the message may be something covert. He opened it.

U need 2 hear wot hppnd 2 Grace @ da hotel, the message read.

'Look at you kids,' grumbled a passer-by. 'Heads in your phones all the time. Why don't you actually talk to each other instead?'

The three of them looked up at the sound of the admonishment.

'*Dwi ddim yn deal*,' Lucy immediately said, in an accent that sounded more Trinidadian than Welsh.

With a comment about 'ruddy foreigners', the outspoken local wandered off. They watched her go.

'What the hell was that?' Grace asked.

'*I don't understand*, in Welsh. Even living in Wales, it comes in handy at times.'

Grace laughed. 'Hashtag lol.'

Oh, good grief! We're back there again, Alistair thought. He announced, in his plumiest tone, 'Congratulations on nailing the accent, too.'

Lucy sneered at him with affection. The content of her text suddenly hit home. Alistair hadn't heard the girls talking while they'd been walking, and the answer was, unfortunately, obvious.

'Have you two been walking along and chatting to each other by text?'

The girls nodded to him as if this was the most normal thing ever. Alistair spared an apologetic thought for the local lady who was just now crossing the road further up Fore Street.

'Fine. But do you mind if we actually talk, though?'

Grace shrugged. 'Sure. What about?'

Lucy asked Grace to tell Hobo everything that had happened at the hotel.

'You'll think I'm going mad. Or imagining it.'

Alistair tried to sound reassuring. 'No I won't.'

'Hobo's sound,' Lucy confirmed.

Grace nodded and took a deep breath. 'It was just really, really weird.'

She explained what she'd found going on there, and how the old man had made her feel really uncomfortable. Alistair listened, careful not to comment in case it be perceived as casting judgment in some way.

'When I realised I could move my feet again, I just knew I had to get away. So, I ran. And that was it.'

'Thank you, Grace. You didn't get a name for the old man?'

'No, no one said his name. But—'

'Go on?'

'He said "we" instead of "I", and he talked about the Traveller. But I don't know who that is.'

Alistair tried not to express the deep concern he felt. Lucy, he noted, was virtually glowing with excitement. Had she heard the name during her vision as well?

'And these fits the old man had. When did they happen, roughly?' Alistair asked.

'One was before I arrived, but not too long before I don't think. The other was just before I left to find you again. Why?'

'Just wondered, that's all.' Alistair thanked Grace and glanced at Lucy. It was clear to him that she was having similar thoughts; the timings of these 'fits' were closely aligned to the psychic attacks he and Lucy had received. Too closely aligned for it to be coincidence. And the name, also.

They needed to find the old man, speak to him. And all this time they'd been walking away from him. But they couldn't take Grace back there again. The experience had clearly freaked her out.

A loud cheer from most of the football crowd distracted them.

'That's Jerome!' Grace squealed, pointing to the showboating goal scorer by the corner flag. 'He goes to my school. Fit as. He said *hi* to me once.'

'Yes, well, let's carry on, then,' Alistair said, suddenly feeling very much out of his depth once again.

Alistair could see the village green waiting for them at the end of Fore Street. They'd be able to picnic on the grass there, or possibly grab one of the bench seats that dotted the perimeter, usually dedicated to some deceased resident or another. He turned to tell the girls, but they'd stopped several feet back. They were standing close together, looking back the way they'd come.

'What's the matter?' he called.

The girls slowly turned their heads to look his way. Grace, in particular, made him involuntarily shiver. She had the hallmarks of the hunted about her; she looked washed-out and terrified.

He jogged back to them.

'We're being followed,' Lucy said.

Grace grabbed his arm. 'I want to go home, now.'

He turned to Lucy. She already had her phone in her hand and she raised it to her ear.

'Voicemail,' she said after a few seconds. 'Where should Mum pick us up?'

'The village green, just up there.' He pointed the way they'd been heading.

'Hi, Mum. Can you come for us ASAP? Bledoe village green, Fore Street.' She hung up.

Alistair asked, 'Is it anyone you recognise?'

Grace nodded. Lucy placed an arm around her shoulders.

'Mum won't be too long, I'm sure. Grace thinks it's the old man from the hotel.'

Well, that may save us a walk, thought Alistair. 'You've seen him, Grace?'

'Flashes of white hair, that's all.'

'How long since you spotted this?'

'When we were up on the moors.'

Alistair nearly screamed with frustration. 'Why didn't you say something before?'

'All right, keep your hair on.'

'Grace,' Lucy chided. 'That's low.'

'Sorry, Hobo. Look, I thought I was probably imagining it. But this time when I checked behind us, Lucy saw him too.'

'I saw *something*,' Lucy confirmed.

The three of them stood there, watching for any movement. There was nothing. When Lucy's phone beeped it startled them all.

'Mum's on her way.'

'Let's head along to the green, then,' Alistair said. 'At least there we can grab a bite to eat while we keep watch and wait.'

They moved off again, slowly. Each of them peered over their shoulder every few steps, but no stalker was evident. Alistair began to think maybe it was Grace's fevered imagination after all.

With the two girls still trailing some paces behind, Alistair entered the village green without any further sign of them being followed. The old telephone box greeted him, like a bright red beacon. Alistair knew it only contained tourist information now, not a payphone. Plenty had changed about Bledoe since he was a boy, but not much had changed since he'd last been there. The adjacent post box was still in use, which was a relief since the village had lost its post office back in the purge of the 1990s.

The lichgate by the parish church graveyard was the same ornate iron replacement he'd seen plenty of times since the 1970s, although he was thrilled to see it now threaded with roses. Through the gate walked a familiar figure, albeit somewhat more bent now with age and requiring the use of a walking stick. Edwin Stone, the village Pastor, as was his father before him. He was still clinging to his calling long after retirement age.

Alistair lazily assumed Edwin was headed for the rectory before recalling that the rectory was now *The Old Rectory*, a tea shop. It was closed. Edwin hobbled past, with a chirpy acknowledgment to the three of them.

'Is everyone here ancient?' Lucy asked.

Alistair nodded and pursed his lips. 'It does look that way, yes.'

He could see Tuck Shop Thompson's old family shop, latterly owned by the Vines, just off the square. This was now *Bledoe Gifts*. He recalled Doris looking in there once, for a gift for a friend. *Full of tin-mine tat and Cornish Fairings*, was her assessment. He grinned at the memory.

'We eating then, or what?' Grace asked, dragging Alistair out of his reverie.

He indicated a nearby bench and they seated themselves.

'Still wanna keep watch, though,' Grace continued.

Alistair opened the packet of mini pork pies he had and handed them around. The three of them then spun on the spot to make sure they had all the approaches covered.

Alistair found himself looking back the way they'd come. The football match must have finished as there were a number of people heading their way from the sports ground. No doubt off to *The Rose & Crown* for celebrations or commiserations. If anyone had been following them it would be easier for them to blend in now.

He heard a muted yelp from Lucy, who was seated behind him facing the wrong way, her legs threaded through under the back of the bench. Alistair turned to see what the matter was. Grace turned, also.

'Sorry,' Lucy said. 'Took me by surprise, that's all. I wonder who did it?'

She pointed to the small brass plaque on the back of the bench, and Alistair's earlier thoughts about dedications came back to bite him.

In memory of Brigadier Sir Alistair Lethbridge-Stewart,
former local resident. Family man, friend and hero.
22nd February 1929-16th December 2011

His actual date of death!

Lucy photographed it with her phone. 'Gonna WhatsApp this to Con and Gordon straight away.'

Grace frowned. 'Lethbridge-Stewart. I know that name from somewhere.'

'My family,' said Lucy with pride. 'And this was my grandad.'

'Cool!'

Just then the honk of a horn told them that Tamara had arrived. Lucy looked at Alistair.

'Are we staying?' she whispered.

Alistair nodded numbly, still grasping the reality of knowing when he was going to die.

Tamara pulled up. Grace quickly claimed the front seat, looking smug. When Alistair and Lucy didn't move, Tamara lowered the passenger window and called through.

'What's up?'

Lucy indicated where they'd been sitting. 'This bench is dedicated to Grandad!'

'How special. Take a photograph and we'll show your dad. Come on, then, get in.'

Lucy shook her head. 'We're gonna stick around for a bit longer, got a few more things to do.'

Grace looked dismayed. 'Oh, great. So, it's just me and your mum?'

'You said you wanted to go home.'

'Yeah, but, that's cos...' Grace stalled. She was clearly not wholly convinced that they had been followed after all.

'Cos what, love?' Tamara asked.

'Nothing, sorry.'

'Why don't I park up somewhere and we can wait for you, Luce?' Tamara suggested.

That was the last thing they needed. Alistair wasn't sure what Tamara knew, but if Anne fulfilled her promise properly, then she'd not know anything. Which meant he couldn't have her being involved now.

'It'll be really boring for you, Mrs Wilson, I'm sure,' he said.

'I can have a look around the place,' Tamara said. 'I've not been here since your grandad's funeral.'

Lucy looked at Alistair, somewhat aghast.

'Mum! Don't be so... morbid.'

Alistair couldn't help but smile. Did that mean he was buried alongside his mother and brother? For some reason that filled him with a strange sense of calm.

'Besides,' Lucy continued, 'Grace got a bit freaked out by some old boy having, like, an epileptic fit earlier. She needs home comforts. We'll give you a call when we're done.'

Tamara turned to Grace. 'You poor thing. Do you want home comforts, or a browse in that large Matalan not far from here? Your mum did say retail therapy, after

110

all. I was gonna take Lucy, but since she's being so single-minded I'll buy you something nice instead.'

'Hey!'

But Lucy's protest fell on deaf ears. Tamara gave a wave and raised the window. As the car pulled away, Alistair saw Grace press her face and hands to the window and stare back at them, looking horrified.

'What was that all about?' Alistair asked.

Lucy's phone beeped. She looked at the screen, then looked behind her.

'Ahh. Grandad, I think Grace spotted the person who's been following us.'

Alistair turned to find a wispy-haired old man behind them, riding a mobility scooter.

'Yes,' the old man said with a nod. 'I thought it was you two. Although how, I don't suppose I'll ever know.'

Lucy was the first to find her voice. 'You know us?'

'That I do. Lucy Wilson and Hobo the Hairless Wonder.'

Alistair realised it was one of the old Bledoe Cadets before him. 'As I live and breathe, it's Smiffy Gloyne!'

The old man nodded again. 'And I've not seen you two since May 1st, 1937.'

Lucy looked at Alistair. He raised his hairless brows.

'You two haven't aged a day. You even have the same clothes.'

'You remember us that clearly?' Lucy asked.

'And so I should.' Smiffy suddenly looked incredibly distant and sad. 'That was the day Nobby Clarke died. The day I went mad.'

Alistair had been reacquainted with Smiffy back in 1970, and although he tended to keep himself to himself, Alistair had seen him around Bledoe on his visits over the years. But the sight of him now, mid-way into his nineties, so soon after seeing him as a virile youth still came as quite a shock. If Smiffy had indeed followed them down off the moors, it was almost certainly because he thought he recognised the children. Although Alistair could tell that Lucy didn't completely believe him, she had agreed to send Grace a reassuring reply to her text, telling her that the old man was a friend of her grandad's and they were all right.

But what was this about Nobby Clarke? Dead? And on the same day that Alistair had been there; the same day that Lucy and he had popped up in the circle.

Another death he'd forgotten about. Alistair wondered how many more deaths may have been concealed from him in the frazzled mess of his memory.

Lucy and he had followed Smiffy, at his insistence, from the village green and along to his home.

Alistair stood gazing at the tumbledown wreck before him; all that remained of Smiffy's forge. The years had clearly not been generous to the building; like a pumpkin left outside from Hallowe'en until Christmas, the structure had started to sag and lean, and bits were missing at the edges. It sat between two pristine neighbours who probably wondered who would go first: Smiffy or the house.

The forecourt, where Smiffy and the generations before him plied their trade, was full of junk. Alistair was unable to hide his sense of regret; the canopy roof above was now rotten and had fallen through in places. There was a makeshift ramp covering the small step to the front door, which was open.

'I won't invite you in,' said Smiffy. 'The place needs a bit of a tidy.'

Alistair smiled at the polite understatement, but it was lost on Lucy.

'Where's social services?' she asked under her breath, with a frown.

Smiffy hurled a small dead animal – presumably a

rabbit or a pheasant – through his doorway. 'Something for the pot,' he said with a wink and a chuckle. 'Old habits die hard.'

'I don't trust him.'

Alistair looked at Lucy. 'He's an old friend.'

'Can you always trust old friends?'

He looked away. Unfortunately, she had a point.

Lucy continued. 'And he said he was mad.'

'In my experience, mad men do not know they're mad. Poor Smiffy here… Well, it sounds to me like a self-diagnosis based on the unfortunate opinions of others. He's always been a little moody, a little socially awkward, prone to random emotional outbursts, perhaps. But not insane.' Alistair paused. 'Poor bloke, his mother died when he was young. I don't remember why. His father had no love in him, except for alcohol. If anything, the fact that Smiffy's still alive at his age is testament to his amazing spirit.'

'What about what Grace said? If he's possessed or calling himself the Traveller, that could be perceived as madness.'

'We'll have to find out.'

Smiffy manoeuvred his way back off the forecourt. Alistair wasn't sure the old man hadn't heard Lucy's comments when he spoke.

'Where's that other girl, then?'

'She went home. Didn't you see her go off in the car? You scared her.'

'Good. Didn't recognise her. Don't trust folk I don't know.'

'Do you trust us?' Lucy asked.

'I think I know what you are.'

Alistair took a deep breath. 'Smiffy…'

But Smiffy trundled past them and onwards.

'Where are you going?' Alistair called.

'River,' the old man answered. 'Nicer there. Better

113

place to die.'

Alistair looked at Lucy. 'What did he just say?'

The two of them followed Smiffy through one of the newer housing estates.

'This all used to be farmland,' Alistair told Lucy, but her mind was elsewhere.

'Grandad, I don't like this. He's calling the shots and we're following blindly. He could be leading us into a trap.'

'I don't know. He thinks he's going to die.'

They paused. Ahead, Smiffy had stopped at the side of the river, like he was poised, waiting for something.

'Ohmagod, is he going to jump?'

'It's barely a foot deep here,' Alistair said dismissively. 'At least it used to be, at this time of the year. More like a stream. Gets deeper in winter.' He placed a cautious hand on Lucy's shoulder. 'If anything goes wrong, we have your ring.'

'Yeah, but we don't want to travel through time... Oh.'

Alistair watched the realisation as it dawned on Lucy's face.

'May 1st, 1937, Smiffy said. Wasn't that the date you mentioned earlier? And wearing these clothes.'

'Exactly. Let's see what Smiffy can tell us first.'

They joined Smiffy on the paved riverside promenade, with its benches, floral baskets and fenced barrier. Alistair figured that the stylish landscaping must have been part of the residential development. He watched the shallow river trickling along beneath them. It felt like a conveyor belt, floating childhood memories past him; innocent times spent splashing about, building rafts with Raymond, Jemima and the other Bledoe Cadets in the winter months when the flow swelled.

The lower farmlands would flood. Cattle would come

down to the river to drink, and often the Cadets had to rescue a careless calf or sheep that had trodden too far and got stuck. There was also that time Henry's raft got caught up in a sudden rush of current and they found him half a mile downstream, beached up the muddy river bank among the shattered remains of his raft, laughing like there was no tomorrow. Happy times. Innocent times. But by then James had gone. And the war was on. And then his father… Maybe not such happy times after all.

'Beautiful, isn't it?' The ancient voice dragged Alistair back to the here and now.

He looked at Smiffy, parked next to a bench. 'Any more of the old Bledoe Cadets still about the village?'

'A few,' the old man replied. 'Ray's still over at Redrose, Ed Stone is still clinging to his faith, Jason Starling has passed his practice onto his daughter… None as was around the day you were, though.'

Alistair was about to correct Smiffy, but fortunately remembered he was in Hobo's body. Still, he was happy to hear that Ray was still around enjoying his late in life marraige.

'So, Smiffy,' Lucy began. 'That day in 1937…'

They heard a sniffle. Smiffy's shoulders were heaving.

'I'm sorry, I…' Lucy looked at Alistair, lost for words.

'Why haven't you aged?' the old man asked through his tears. 'Why haven't you changed at all? And why have you come to me now? Is this it? Is my time up at last? Do you always appear when a Bledoe Cadet is about to die? You were there for Nobby. Did you come back for Henry? For Terry? For Alistair?'

'Smiffy!' Alistair's retort was harsher than he intended. He amended his tone. 'Smiffy, calm yourself. I can't explain why we appear to be exactly the same now as we were in 1937, but I can assure you we're not any kind of Grim Reaper. You'll just have to accept us as we

115

are. Can you do that?'

The old man blew his nose. That appeared to be all the confirmation they were going to get.

'We've been up Redgate Smithy this morning,' Lucy told him.

'I know, girl. Seen you, didn't I?'

'Some of the stones looked like they'd been damaged by fire years ago. We've been investigating —'

'You know what happened. You were there.'

'What, May 1st, 1937?' Lucy looked at Alistair, who nodded.

'The thing in the sky, the buzzing in the ground, the fireball, the strangers – you!'

Thing in the sky...

Alistair's mind turned to the story he'd seen on Hobo's phone. The asteroid.

The old man suddenly roared. 'Told enough people, enough times! Said I was mad, seeing things; not right in the head. Wouldn't let me fight in the war. Labelled. Unstable. Stuck here with a drunken sot of a father. No woman would have me.' He paused in his charged reflections. His extended bottom lip quivered. 'Loved playing football, you know? Wanted to play proper. Couldn't play at all after the fire... After the fire.' The river glistened, reflected in the tears that rolled down Smiffy's cheeks.

Alistair placed a comforting arm around Lucy's shoulders. 'Sorry, Smiffy.'

'Ohmagod. Look at him. Did we do that? Grandad, are we responsible for Smiffy's problems?'

Alistair led her a few paces away. 'I can't say, Lucy. I'd hope not, and again this sounds like a perception problem. He's seen or experienced things that his mind has struggled to comprehend, and others have abused that.'

'Then we need to find out more, make sure that when

116

we go back to 1937 we do the right thing, make it better for him.'

'No, it doesn't work that way. We can't know too much.' Alistair was reminded of something he'd once been told. *You never did understand the interrelation of time.* It was true back then, but he'd seen a lot since. Lucy's expression showed him she hadn't. 'Another interpretation of the Blinovitch Limitation Effect. Once you become a part of events... Haven't you used the ring yet?'

'Not properly,' she admitted.

Alistair nodded slowly. 'Then listen. If we knew exactly what was going to happen when we travelled back through time, we'd end up trying to craft or manipulate events so that they happen our way when perhaps they shouldn't. It's better to travel without any preconceptions and just allow things to take their natural course.'

'But you were there, you've already lived through it. Doesn't that also count?'

He rubbed his hand over his mouth. 'Not in the same way, no. Besides, my childhood memories are pretty shot to pieces, even now. I was stuck in my eight-year-old self only the other day and I didn't have a clue what was going on.'

'Okay, but...' Lucy looked over Alistair's shoulder. Smiffy had gone.

Alistair turned with a frustrated growl. 'I never asked him about the Traveller.'

Alistair and Lucy had a chocolate bar each as they strode back to Smiffy's forge. He wasn't there, but then Alistair hadn't expected him to be. The nonagenarian was a loose cannon and a law unto himself, it seemed. Lucy was clearly struggling with feelings of guilt from what Smiffy had said, balanced against her lack of trust in the old man.

'Shouldn't we try the hotel?' she suggested.

'Why would he be there, though? That's a fair old jaunt from here.'

'Not when you have a mobility scooter. It's where Grace met him.'

'Possibly met him. I'm not wholly sold on that, yet.'

'All right, but we know he was up on the moors; he followed us down.'

Alistair wasn't convinced, but aside from trawling the whole of Bledoe it was the only lead they had.

Sometime later the two of them were approaching the forecourt to the Redgate Smithy B&B. There were a number of mobility scooters parked outside the main entrance, any or none of which could be Smiffy's. They walked through the large doors. It was very quiet inside and smelled of pine cleaning products.

'Can I help you?' asked the receptionist.

Lucy nudged Alistair forward.

'Hello, yes. We believe you had a guest, or a visitor taken ill here, this morning.'

'Yes.'

'Can you tell us his name, please?'

'Not without compromising visitor confidentiality. Are you relatives?'

'Yes, we are.'

'Then you'll already know his name, won't you?'

Alistair cursed internally. She'd made a prize fool of him. 'His name is Raymond Gloyne.'

The receptionist shook her head. 'Nope, sorry.'

'Who's Gee Saint John Mills?' asked Lucy, very obviously reading the guest signing-in book upside-down.

'*Sin-jun* Mills,' Alistair corrected her.

The receptionist deftly closed the guest book.

Lucy smiled at her. 'What we're really after, miss, is

someone known only as the Traveller.'

'Ooh.' The receptionist chuckled. 'The Traveller, is it? Very enigmatic.'

Lucy nodded. 'Anyone staying here under that pseudonym? If so, can you tell him that the Bledoe Cadets want to speak with him, please?' She winked at the receptionist and tapped the side of her nose. It didn't work.

The receptionist looked at them both, stonily.

'Do I have to get one of the porters to come and show you two out?'

'Can we have a quick look around, first?'

'Out! Now!'

Sometime later, Alistair and Lucy were back in the stone circle, sitting on the altar stone, staring at the black rock embedded in the moorland beneath them. Lucy was thinking aloud.

'This has gone so far beyond researching burn marks on old stones. We've got death, personality disorders, a potential alien encounter to look forward to. What do we do next, Grandad?'

Alistair was about to speak when Lucy's phone beeped. It was a text from Grace. The network signal was intermittent at best, so it may have been sent a while ago. Lucy read the message and raised her eyebrows.

'Wow. Grace has been doing some online research at home for me. She's also got a top from Matalan that totally rocks, thanks, *Mum*. But listen to this: *found old local newspaper article in online library. Fire in the stone circle, night of May 1st, 1937. People died.* Cool! I mean, obviously not cool, but… you know.'

Alistair let out a hmm, and pulled out Hobo's phone. He tried to bring up the news article which had interested him during yesterday's journey to Liskeard. He had to stand up on the stone and reach at full stretch to get a signal.

'To infinity and beyond!' said Lucy with a chuckle.

Alistair smiled and rolled his eyes as he sat back down. 'Right, listen to this. *Huge flying rock, first spotted 1936 on its last approach…*' He pointed at the screen. '1936. This registered when I read it yesterday; too close to the temporal location of my last jump. And now what Smiffy said about the thing in the sky…' He returned his attention to the phone. '*…recently been mapping the asteroid's path further on its 81-year journey.* But when did it actually pass by? Suppose the article is wrong, and it was 1937 instead…? Plus eighty-one makes it 2018.'

'Obviously didn't land in 1937.' Lucy waved her arms in a wide gesture. 'No huge crater here, humans not killed off like the dinosaurs, you know, stuff like that, bit of a giveaway.'

'Yes, thank you, Lucyloo. We know it didn't land, as it's due to come around again this year, remember?' Alistair beckoned her to follow him out of the stone circle. 'But meteorites, the bits that break off from comets and asteroids, do often land.'

'You mean that black rock there?' Lucy pointed at the rock poking out of the moorland by the base of the altar stone. 'The one you said wasn't there in 1937.'

'Very likely.' Alistair waved the phone around.

'What are you trying to do?'

'I want to look up the date that the asteroid last passed by. 1936, or 1937…?'

Beyond the circle their network signal improved a bit. Lucy replied to Grace and asked her if she could search out any articles about the asteroid from years ago.

Alistair was rather getting the hang of Hobo's smartphone now, and he quickly found what he needed. 'Here we are. *The Times*, Monday April 26th, 1937. Headline: *Asteroid arrives for May Day*. The day after I left 1937.'

Lucy nodded. 'The day after we arrived there, too?' Her face lit up with excitement, tempered with apprehension. 'Time we went back?'

'I think so. The Gnome didn't bring me here to just take a tour of my old stomping grounds.' Alistair smiled reassuringly, and Lucy lifted the chain from her neck. 'How does this ring of yours work, then?'

'Dame Anne said it's linked specifically to Lethbridge-Stewart DNA.'

'Of course it is.' Alistair pursed his lips into a smile. 'Mount Jampa,' he muttered, and then more clearly, 'She always was very clever. Used to belong to her father, you know.'

'He wasn't a Lethbridge-Stewart, though.'

'I know. Like I said, Anne Travers was always very clever.' He looked Lucy in the eyes. 'I've known my end was close for months now, and I asked her to look after your... family.'

Lucy frowned. 'Why? Mum and Dad have almost nothing to do with the Lethbridge-Stewart side of the family.'

'I know.' It was a sore point. He and Albert had never become as close as he'd hoped, and after 2004... Well, the distance just continued to grow. If it wasn't for Tamara and the kids, Alistair felt sure Albert would have ceased contact completely.

He considered his granddaughter. Almost seven years since he'd last seen her, and here she was. Being more of a Lethbridge-Stewart than his son ever could. Alistair wanted to tell her, tell her what he knew, but how could he betray the promise he'd made? Later, he decided. He would tell Lucy later, before he returned home.

'The point is, Anne clearly fixed the ring so you could use it, and only you. Not even she can use it, I expect.'

Lucy nodded. 'Or another Lethbridge-Stewart?'

121

Alistair smiled, glad to see they were thinking the same thing. 'So, what do you do to make it work?'

'You just think of the place and the time where you want to be, and shazam, you're there.'

'Shazam. A real marvel, eh? Well, I know the time and place. But… it won't work for me, since this is Hobo's body, his DNA.'

'It won't work for Hobo, no. But that is you in there now, Grandad, so… I don't know, it might be enough to confuse it.'

'Only one way to find out, and we know that you and Hobo end up there…' He held out a hand, and Lucy removed the ring from the chain.

Alistair looked at it for a moment, then placed it on his finger. It was a little too big. No wonder Lucy kept it safe around her neck.

'Ready?' he asked.

Lucy smiled and nodded. 'Ready.'

He offered his hand, and Lucy took it. With a smile, he closed his eyes and thought of 1937.

CHAPTER EIGHT
Strangers When We Meet

THEY WERE STANDING IN EXACTLY THE SAME SPOT AS they had been in 2018, although 1937 was currently cloudier, just as it had been yesterday. Which was today…

Time travel, although not completely uncommon to Alistair, was never something he'd truly get his head around.

It never occurred to him before, but with the sudden shift of eighty-one years, he realised the air was different as well. It smelled… sweeter. Not purely the reserve of childhood remembrances, after all. He was also struck by the sudden change in background noise. Even though Redgate Smithy was only surrounded by relatively small rural villages, the sound of distant road traffic had still been almost constant in 2018. Here all was quiet, as if someone had flicked a switch.

Lucy wore an exhilarated grin. 'All right?'

He nodded his response, unwilling yet to trust his voice.

'Shall I take the ring back, for safe-keeping?'

Still without a word, he slipped the Kontron crystal ring from his finger and returned it to Lucy, who threaded it back onto the chain around her neck. She headed immediately to examine the standing stones.

No time travel shock from her. Alistair smiled. Lucy was a natural at this, and a sudden sense of pride welled up in him.

'None of that burnt mottling,' Lucy called over her shoulder.

Alistair took a quick look to either side. 'More stones than in 2018, too, of course.'

'The smugglers?'

He nodded and approached the nearest obvious fake, prodding and poking at its egg box-like shell. 'Look at this. One good downpour and they'll start to dissolve.'

Lucy joined him. 'I guess it's easier for the police to leave them up here and let them rot. It's not National Trust or anything.' She squatted down to check the hatch area. 'Ewww. Yep, no goods here, just the ballast.'

'No brandy or chocolates for us then.' As he said this, Alistair had a sudden sense of *deja vu*.

'Too late, mate,' said a voice a little way behind him. 'Coppers cleared all that out earlier.'

Lucy stood. Even though Alistair had already experienced this moment, seeing it through a pair of different eyes left him momentarily disassociated. He turned around slowly.

Yet again, he had the strangest sensation that he was standing in two places at once. He was there, looking through the eyes of Hobo, and he was also *there*, in the body of his child-self. He could feel his brother's protective hand on his shoulder in both places.

His young-self's hand reached out as if to touch him. *No*, Alistair thought, *not again*.

And then, like the stretch and snap of elastic, the feeling was gone. He was Hobo and young Alistair Lethbridge-Stewart was simply one of the faces staring with suspicion at him and Lucy.

'We're nothing to do with the smugglers, if that's what you're thinking,' Alistair said hastily, as he and Lucy felt themselves herded towards the altar stone. The Bledoe Cadets and their hangers-on surrounded them. In Hobo's body he was slightly taller than James, which

124

was more of a shock to him than the time travel. 'Neither are we Willie Blackmore's sheep,' he added, looking his brother in the eye but being careful not to appear confrontational.

The familiar name of the farmer made James pause. He looked the two strangers up and down.

'You're a bit too closely sheered, if you are.' There were a few chuckles. 'Why haven't you got any hair?'

Alistair took a deep breath. 'It's called alopecia.'

There were mutterings within the group.

'Hello what?'

'Alo-pecia. It's a condition. It means I'm completely hairless.' He rolled up a sleeve to show off a smooth arm as well. Some of the children backed away. 'It's not catching or anything.' He tried to sound reassuring.

Lucy gave a tiny squeal and Alistair figured she'd just picked his young-self out of the group. He looked from James to little Ali. He was able to check him over properly from the outside this time. His eight-year-old self, only recently released from inside one of the fake stones behind them, was fresh-faced and rosy-cheeked; his hair a mess and his body seemingly full of boundless energy. Unsullied, unspoilt, his whole life ahead of him. Full of possibilities, full of potential; just waiting – quite literally – to take on the world.

Should he avoid all physical contact with his young-self? Did the Blinovitch Limitation Effect matter when it was only your mind in the other body?

The ringing of approaching bicycle bells broke the moment. As the locals turned to see who was riding towards the circle, Sir Alistair motioned to Lucy and the two of them squatted down, using the altar stone for balance.

'Right. We're here to witness what goes on in the circle, but Grace said it happened late, so I say we go along with whatever the Bledoe Cadets are doing for

125

now, agreed?'

Lucy nodded. 'The Bledoe Cadets, your old gang, eh?'

'Yes, although my other self is too young to join at the moment, so officially I'm not supposed to be here today. We know from Smiffy that the Cadets are involved somehow. Or at least Smiffy is, anyway.'

'Yes, I think I recognised Smiffy. And your brother. Which one's Nobby Clarke?'

Sir Alistair paused, listening as others started to speak. 'I think he's just turned up,' he said.

They tentatively stood to see what was going on.

Nobby and a very puffed-out Tuck Shop had ridden into the circle, right up to the wall of Bledoe Cadets.

'I say,' Nobby said between breaths. 'Didn't you chaps hear me calling? I see you're all right, after all. Thank heavens!'

He was met with stony silence.

Nobby continued, regardless. 'We were keeping a watch from over there.' He indicated a vague direction. Sir Alistair was very doubtful of the truth of the claim. In fact, no one appeared to give it any credence whatsoever. Nobby visibly gulped, then looked to get some back-up from his accomplice. 'Weren't we, eh, Tuck Shop? Tell them.'

Tuck Shop nodded. He was sucking on a sweet between gulped breaths.

Nobby looked for support along the whole line of the Cadets, even little Ali, but his main focus was James. There was a long, awkward moment before James finally spoke.

'You both got away on your bikes.'

'Yes, we—'

'And hid?'

'Err, yes, and—'

'Did neither of you think you should try to get help for those of us left behind? Or call the police?'

Nobby huffed and harrumphed before looking at Tuck Shop and inclining his head. 'Go on, Thompson, tell him our plan, tell him what we did.'

Tuck Shop wiped his mouth on his coat sleeve and nervously explained how they'd intercepted Janet and Nancy as the girls had cycled off and instructed them to get help, while he and Nobby stayed where they were as cavalry backup in case they were needed.

This brought much sniggering from the group.

Lucy tugged on Alistair's sleeve. The meaning of her look was obvious; she didn't believe them. Neither did he.

It was strange watching the interaction of the Cadets. For him it'd been well over twenty-four hours since the police had left, since Nobby and Tuck Shop had scarpered. But for the Bledoe Cadets... little over an hour had passed. It was like pausing a DVD in the middle of an exciting scene, then coming back to it late the following day.

James circled the two Cadets. 'And just when were the cavalry going to sweep in and help us out, eh?' He leaned forward intimidatingly. Neither Nobby nor Tuck Shop would look his way. 'While we were being chased by slavering dogs, perhaps? Thrown from the tops of the stones, perhaps? Threatened with knives?'

'We couldn't see any of that from where we were,' said Nobby, frustration edging into his voice.

'Of course you couldn't!' Nearly everyone jumped at James' sudden yell. 'You were hiding! You're a coward, Clarke. A filthy coward. You too, Terry. You ran away and let us all down. You don't belong in the Bledoe Cadets.'

'Just because your little brother was—'

'No!' James shouted, shutting Nobby down. 'Don't you dare bring him into this.'

Little Ali backed away behind the others, as he always

did when faced with confrontation.

James continued. 'This isn't about family. It's about honesty, duty and doing the right thing by everyone. It's about what the Bledoe Cadets stand for.'

Before Alistair realised, his younger self had walked back into him. Physical contact. His insides churned momentarily, but the world didn't explode. It was all right. He relaxed.

Little Ali looked up at him. He ruffled the young boy's hair and offered him a reassuring smile.

'Sorry, baldy,' said little Ali.

Sir Alistair's smile dropped.

Smiffy called out, 'Smack 'im, James.'

Nobby scowled but James shook his head. 'He's not worth the effort.'

Jemima clearly tried to whisper, 'I would,' but failed to actually whisper it. She appeared shocked at her own clumsiness, and there was a ripple of amusement among the boys.

Lucy smiled at Jemima and nodded her agreement.

'Since you're not a Bledoe Cadet, Jemima Fleming,' James said, looking her way, 'I have no jurisdiction over what you do.' He turned back to Nobby but kept addressing Jemima. 'But I'll tell you this much, you've been ten times the Cadet today than Clarke has. Shame you're too young.'

'And a girl,' Henry added.

Alistair wished he hadn't. He felt Lucy tense up next to him. A girl from 2018 being confronted by the sexism of the 1930s…? It was never going to end well.

'Oi. What's wrong with being a girl?'

The line of Cadets parted, suddenly exposing Alistair and Lucy. It was almost as if they'd been forgotten. The anger and suspicion that had originally been aimed their way, which had been displaced by the arrival of Nobby and Tuck Shop, was now returned to them.

Henry didn't answer Lucy's challenge. Instead he gave one of his own.

'Funny-looking pair, aren't they? What exactly are you doing here?'

'We're on holiday,' Lucy told him.

'From where? Africa?' Nobby asked, scoffing.

'Hey! Mind your manners, Clarke,' James spat in response, and Alistair glowed with pride. As James turned back to the two apparent strangers, Nobby waved his hand in a dismissive manner.

You'll get yours, thought Alistair. Then he remembered what old Smiffy had said about the fire and felt awful.

'We're from Wales, Ogmore-by-Sea,' Lucy said.

'You don't sound Welsh.'

'I'm not. I was born in London. I'm Lucy Wilson. This is Hobo.'

Alistair gave a small wave.

'Lucy. That's not a darkie name,' muttered Nobby.

'It's a British name. I'm British, born in London to a *British* family. What's the matter, you think I should be working on your plantation somewhere? Who shoved a plum up your butt and made you Lord of the Manor?'

'She's got you nailed there, Nobbo,' said Smiffy, with a raucous chuckle. He was at the side of the group, doing some keepy-uppies with his football.

'Is that how girls dress in London, then? Or Wales?' Raymond asked. He was particularly staring at Lucy's trousers. 'Don't dress like that around here.'

'We just happen to be a little more *modern* than most.'

Smiffy lost control of the ball and ended up volleying it in Sir Alistair's direction. Although a rugger man for much of his life, he knew how to handle a football. He took the approaching ball, controlled it smoothly and volleyed it back. The group dynamic immediately shifted again, as if Alistair had undertaken a rite of passage. Immediately Smiffy, Henry, Raymond and James spread themselves out within the circle and started to volley the football between each other.

'Oi, Hobo,' Smiffy called out to Alistair. 'You joining in then, or what?'

Alistair didn't have to be asked twice. He couldn't believe it. Here he was, looking like a complete stranger, having a kick around with his brother and his brother's mates, while his younger self and his granddaughter looked on.

The bonding power of the so-called beautiful game.

Little Ali sat on the central stone and tried to gather his thoughts. He was glad that he hadn't been whisked off home to his mother's arms and mollycoddled. The shock might have hit him more heavily, then. There was no denying it had been a whirlwind afternoon so far, and his involvement had largely been his own fault. But if this was what life was like as a Bledoe Cadet, then maybe he shouldn't be too eager to join up, after all? He told himself that was rubbish, of course he still wanted to join. If only they'd let him.

The smugglers and the police had been excitement enough, but then immediately afterwards these two strange-looking older children had appeared as if from nowhere, and now the bald one was off playing football. Ali thought the girl had been a boy at first, but it was just that she was wearing trousers. She was coloured and had huge hair. There was no one like her where they lived. The girl grinned at him and he found himself smiling back automatically. There was something about her that he decided he liked; something that made him feel special.

Ali was about to start talking to her when Jemima sat in between them and took the new girl's attention away.

He decided he'd leave them to it. *But Jemima had better not be pretending she's a Bledoe Cadet*, he thought. Tuck

130

Shop was still standing around, holding up his bicycle, like a spare part. Ali went over to him and asked for a sweet.

Jemima had never seen a girl like this one before. What had she said her name was? Lucy something. She was smiling at James' annoying little brother. Jemima wasn't having that; she wanted the new girl for herself. Before little Ali could start up a conversation, she plonked herself on the stone between them.

'Hello. Did you say your name's Lucy? I'm Jemima, Jemima Fleming.'

Lucy grinned at her. Jemima took in her wide, intelligent eyes and that wonderful smile that seemed to shine with its own light.

'Hi, Jemima. Not many girls in the group, I see.'

'My two friends ran away earlier when the smugglers came after us.'

'Yeah, I heard. But you stuck around and showed them that girls are as tough as boys. Nice one.'

Jemima felt her cheeks redden and stuttered out an acceptance. 'Can I touch your hair?' she asked, suddenly.

Lucy smiled again, pulled her woolly hat off and leaned forward. Jemima touched the black, wiry hair. It was springy, and she realised she'd expected it to be more solid than it was.

'Not many people of colour live around here, then?' Lucy asked.

'None at all.'

Lucy sat back upright. 'Does that make me cool and unique, then?'

Jemima was crestfallen. 'I don't know what those things are. I'm only eight. Nearly nine.'

'Bless. Well I'm nearly thirteen. And don't worry, there's nothing "only" about being eight. I can tell you, honestly, I *am* cool and unique. So is Hobo over there.

131

And you know what else? I reckon you probably are, too, Jemima Fleming. You were the only girl who stuck around to face the smugglers.'

She felt amazingly pleased with herself at this. Lucy continued.

'So, what do you lot *do* in Bledoe, then? D'you just hang out and stuff, yeah? Cos, like, you haven't got TV or anything, yet, have you? So, I mean, do you just gather by a candle and read books in the evenings, or – hey, you've got radio, yeah? Is it candles, or do you have electricity? Oh, man, have you got an outside toilet? I heard all old houses used to have outside toilets. What's with that? What happens at night or when it's snowing? Do you end up, just, like, having a wee out of the window?'

Lucy finished with such an odd look of disgust mixed with confusion, that Jemima could do nothing but laugh madly at her.

Little Ali walked past and sat back on the stone. He was chewing on a sweet from Tuck Shop.

'Why do you wear trousers?' Jemima asked Lucy.

Lucy smiled again. 'What is it with you lot and these trousers, eh? They're comfortable, and practical and warm, that's why I wear them.'

'I asked my mum if I could wear trousers, once,' Jemima admitted. 'Mum reckons that only *peculiar* girls wear trousers. Are you peculiar?'

Lucy looked at her a bit oddly, and Jemima realised she may have said the wrong thing.

'Peculiar? Do you mean, like, gay or trans or something? It doesn't sound very progressive.'

Gay? Jemima didn't understand why Lucy would think being happy was peculiar, so she decided it was best to leave it and move on. Especially as she didn't know what 'trans' meant.

'Mum said as long as I'm her daughter, I would be a nice girl and wear pretty clothes.'

The clink of glass jars and the sound of Nobby Clarke chuckling curtailed any further conversation between the two girls. They looked up. The public schoolboy was just leaning his rucksack against the end of the stone and looked amused.

Jemima was about to make a comment to Lucy, but the older girl spoke out instead.

'Something funny?'

'Only the hypocrisy of ignorant mothers.' Nobby looked Jemima in the eye. 'Where are your two chums, then?'

Jemima didn't have an immediate answer, but Lucy did.

'Worried they won't support your story, eh, soldier?'

The boy removed his glasses and rolled his eyes dramatically. 'Oh, how tedious. Please sit back and keep your feet up and out of sight. I have a job to finish and you're blocking my light.'

Nobby held up the camera hanging on a strap around his neck and squatted.

'What's he doing, exactly?' Lucy asked Jemima, in between the clicks and the ratchetting of the film being wound on.

Jemima finally found her voice. 'School project, he says. *Daddy*'s paying for an exhibition.'

Nobby was apparently ignoring them, but the angry curve of his mouth showed that he took in every word they said.

Jemima turned to check on little Ali, sat behind her. He smiled at her, but she didn't return it. How much less a boy he was than his brother, and not just in age.

'Hey,' said Lucy, suddenly. 'He was right. The stone's not there.'

Jemima spun back around to find that Lucy was standing on the alter stone and was peering over the edge at the ground all around.

'What stone?' asked Jemima.

Ali stood up and started looking as well, so Jemima did too.

'Small black boulder buried in the ground, should be just here.' Lucy jumped down and indicated the location, startling Nobby.

'Do you mind?' he said, brusquely. Lucy smirked and pretended to ignore him, with a wink at Jemima.

'Never seen a buried rock there,' Jemima said.

'Me neither,' added little Ali.

They then watched as Lucy scraped away at the ground with her hands and muttered to herself.

'Oh! For the love of — Can you *not* do that while I'm working here, *please*?' Nobby groaned.

'Unless it's buried really deep. But then, that much erosion over eighty years? No way. Unless… it *is* part of the…?' Lucy sat back on the ground suddenly, then looked about herself with a self-conscious smile. She wiped her hands on her trousers. Jemima shook her head and laughed.

Yes, this Lucy girl really was something else.

Sir Alistair followed as Smiffy started to dribble the ball towards the Cadets' usual goalmouth. Having just spent time with the blacksmith's son as an old man, it was joyous to see him so young and virile. He was yelling that they should have another Cup Final knockout. This was met with groans from Henry and Raymond and a laugh from James.

As Smiffy approached the goalmouth, however, from the other direction chugged the familiar shape of Farmer Dury's tractor. The vehicle stopped almost exactly where it had pulled up not that long before, although this time the farmer wasn't carrying a squad of policemen. All the children stopped their activities and gathered together for protection inside the circle, waiting to see what would transpire.

Henry called to James. 'Hope he's brought our bikes back.'

Lucy appeared by Alistair's shoulder as he loitered at the rear of the huddle. 'Hey, you were right about that black rock. I scraped at the ground in case it was buried.'

He turned to her. 'I'm not sure if that's a good thing or a bad thing, to be honest. It *must* be part of the asteroid then. Only thing that makes sense.'

'What shall we do next?'

'Let's keep a low profile for now, try not to draw any attention to ourselves, all right?'

'Grandad, we couldn't stick out more here if we tried.'

That was true. 'Okay,' he said, 'just do the best you can.'

He didn't want to tell Lucy about the photograph at the home. Clearly, somehow, they managed to blend in fine. Enough to have their photo taken outside Redrose Cottage, at least.

He pulled a woolly hat from Hobo's backpack, which helped him feel less like a beacon.

Janet Hoyle and Nancy Pardew were the first down from behind the tractor. They eagerly reported to both James and Nobby that, as instructed, they had raised the alarm.

'I called the police,' said Janet. 'They told me they already knew about it and had a squad on its way.'

James looked momentarily confused as he turned to Henry.

'Isn't that what they told you, too?' Henry nodded, and James shrugged.

'And I told Jemima's parents,' Nancy announced proudly.

Jemima's face dropped at this. It dropped even further when she saw her parents dismounting from the trailer.

Lee and Lesley Fleming were furious that she'd strayed so far from home. Rightly or wrongly they blamed the boys for this, not her; that and the fact that she'd been placed in danger with the smugglers. That was unfair, and Alistair wanted to speak out, but Jemima's father wasn't having it any other way. Interestingly, it was Nobby's parents who came to the boys' rescue.

Leonard and Greta Clarke were almost upon the group before Alistair even noticed that they'd been on the trailer too. Nobby sounded exceptionally put-out when he asked them what they were doing there. His father was tall and stout when not seen behind the wheel of a speeding car. He looked and sounded every inch the posh private practitioner that local gossip painted him. He happily announced to the whole group how Lee Fleming had rushed to their house after the alarm had been raised, asking if someone could drive him up to Redgate Smithy, *poste-haste*. (Clearly an affectation; Alistair sincerely doubted Lee Fleming would have used such a phrase.)

'We were the nearest family they could find with a motor car,' Leonard Clarke concluded.

'Three motor cars, in fact,' said Nobby, with a smug grin.

'It does not become us to brag, Graeme,' said his mother.

'Of course, I had to take the Rover,' Leonard continued, clearly of a similar mind to his son. 'We stopped in the lane just as Mr Dury, here, was disgorging a stream of police and some ruffians back to their van. What's that other van down there, by the way? Its rear tyres are flat.'

'Must belong to the smugglers,' James said.

Leonard gave a hearty laugh. 'Top quality felons there, then. Perhaps the judge will hang some sense into them?'

Alistair did not appreciate the sick joke, and he felt Lucy tense up at his side.

Greta quickly took up the story and explained how much she'd tried to reassure Lesley Fleming that Jemima would be perfectly safe as long as their Graeme was present.

Alistair noticed how Greta very specifically called Jemima's mother 'Lesley', in the patronising way that people often talk to infirm elderly relatives. He wondered if anyone else had picked up on this? Jemima's mother hadn't. She smiled back and nodded.

Greta continued, 'And I was right, wasn't I? Graeme and his little Cadets looked after Jemima.' She cuddled up to her son. 'Mummy's special hero.'

A ripple cascaded through the gathered children at Greta's words. They definitely weren't *Graeme's* little Cadets.

'Come on, then,' Greta announced. 'I think it's high time you all went home for tea.' She gestured towards the idling tractor and waved at Farmer Dury.

'Oi, missus,' Smiffy yelled. 'James here's in command, not your twit in tweed.'

There were mutterings of agreement from Henry and Raymond.

Lucy whispered, 'Go for it, Smiffy.'

'Leave it, lads,' said James. 'It's not worth it. Let's just head home, like the lady says.'

But Smiffy wasn't backing down. 'I'll tell you what *mummy's special hero* did. He heroically ran away and hid, sent a couple of young girls off to do what he should have done, then even more heroically popped back after everything was cleared up to see what was left. I may not be the brightest button in the tin, but I sure as hell know what makes a hero, lady.'

'You watch your manners, boy,' Leonard Clarke

137

boomed, striding forward and forcing Smiffy to back away. Alistair saw his young-self squeeze in behind James. 'I'll tell you when you can criticise anything your betters say. When you can afford to wash and change your clothes more than twice a year. When you can write your own name. And when your name actually means something in society.'

Leonard prodded Smiffy sharply in the chest to punctuate each point. The boy staggered further back, eventually colliding with the central stone, his arms windmilling to keep his balance. When he stepped forward again, he pursed his lips and bunched his fist. But James intercepted him, growling 'Leave it, leave it,' into his ear.

Alistair held on to Lucy, knowing that her sense of social justice would have been riled by what she'd witnessed. He felt her pull against his grip.

'Look at us,' he hissed in her ear. 'We step forward now we'll be given even worse than Smiffy. We can't afford to be outcasts.'

Her eyes told him how disappointed she was, but he knew in his heart that he was right.

The Clarkes were showing no sign of leaving. Instead, they stood like stewards, watching everyone file out of the stone circle towards the tractor. Farmer Dury motioned to the Clarkes, but Leonard waved him on.

'We'll walk back to our car. Get some fresh air while we're up here.'

Someone called out from the trailer that the police had already cleared out all the loot. Alistair wasn't certain, but it sounded very much like James. It made him smile.

The Clarkes appeared to ignore the jibe. Nobby presented his father with his bicycle.

'Mr Dury?' Leonard called out. 'Don't suppose you could take Graeme's bicycle, could you? Don't want to spoil the Rover's interior. Perhaps you could drop it by our house? One of the staff will be in.' He held out a ten-shilling note, which the farmer readily accepted. Leonard then looked around to see if anyone was left, and finally noticed Alistair and Lucy.

Alistair hustled Lucy over towards the tractor. 'Come on, quickly.'

'I say, what uncommon curiosities do we have here?'

'Visiting,' Alistair said, without looking at Leonard Clarke. The man hefted up Nobby's bicycle as they hastily clambered aboard the trailer.

'All right, then, that's your lot.' Leonard gave a wave to Farmer Dury. He then made a half-hearted apology to the Flemings for not being able to take them home in the car. Lee thanked Leonard anyway, and Lesley promised Greta she'd bake them a cake and pop it over after church the following day. Greta smiled and nodded, with a little wave, but as she turned away Alistair heard her mutter that the staff could have that.

Horrid people, he thought.

Alistair watched the Clarkes waving to the departing tractor for a good few minutes until they were hidden by the moorland. He turned to Lucy, thoughtfully.

'Interesting that they wanted to remain behind.'

'Fresh air and exercise. It's what the doctor ordered.'

'Yes. Somehow I don't entirely believe him.'

The journey into Bledoe could have been an awkward experience for Sir Alistair and Lucy. They were much more exposed, sitting around the perimeter of the grubby trailer with everyone else. Fortunately, the presence of Lee and Lesley Fleming meant that no one was interested in much beyond their own laps.

They trundled along Fore Street and into the centre of the village. Alistair watched Lucy's wide-eyed wonder as they largely repeated the journey the two of them and

139

Grace had done a little earlier that day – give or take eighty-one years. Farmer Dury eventually parked up outside *The Rose & Crown*.

'Dunno 'bout the rest of 'e, but I'm off for a drink,' the farmer said, dismounting and heading for the pub.

James called out after him. 'What about Nobby's bicycle?'

The farmer turned, holding the ten-shilling note between his thumb and index finger. He grinned, mischievously.

'Said I'd drop it off at their house. Didn't say when, though.'

Smiffy howled with joy. Henry nodded a brisk farewell to all and jumped down also. James handed him his bicycle.

Alistair saw Henry's father, Jonathan, standing at the door to the public bar to welcome them. Word had probably got around about the smugglers by now. The Flemings set about getting themselves off the trailer, along with Jemima, Nancy and Janet and their bicycles. Raymond helped. Tuck Shop clearly felt that now was the best time to make himself scarce too; one moment he was there, the next he'd scarpered.

The others, meanwhile, found themselves drawn to watch Jonathan Barns. He was a sturdy man, typical pub landlord, and with a dry wit which endeared him to many of the village's older residents. But he currently wore a scowl.

'Been a bit of a hero, your 'Enry,' called the farmer as he hobbled to the door.

'I'll be the judge of that, Old Sam.'

The children heard Farmer Dury chuckle raucously as he entered.

Henry leaned his bicycle against the side wall of the pub, and paused before entering himself. Alistair couldn't hear what he said, or his father's reply, but he could read Jonathan's lips: something about being 'too nosy for your own good,' and then the door was shut behind them.

The closing of *The Rose & Crown* door triggered the others into action. They all dismounted to head their separate ways. Alistair picked up Raymond's bicycle to pass it down; as he did so he spotted Nobby's Leica camera. It must have been with the bicycles when they were piled on at the stone circle, and the strap had got entangled on Raymond's derailleur. It was a few minutes work for Alistair to release it. James took it from him and examined it.

'Smart, very nice.'

'Shall I take it? My mum can pop it round tomorrow with the cake.'

This was Jemima, and only then did they notice that she was still there, on the road. Janet and Nancy flanked her.

Smiffy jumped down. 'Thought you'd gone home with your mum and dad, after the effort they went to.'

'Told them I wanted to go home with Janet and Nancy first, thank their mums and dads for helping save my life. Not going to, though.'

James laughed as he jumped down, then reached up and swung little Ali down too. 'So, what are you going to do instead, Jemima Fleming?'

'I want to spend more time with her.' She pointed up to Lucy on the trailer.

Janet and Nancy grumbled that they'd rather have their tea and walked off.

Smiffy grabbed the camera from James and grinned like a lunatic. 'Before this gets returned I reckon we ought to have some fun. Teach Nobby to take more care with his expensive toys.'

They watched as he ran off and took photos of dogs' mess on the pavement, and a dead rat in the gutter.

'James, Raymond,' Smiffy called back from around the corner. 'One of you want to come and photograph my bare bum?'

Alistair almost shook his head in disbelief, but Lucy exploded with laughter. He looked up at her, and before he knew it, he too was laughing.

CHAPTER NINE
Here Today, Gone Tomorrow

THE DAY WAS PUSHING INTO EVENING NOW, BUT WITH the sky clear of cloud there was enough sunlight to keep the streets of Bledoe bright, even as the shadows lengthened. Alistair was starting to feel the effects of a long and active day. Raymond had confiscated Nobby's camera for safe-keeping. He was wheeling little Ali along on his bicycle, to the younger boy's joy. There were the beginnings of a firm bond on display. No wonder he and Raymond had got along so well after James...

He paused in his own thoughts. *Yes, after James.*

Alistair offered an unspoken 'thank you' to the Accord for granting him this opportunity. There was James; his brother. The brother he had completely forgotten for so many years. The brother he had fought against as General Gore, the brother he had seen bleed to death at Eastchester. The brother he had seemingly encountered in so many ways other than that in which he should. And even here, now, they were passing acquaintances yet again. But somehow this time it felt different. It felt... *better.*

Yet still his enjoyment was tinged with guilt. Not because he couldn't reveal his true identity to James. No, the guilt was his and his alone. An irrational guilt. The kind that said it was his own fault that the Intelligence had wiped his memory of James for so long. The moments he was now experiencing were special, but he knew, on reflection, that they could never provide the peace of mind he'd need to forgive himself. That was something he would carry with him to his grave.

After a short while, it struck him that Smiffy had stayed with the group of odd acquaintances, despite the blacksmith's not being far from the pub where they started. Smiffy's mood noticeably swung between playful and morose, the beginnings of the man they had recently encountered in 2018. There was a sense that the others had quickly grown tired of him.

By now James wouldn't get off his bike; Raymond had grabbed little Ali to look after as an excuse. Lucy and Jemima were staying well back and talking between themselves.

Alistair recalled what Smiffy had waiting for him at home; probably by this time on a Saturday a drunken father, little in the way of food, or care and affection, just a beating for having been out with his friends. The least Alistair could do was to try to make the boy's free time a little more bearable, and he needed to do something to perk himself up again, too.

He called across to Smiffy and indicated the football. Having a kick around as they wandered along was definitely Smiffy's medicine of choice and both boys perked up immediately. There was no danger from traffic, since there was no traffic. James even joined in with an occasional volley as he rode around them.

Today had been wonderful for Jemima in so many ways. She'd got some nasty bruised ribs (which hurt more now, but that's because she'd been laughing so much) and there had been real danger with the smugglers. But James had done a lot to protect her and she'd never felt threatened at all. She wondered if maybe she'd be allowed to join the Bledoe Cadets at some point? James had said how much she'd proved herself, after all.

James Lethbridge-Stewart; what a boy he was. None of the others could shine a light on him. Shame his little brother was so annoying, though; and always there, too. Jemima would be trying to walk with James now, back to his home, except for Lucy Wilson.

Lucy was funny, outlandish, full of energy and like no one else she'd met before. She talked back to boys more freely and aggressively than Jemima did. And Jemima had been chastised by her mother often enough for being spiky. *Don't back chat the boys like that*, she'd say, *you'll get a name for yourself and they won't like you.*

'I love these old cottages and the thatched roofs,' Lucy was saying. 'And these street lamps are dead snazzy.'

Like much of what Lucy had said to her so far, Jemima didn't know what this 'dead snazzy' was, but it sounded impressive.

'A man comes along with a stick and lights them when it gets dark enough. If he remembers, anyway.'

'It's all automated where I come from. We take it for granted, which we probably shouldn't do. And there's these tired old multi-coloured stereotypical seaside lights along the side of the big car park facing the sea in Ogmore. Ooh, sea, side, seaside! And it's like faded splendour from the nineteen fif— *Sometime* in the past, and Hobo and I are all like *blurgh*! Come on, get with the tech, it's— Yeah, you know?'

Jemima smiled and shook her head. 'No. Mum wants Dad to save up for a radiogram, if that's what you mean?'

Lucy laughed for the umpteenth time. 'Smart. So, you got any brothers or sisters, then?'

'A sister. Joy, but she's only seven. What about you?'

'I've got two older brothers, me. One lives with his partner in London, one's away at university.'

'Does the one in London own a shop? The one who lives with his business partner? I've heard my dad mention that this is common in bigger towns.'

Lucy didn't answer, she just smiled and stroked Jemima's hair from her eyes. Jemima continued.

'That's why you wear trousers, yes? Hand-me-downs from your brothers?' She peered down at her own fading pinafore dress and red cardigan, the usual attempt by her mother to make her look 'pretty'. One day she'd build up the courage to ask who she was supposed to be looking pretty for.

'Yeah, I guess so. D'you know where we're going?'

'Redrose Cottage, probably. It's where the Lethbridge-Stewarts live. Where are you and Hobo staying?'

'Oh, locally. Not far. You'll get into loads more trouble with your mum and dad for coming here, won't you?'

'Maybe. But life in Bledoe is pretty dull, so it's worth the risk. That's why I escaped up to the moors in the first place. Not like all the mad things you've seen, like tube trains and bendy buses and DBBs and Chinese takeaways.'

'Can't be that bad. Come on, give me an average day in the life of Jemima Fleming. What do you have for breakfast?'

'Toast and jam. And a glass of milk. Sometimes a boiled egg instead.'

'Wild. No Pop Tarts? Shreddies? Probiotic yoghurt?'

Jemima laughed. 'You make these words up, you must do!'

'Ha! So, go on, does your mum make you get dressed before breakfast, or can you bum around in your PJs? What time does school start? I have to be there for ten to nine. I get the bus with Hobo most mornings.'

Jemima burst out laughing again. Lucy came out with such odd phrases and wild ideas. She wondered if this was what it would feel like to have an older sister?

It was clear to all that they'd been taking a meandering

route towards Penhale Meadow and the Lethbridge-Stewart family home. On the final stretch, James put on a burst of speed and cycled ahead.

'Heads up!' Alistair called, and hoofed the ball after his brother.

'Hobo!' Smiffy yelled as the ball bounced right over James and on into the front garden of Redrose Cottage.

'Oops.'

It caught the wall near one of the front windows, which rattled precariously in its frame. The ball bounced off into their mother's flower beds.

There was a moment of horrified silence, then the front door opened, and Mary Lethbridge-Stewart emerged, wiping her hands on her floral pinny.

'Clear off out of it, you lot! You break my windows I'll have your hides, I will!'

'Sorry, Mum,' James said. 'Just got a bit carried away, that's all.'

'James, you monkey! You've been galivanting off up the moors again, getting into trouble. And you, young man.'

She took a faint swipe at little Ali as he nipped in through the gate and fished the ball out of the flower beds. He threw it back to Smiffy who grabbed it, then turned tail and ran off. Mary watched the blacksmith's son go, then she spotted Jemima.

'If you know what's good for you, Jemima Fleming, you'll get yourself home immediately an' all. The worry you've put your poor parents to, today.'

Jemima gave Lucy an apologetic shrug and ran off after Smiffy. They'd both be home in no time at that pace.

Alistair saw Raymond flinch as Mary's gaze in turn rested on him

'Raymond Phillips, have you come for tea?'

His response was almost comical as he realised he wasn't being lambasted. He fumbled his way through an acceptance.

Predictably, Alistair felt Mary looking him and Lucy up and down next. There was deep concern on her face.

'We should go, too,' he whispered. Lucy had other ideas.

'Hello, Mrs Lethbridge-Stewart,' she said. She stepped forward to the gate and offered her hand. 'I'm Lucy Wilson, and this is Hobo.' The hand was not accepted.

'They're here on holiday, Mum,' little Ali said.

'You three.' She pointed at James, Ali and Raymond. 'Inside. Now.'

The front door was slammed shut without further ado. The front window rattled again in its frame.

'Suppose we're going around the back, then,' James muttered.

There was a moment of silence, then Raymond called out, 'Oi, you lot!'

Alistair, Lucy, James and little Ali all turned around and *click*! Raymond had consigned them all to celluloid history.

'Perfect!' Raymond said. 'And still just enough light.'

Alistair felt a wash of wooziness come over him. After all this time, to finally find out exactly how that photograph had come to be.

'Come on, then,' James said. 'We'd better go in. You two around tomorrow, after church?'

'Maybe,' Alistair said, with a vague nod.

'Maybe see you then.'

'Raymond Osbert Phillips!'

They all turned to look up the road. Raymond's parents were standing there.

Osbert? Good grief! Whatever you do, don't laugh, Alistair thought.

'Uh oh,' said James, failing to contain his mirth.

'Shut up, James,' Raymond spat, which only made

James laugh harder. 'Al? Looks like I'm not staying for tea,' he muttered. 'Thank your mum for me anyway.'

He ran off. Lucy released the laughter she'd been holding in. Alistair succumbed to a chuckle as well.

'Osbert?' Lucy said between breaths.

James nodded. 'After his mum's grandfather. At school he insists he doesn't have a middle name. *Hates* it! Anyway, better get in. Maybe see you tomorrow.'

With a wave, James led his little brother around to the back garden.

Alistair watched as they disappeared out of sight, wondering if he'd just seen James for the final time, wondering if he should have said a more meaningful goodbye.

'It looks a lovely cottage,' Lucy said. 'It should be a heritage site in my day.'

Alistair smiled at Lucy's sentiment. 'It was, Lucy, yes. A lovely cottage. A lovely family home. Events just spoiled it for Mother. Too many memories. You get that when you're older. It becomes more difficult to spring back; more appealing to move away and start again somewhere else.'

'Grandad,' said Lucy, gently touching his arm. 'Come on, we need to get back up to the stone circle. It's getting dark already.'

It was, too. Alistair hadn't realised quite how low the sun was until he looked up at the sky. They needed to move. He tried, but something kept pulling him back to the cottage.

'You couldn't have said goodbye any other way.'

He turned and looked at Lucy. She knew what was troubling him. It was probably troubling her too; this was her heritage as well, after all.

'They have to think of us merely as people,' Lucy said. 'They can't suspect otherwise. Although I'll admit, I thought I might get to have tea with my great grandmother first.'

Alistair smiled, and finally found the strength to walk away, slipping a hand into Lucy's.

'I think Mother almost certainly assumed we're gypsies. I recognised the expression on her face: not welcome.'

'But Raymond took the photograph. I'd totally forgotten about it until then.'

Alistair blinked. He'd never shown the photograph to her.

'Like I said, I haven't properly used the time ring before, but I kind of did when I first got it. Took me back to the old home…'

'I think I would have remembered that.'

'It was more of an out-of-body experience.'

'I see. Go on.'

Around them, as they walked, the village had grown silent as the sun set.

'Not long after we moved to Ogmore there was a bit of a… situation. The Great Intelligence saw your legacy in me and tried to set a trap.'

'Yes, I saw something of it in Hobo's memories.' Alistair thought about all his children and grandchildren. 'What have I saddled you with?'

'The most amazing thing ever, Grandad, that's what. And we won. We still win. Because we're Lethbridge-Stewarts and that's what we do.'

Alistair smiled. 'That's my girl,' he said.

'Anyway, I used the ring, and kind of visited you at the home. You didn't see me, and I was only there for a moment or two, but I remember seeing the photo… Never noticed it before.'

Alistair chuckled. 'I've had it for a while, a memento from Ray. It's only recently, as I've seen you grow, that I realised it was you.'

Lucy smiled up at him. 'And now you know who else

is in it.'

'Yes,' he said. 'Yes, I do.'

'Good job we rationed lunch,' Alistair said, as they tramped back across the moors towards the stone circle. 'We'll have the last of it when we get there. I'm starving.'

Lucy laughed next to him. 'Grandad, the lunch Grace's mum sent us off with could have fed us and the Bledoe Cadets combined. It was rationed through necessity; no one can eat that much!'

Their eyes had adjusted to the near-dark conditions, but they had to tread carefully on the uneven ground. There'd been no traffic on the lanes, except the smugglers' van parked up with its flat rear tyres. There were no lights in or around the stone circle, nothing to guide their way except the silhouettes of the tops of some of the stones above the moorland behind. If the Clarkes were still there, if there was anything going on, it was being done in the dark.

'Grace's text didn't give a time for the fire, did it?'

'Don't think so, no.' Lucy produced her phone. '*Fire in the stone circle, night of May 1st, 1937. People died.* That's all it says. And we know from old Smiffy that one of those people is the charming Nobby Clarke.'

'Yes, Smiffy. Presumably he'll show up again at some point, too.' The final word turned into a shocked breath. Alistair hissed, 'Drop!', grabbed Lucy and threw them both to the ground.

'Ow! What's up?'

He pointed ahead. Two figures, adults, were just visible, approaching from the direction of the stone circle. As he and Lucy lay there, the figures strode confidently by. After a few minutes, Alistair risked standing.

'Who was it?' Lucy asked.

He shook his head. 'Didn't recognise them. Too dark.'

'Not Nobby's parents, then?'

151

'No, I'm sure of that. Leonard Clarke has a recognisable silhouette.' He patted his stomach for effect. 'I think we should keep our voices low from now on, though. Sound travels in odd ways across these moors.'

Lucy nodded. 'Come on then, let's see if those two were up to anything suspicious.'

Remaining as silent and inconspicuous as they could manage, Alistair and Lucy carried on along the rough moorland track.

The stone circle appeared to be empty when they arrived. Alistair held Lucy back and they sat watching the area for ten minutes before they risked entering. As they became more exposed to the elements, they both took the opportunity to add some extra layers of clothing from their backpacks. Lucy rather smugly pointed out that it was her idea to bring spare socks and an extra t-shirt.

When they agreed it was safe to proceed, they still crept around the circle cautiously. But it was clear that no one was there, and nothing was going on.

'Not yet, perhaps,' Alistair said. 'But something is going to happen.' He looked up at the dark sky. 'And soon, according to Grace's research.'

Lucy climbed on top of the altar stone and sat. With a shrug, Alistair joined her.

'What next, then, Grandad?'

'What would you suggest? I'm only your scientific advisor, remember?'

'We're gonna have to play the long game, aren't we? Sit it out and wait for things to happen.'

'How about we have some dinner while we wait?'

They both took a packet of crisps, an apple and the last of the mini pork pies. Alistair shook his water bottle. It was almost empty.

'Should have found somewhere to top this up.'

Lucy shook hers. No better.

They looked towards Bledoe. The village was little more than a few distant twinkles on a charcoal backdrop.

'Better not tell Grace's mother we've been eating on her heritage site,' Alistair said with a grin, feeling a bit like a naughty child.

'Can you imagine?' Lucy laughed. 'We shouldn't stay here in the middle, though. It's too exposed.'

He agreed.

'Let's go to opposite sides, keep to the shadows of the stones,' Lucy suggested.

Alistair didn't like them splitting up, but he also knew that he wouldn't like any plan that placed his granddaughter at potential risk. They kept each other in view as far as possible. Deep down, Alistair was certain that Lucy could look after herself. Certainly that was the sense he got from Hobo, buried as he was deep within.

In the dark, seated on the untidy grass, Alistair found it easy enough to be concealed simply by sitting with his back to one of the stones, keeping his legs out straight before him. He could just see Lucy, opposite. She'd done the same. He waved to her.

And now, he thought, *we wait.*

Alistair saw a bright light somewhere in the distance. It was growing larger, getting closer. A tunnel?

Could this be it? The end? Chin up, Alistair, old chap, face it like you always said you would, square on, giving as good as you got –

He reached instinctively for his trusty service revolver. It wasn't there. He tried to look down, to see where it was.

With a jolt his head jerked up and his eyes sprang open.

'All right there, Hobo?'

Bright light shone in his eyes again and he shielded his face with his hand.

'Here he is, James,' the voice called out. 'You fell asleep, you wazzuck.'

Hands gripped his arm and yanked him upright. Boy, was he stiff. There was a strong smell of paraffin. He saw Smiffy, the owner of both the voice and the lamp. Torches were also flashing and shining haphazardly in the pitch blackness. The two of them were joined by a groggy Lucy, who'd clearly also fallen asleep. James was there – and little Ali, too. Both the Lethbridge-Stewart boys held an electric torch each.

'What's going on then, eh?' James gently yet firmly positioned Lucy next to Alistair.

Lucy looked at him, then back at James. 'What d'you mean?'

'Must be up to something, you two. No one comes up here at night unless they're up to something.'

'You came up here.'

'Ali and I watched you from his bedroom window; overlooks the moors. Saw you come up, didn't see you come back down again.'

Lucy glared at James. 'Worried, were you, *Uncle James*?'

James narrowed his eyes, glanced at Alistair. 'Suspicious, more like,' he said. 'Especially after today.'

'Although Mum'll go mad if she finds out we're up here in the dark. Probably tell Dad too.' Little Ali was clearly thrilled to be out on another adventure, yet the paisley pyjamas sticking out from under his coat and trousers were a reminder of where he ought to be.

Alistair looked at his young-self and couldn't resist a smile. He still had no recollection of these events, although he did remember the electric torches. They were a present from their father.

Alistair cleared his throat. 'What's Smiffy doing here, then?'

Smiffy stepped up and met him eye to eye. There was

a hard edge to Smiffy's glare that Alistair hadn't spotted before. Suspicion overrode any bond they'd developed earlier, it seemed.

'Trapping,' he said, and opened his coat to reveal a dead rabbit. 'Old man like mine, no meat in the pot otherwise. Saw these two, said I'd come along and help. That's what friends do. Not that that's any of your business, mind. It's you under suspicion, *baldy*, not me.'

Alistair held Smiffy's glare for a few moments, until he felt Lucy's hand on his arm. He backed up a few paces and tried to sound affable, splitting his gaze between Smiffy and James.

'Well, as you discovered, we came up here, had a look around and then fell asleep; that's why we didn't come back down. All perfectly innocent.'

'Yeah, fell asleep,' Smiffy said. 'On opposite sides of the circle, as if you were looking out for someone.'

Little Ali looked between Smiffy and Alistair. 'More smugglers!' he burst out.

Smiffy turned at James. 'That *was* when they turned up earlier, and we don't know nothing about 'em. They could be part of it all, and we've just been taken for a ride all this time.'

'We're not smugglers,' Lucy insisted.

James' face showed conflict. He licked his lips, as if unsure of what to do or say next.

'What's going on here, then?'

They were surprised by a warbling voice and a wobbling torchlight. As they watched, Nobby Clarke rode unsteadily into view.

'You got your bike back, then?' Smiffy wasn't impressed.

'Found it, you mean. Still on the blessed trailer, outside the pub of all places. A common courtesy, that's all Father asked for.'

'Paid for,' James corrected him.

'And knowing Old Sam Dury,' said Smiffy, with a laugh, 'he got his money's worth, too.'

Nobby ignored them. He dismounted and chuckled at the scene before him. 'I say, chaps. Is this a good, old-fashioned lynching? You going to sacrifice the strangers?'

James deliberately dazzled Nobby with his torchlight, much to the muted delight of the others.

'Never mind what we're doing, Clarke. Why are *you* up here this late?'

Little Ali piped up. 'Dangerous on your own, up here in the dark.'

The Cadets laughed.

'Don't you worry, young Ali,' said Smiffy, ruffling the boy's hair. 'The Beast of Lanyon Moor don't eat tweed.'

Nobby was doing his best to dodge the torchlight in his face. 'Yes, haha. Erm. As a matter of fact, I'm looking for my lovely Leica camera. Must have left it up here when the farmer herded you all back to the village earlier. Father went berserk when I realised.'

James told him he'd had a wasted journey. Raymond clearly still had the camera, although James wasn't going to tell Nobby that.

The torchlight picked up Nobby's face again; he wore a scowl, but it quickly morphed into his distinctly unpleasant smile.

'Are you lot sticking around here now, or heading… back?' Nobby accompanied the enquiry with a vague waft of the hand.

'We're all right here for now, thanks, Nob,' Smiffy said.

Nobby clicked his tongue a few times then, when nothing else was said he sucked his teeth, shrugged and remounted his bicycle.

'See you all at Church tomorrow, then, no doubt?'

He waited for a response. None came, save for a quick

nod from James. With a nod himself, he swung his bike around and headed off. They watched him go, his torchlight bouncing around as he trundled across the uneven moorland.

'He's up to something,' Lucy murmured.

'Hey, look!' Little Ali pointed to the sky. There was a shooting star, so crisp and clear in night sky. 'Everyone make a wish.'

Alistair looked down at his younger self, spellbound by the sight. He tried to recall what that wish had been. It would be very different now. In his advanced years he was more inclined to tell people to be careful what they wished for.

'Oh, to be that young and innocent again,' he murmured.

'Yeah, all right, Grandad!' Lucy chuckled next to him. Realising what she'd said, she quickly turned it around. 'He's, what, five years younger than you, Hobo? Jaded old teen, you! By the way,' she whispered, confidentially, 'was that the asteroid, do you think?'

'No, too close. It shouldn't leave a trail like that. That was atmospheric.'

James interrupted them, with his torch beam. 'So —'

There was the sound of a stumble, a light female giggle and a muted clink of glass from somewhere not too far away. The children froze instantly, eyes and ears scanning around them. At a motion from James, they turned off the torches and Smiffy hooded his lamp, leaving them all in complete darkness. Gradually their eyes adjusted. The bright moon and clear sky bathed the circle with an ethereal light.

There was an audible shush, then a howl like a wolf not too far away. They were definitely not alone.

'Anything to do with you two?' James asked.

'No,' Lucy whispered vehemently.

'Is that the beast?' Ali asked with a whimper. 'I'm

157

scared.'

'Don't be,' said James. 'Sounded to me like a person pretending to be a wolf.'

Alistair agreed on that front, but despite the pretence they needed to take action, and quickly. He stepped closer to James. In the faint light his brother looked so much like General Gore, it was unnerving. He quickly pushed that thought away.

'James,' he said, his tones hushed and controlled. 'Believe me, this is nothing to do with Lucy and me. I know we can't prove anything, but I think we might be in some danger here. We need to leave the circle – now.'

James appeared torn again. His eyes glistened in the moonlight.

'Come on!' hissed Lucy.

James finally nodded and gestured for them all to head off. Smiffy wasn't convinced. He blocked Alistair's way.

'Why?'

'Because who or what made those noises may be dangerous.'

'Your friends? We'll take 'em on.'

'I don't know who they are any more than you do!'

James turned to the young blacksmith, gesturing sharply at little Ali. 'I am not risking my brother, Smiffy. Not again. Now come on. We're sticking together this time. Lights on, off we go.'

Smiffy gave a grunt of resignation. The three local boys turned their lights back on and all five of them headed off at a jog, back across the moorland as if they were heading for Bledoe.

After a short while Lucy sprinted to the front, held out a cautionary arm and they all stopped.

'I don't want to go too far. We need to see what's happening in the circle.'

'You think something's going on back there?' James

asked.

'I know it sounds suspicious, but we've been warned.'

'And we can't reveal our sources, sorry,' Alistair added.

James nodded. 'You're right. It does sound suspicious. But if there's stuff going on, we need to know about it. All right, lights off again,' he ordered.

Smiffy yet again challenged the decision. 'Why's she calling the shots?'

'She's not,' James spat back. 'I am. Let's head round and up as if we were going off to Higher Tremarcoombe. There's a small lip at the top of the slope on that side of the circle. We'll be more sheltered for spying there.'

Alistair loved every instance he had of watching and hearing James in command. It was such a natural role for the boy – unlike himself, who'd had to really work at it in his formative years. Again he reflected on what might have happened had James lived. He always imagined that James would have gone into military service, maybe joined the Coldstream Guards like his alter-ego had, while he, Alistair, could have gone into teaching like he'd wanted. Watching James now only confirmed his supposition.

Alistair checked on his frightened younger self. 'You all right, Ali?' The lad nodded back up at him, pulled his coat tighter around his neck and followed his brother.

Alistair paused.

'Come on,' said Lucy. He didn't move. 'Grandad, are you all right?'

He nodded. 'Sorry, I was just struck with a feeling… A sudden sense of familiarity.'

'You remember?

He shook his head. 'No. It's more that the situation seems familiar, not the detail.'

'Hey, that's something, at least.'

He wasn't convinced. 'To be honest, Lucyloo, it could

just be a general recollection of being out on the moors in the dark.' He glanced back at the stone circle. 'Something terrible is going to happen. We need to be cautious, not rush into anything. Okay?'

'You can trust me,' Lucy said, and dashed off after the boys.

Alistair smiled, and he was reminded of Kate for a moment. Like Lucy, his daughter had always been fearless.

He caught up with Lucy and the rest of the group. He ignored Smiffy's suspicious glares and grumbles as they reached the alternative vantage point that James had suggested. Alistair's patience was wearing thin with Smiffy, and he had to remind himself what would become of the boy after tonight.

At a sign from James, Smiffy at last fell silent and the five of them lay flat on the cold, tussock grassland, crawling their way up to the edge of an incline which allowed them clear vision straight across to the sarsen monoliths. Alistair felt a tugging on his hoodie and there was a ripping noise. He looked down and saw that his pocket had got snagged on a thorny plant. He'd torn the material as he'd crawled forward and ripped his right-hand pocket open. He gave a silent apology to Hobo, certain the blue hoodie was Hobo's favourite.

The circle sat in silent darkness. There was chuckling nearby. Alistair turned and saw that poor little Ali had fallen asleep; he was snoring lightly and causing the others some mirth. James gently woke his brother, who wasn't happy, but no one was going to take the lad home now.

'Look!' Lucy hissed.

A light could be seen approaching the area within the circle where they'd previously stood.

'Keep low,' Alistair said. It was an automatic reaction, and he was comforted that it was not met with protests from James or Smiffy.

'No sign, they've gone.' The voice floated faintly across to them. Presumably the owner of the torch.

'That's...' Smiffy began.

'Yes,' James said. 'Nobby Clarke. Again.'

'I'll so have him, I will,' Smiffy growled.

'Wait.' James held up a cautionary hand. 'Let's see what plays out, first.'

Alistair felt his pulse thumping in the back of his head. *This is it, then.*

'Looking for his camera, my arse,' Lucy grumbled.

Alistair tutted but couldn't hide a smile. The Cadets sniggered.

'You are just something else, Lucy Wilson.'

'I am indeed, James Lethbridge-Stewart, I am indeed.'

'There's more of 'em.' Smiffy pointed.

Gradually, flaming torches were being lit and figures were emerging into the circle, as if from within the stones themselves. All were cloaked, their features hidden beneath deep hoods. As the children looked on, Nobby passed over his electric torch to one of the figures and donned a cowl and flambeau himself. After some initial chatter and a little giggling, the group formed a rough ring around the central altar stone. A low chant started up, then the group began to move, slowly circling around the altar.

'What the hell?'

Lucy answered James' vague question with another. 'Is this black magic?'

'It's wrong, whatever it is,' said Smiffy, his voice tinged with fervour.

Alistair nodded his agreement. 'I think they're *trying* to be druids, but I'm not sure they're doing a very good job.'

The circle of figures sporadically broke as members lost their footing on the uneven ground, or stepped on the hem of their, or a neighbour's, cloak. Laughter generally ensued. Two of them broke away and started a small fire some distance apart but still within the circle. Once the fire was established, there was a haughty female cry of 'ready', and a live chicken was released, or possibly thrown, into the stone circle, followed by a figure that Alistair immediately recognised from the vision he'd had in 2018.

The figure was tall, its cowl so black that he could detect no definition within it. This was very definitely the leader of the coven. And it wore a horned goat skull for a facemask.

Whatever was going on there, Alistair thought, they were ticking plenty of folklore boxes.

Goat-face carried a salver which glinted in the moonlight. There was something bulky upon it. Was the ceremonial dagger in a knife block? How very middle class. No, there was too much polished metal, too much glistening. When he realised what it was, he didn't know whether to be shocked or amused. It was a bottle of champagne on ice. Someone produced another tray covered with flutes.

Alistair scoffed, 'That's not right at all!'

There was a chorus of shushes from the other children.

'You know about all this stuff?' asked Lucy.

'Well, I've had some experience with stopping it in the past… Well, the future. But nothing quite like this.'

As they watched, the champagne and glasses were placed on the altar stone at one end, furthest away from Goat-face, who was now brandishing the ceremonial blade. The small fire to one side of the coven danced happily to itself, and a kind of spit was being erected across it. As the dancing and chanting continued, Goat-face reached down and lifted up the chicken by its neck. It was still alive, its wings and legs flapping and reaching out for purchase. He swung the bird over the altar stone;

it was clear what was intended.

'No!' Lucy yelled, jumping up suddenly and running across to the stone circle.

'Lucy!' Alistair set off after her, and behind him he heard the cries of James and Smiffy.

'What? Oh no!'

The boys joined him.

Good God, Lucy Wilson, Alistair thought, *what are you doing now?*

CHAPTER TEN
All the Madmen

ALISTAIR SPRINTED AS FAST AS HE COULD, BUT DESPITE Hobo's longer legs, Lucy had too good a start on them all.

'Stop this, stop it now!' he heard her cry as she dashed into the middle of the ceremony, waving her arms and causing uproar among the cowled figures.

'Lucy, wait!'

The three boys quickly followed her into the firelit arena, causing more shrieks and consternation. Lucy ignored everyone else and made a direct line for the knife-wielding, goat-faced leader.

'Let that chicken go.'

'It's that damn darkie girl.' Nobby's voice was very clear from inside his cloak and hood.

There was no confusion over which of the figures Nobby might be; those either side of him turned in his direction. Lucy followed their cue.

As Alistair watched, Lucy approached, then loosed a punch into where, he assumed, Nobby's face was. There was an unpleasant crack, followed by gasps and murmurs all around as Nobby sprawled flat on his back. A pair of bent wire-framed glasses fell from within the cowl to lie on the ground. Alistair moved forward to stand protectively with his granddaughter, who was rubbing her knuckles. Behind them he heard little Ali join James and Smiffy. Whatever would those boys make of all this?

Goat-face raised his hands in a gesture of calm and peace. The chicken and the knife had both been placed on the altar, and the bird was now pecking its way towards the champagne.

'He told us they'd all gone,' said one voice.

'I thought they had,' Nobby complained, standing clumsily in his long gown with someone's assistance. He was holding his hood to his face and by the sound of his voice Lucy had smacked him square on the nose. 'They were nowhere to be seen.'

'We told you your boy was too young to trust.'

'Yes, these damned children,' came another angry male voice and a pointed, cloaked finger. 'If I'm recognised outside this group, it could ruin me, Leonard!'

'Please, please,' came Goat-face's now clearly frustrated voice from inside the skull mask. Leonard Clarke. 'Do not worry, do not panic, anyone. And, may I remind the coven – and especially you, Your Honour – that we do not use proper names around the uninitiated?'

Clarke spoke again. 'Now, girl –'

'Lucy. Lucy Wilson.' She kept her voice level, not showing any fear even if she was feeling it.

'Lucy.'

'Nice to see you again, Leonard. You've had your hair done since earlier.' There was a pause. Alistair suspected that the coven leader was a little taken aback by Lucy's *chutzpah*.

'Thank you for your concern over the chicken. I suspect you and your friends here have all misunderstood our purpose, which is understandable with the trappings we have chosen. But this is merely a game that we grown-ups play. We mean no harm to anyone by it.'

'Except that chicken.'

'The chicken has led a full and fruitful life on the

estate of one of our number. Once we have indulged our romantic fantasies and shed its blood to celebrate Beltane, then it will adorn the spit and be roasted as part of our festivities.' Clarke gestured to the tray. 'See the champagne?'

A voice from the crowd. 'I thought we were celebrating May Day?'

Another voice. 'It's supposed to be Beltane, but I can't make weeknights, so we moved it.'

'Enough!' Clarke barked with a raised hand gesture.

'That's sick!' Lucy spat. 'You use your privilege to laugh and poke fun at other people's beliefs.'

'Oh come, girl,' a female from the crowd piped up. 'These are just stupid pagan rituals. They may be the norm where *you* come from, but here we know it's a load of old tosh and nonsense.' Some light laughter.

'I come from London.'

'Course you do, dear.' More light laughter.

Nobby stepped forward. The blood staining his hood and cloak glistened in the fiery light. 'Give me the knife, Father, I want to make sure she never gets back there.'

Alistair stepped forward to protect Lucy. All this business with knives was not good. They'd been told that Nobby died this night, but they didn't know how. The last thing Alistair wanted was a desperate fight and blood on someone's hands, no matter the provocation. Thankfully for him another of the hooded figures grabbed Nobby's shoulders. A different female voice spoke.

'Graeme, no.'

Lucy surprised Alistair by shirking off his protective grasp. 'Try it,' she said, stepping towards Nobby very matter-of-factly, her shoulders squared. 'You wouldn't be the first no-hoper who's pulled a knife on me. Yeah, life's been tough at times, and I've had to deal with some stuff. Nasty stuff that would make my family worry – my mum, my dad, my brothers. My grandad. But I've dealt with it, and I'm here to tell the tale; a stronger person for it. But you wouldn't know or care about the inner-city struggle, would you? Not out here in the country, with your silver spoons in your mouths. So, come on, *Graeme*, bring it, and maybe I'll break another bit of you.'

Before Nobby could act either way, Clarke called for peace again.

'Lucy, dear,' he said, with unconvincing geniality. 'Where are you and your porcelain pal here staying? Perhaps I could pop by tomorrow and speak with your parents. Offer them some… financial incentive, shall we say, to keep quiet about what you've witnessed up here tonight?'

Smiffy immediately joined them. 'I'll have some of that, then, Doctor Clarke, if you're splashing it around.'

'Ahh, Master Gloyne again. Indeed, I'm sure your delightful father and I could come to some arrangement. A few drinks, maybe, followed by… Ooh, how long is it now since he gave you a damn good thrashing? He's such an attentive parent. Shame your poor mother didn't live long enough to see more of it. But then she saw plenty, I'm sure. We all used to hear the cries.'

Smiffy snarled with pent-up anger and lunged forward. James and Nobby both ran to restrain him, but he'd stopped before they reached him. They still grabbed Smiffy's arms regardless, although Alistair noted that James immediately released him when he realised what the coven leader was doing.

The chicken flapped off the altar in alarm and the ceremonial blade flashed as it was swept up and held, expertly, at Smiffy's throat. Smiffy stood, frozen to the spot as the point of the blade rested below his chin. His panting breath came through gritted teeth, his expression told of the anger, shame and frustration he was feeling. The tears that rolled down his cheeks disappeared off into the darkness at his feet.

'Now who would miss you, eh?' The goat mask tilted to one side, patronising its victim. 'Your Cadet chums? Possibly. Not your drunken wreck of a father, that's for sure.'

Clarke flicked the knife point slowly off the end of Smiffy's chin. Smiffy collapsed to his knees and wept; a broken boy.

Lucy gently pushed through past the boys. 'This isn't a game,' she said, coolly. 'It might be to some of these losers.' She gestured around the group. 'But you? No. You enjoy it. You're just… *evil.*'

'Evil, am I?' Leonard Clarke removed his goat-face and lowered his hood. There was some further consternation around the group, but again he hushed it. 'It's fine. There is nothing to be gained now from concealment. We can deal with this. They are only children, and apart from the Lethbridge-Stewart boys they're all regressive anyway.'

'Who are you to judge us, any of us?' Lucy motioned to the boys immediately nearby. 'People like you make me sick.'

Clarke smiled. Like his son, it was not a pleasant smile. 'Good. There are powers growing in Europe, rising. And when they do, abased creatures such as yourselves…' He pointed at Lucy, Alistair and Smiffy in turn. 'Negroes, freaks, the sick and barely literate underclass – all of you will finally be dealt with.'

'And King Teddy reinstated,' cried one of the coven.

'Hear, hear!' chorused the others.

'And we shall inherit the Earth.' Here Clarke raised his hands euphorically to the sky.

Alistair was sickened. How had it happened that here, in this rural corner of Cornwall where he grew up, away from the hustle and bustle of politics and high society, Nazi sympathisers were able to conceal themselves?

'A toast,' someone cried. 'A toast to bally Beltane, to King Teddy, and to Mr Hitler.'

Alistair's head reeled. He staggered to one side, collapsed to his knees and emptied his stomach onto the ground. Lucy was at his shoulder, with words of encouragement. She was being brilliant, taking all this in her stride. More so than he was. In the background, champagne corks popped, and glasses clinked.

As Alistair crouched there, on all fours, a door seemed to unlock inside his head. He found he was suddenly able to remember – or simply to see – the situation from his younger self's point of view.

Little Ali was separate from the rest, near the fire where it was warmer. He felt bewildered, near panicking. James and Smiffy had left him and joined the girl Lucy and Hobo, the bald boy; but he didn't have a clue what was going on. The bleached white goat skull scared him, but he recognised Doctor Clarke, the man with the posh motor cars, when the mask was removed. The cloaked people started to pour drinks, like they were having a party. Then something caught his eye in the distance; another shooting star – how lucky. But no, this was too close, not a tiny point in the sky. It was heading towards them. Suddenly Hobo stood up, and —

'Everyone, get out of here!' Alistair cried, standing up and dashing from the stone circle. 'James, Lucy, come on!' he yelled, gesturing frantically.

Lucy was next to him. He saw that James had hefted Smiffy over his shoulder, in a fireman's lift. Little Ali was there too. They stopped in a jumble about twenty yards outside the circle and looked back. The coven members remained where they were, clearly pleased to be rid of the interfering children. They continued with their festivities.

'What is it?' asked Lucy.

Alistair looked up, and saw what little Ali had seen

before. A meteorite was falling to Earth through its own fiery orange funnel. It seemed to be heading straight for them. The coven hadn't seen it.

He pointed to it. 'If that isn't the black rock,' he began.

Lucy was spellbound. 'It's beautiful.'

As the children watched, the meteorite slowed its descent until it hovered at what looked to be about fifty feet above the stone circle. Still the coven members didn't look up, but they noticed it soon enough when electric blue tendrils shot from the object. The tendrils connected like arcs of electricity with the tip of each stone in the circle.

Alistair felt a tingling through the ground, like a small electrical current being diffused. The others were reacting to it also.

'Is it attacking?' Lucy cried. 'My feet feel numb.'

'I don't think so.' Alistair found himself having to shout above the crackle of the tendrils and the screaming of the trapped coven members who were unable, or unwilling, to try to breach the perimeter of the stone circle.

'I don't like it.'

James and little Ali huddled together, either the current or the cold causing their teeth to chatter. Smiffy lay on the ground next to them. A blue halo surrounded him, and he jerked and spasmed periodically.

'Look, Grandad.' Lucy pointed to Smiffy.

'It's feeling us,' Alistair said, 'reading us. I'm not sure I've ever felt anything quite like it before.'

But something even more odd was now happening to the meteorite itself. The lightning was connecting with all the stones – even the smugglers' fakes. Where it was impacting on the real stones, the current continued to dissipate through them and down into the ground below. There was obviously some natural connection there. But where the beams were hitting the fake stones, it was causing the structures to smoulder and crackle.

Eventually they burst into flames.

James pointed a finger, and Alistair could see that the meteorite was suffering some kind of feedback effect from this, like the circuit was shorting somehow. It shuddered and dipped to one side as the connections with the fake stones finally blew loose, danced across the ground directly, then broke. At this point the arcs to the other stones disappeared too and the meteorite plummeted to the ground.

Alistair was about to shout a warning to the coven, but the breath was stolen from him as James flung an arm around his throat and dragged him to the ground.

There was a dull *thwmp* sound and the ground, no longer buzzing, shook beneath them. A pause, then loose soil rained down. They lay stationary for a while in case of any further activity, but there was nothing beyond the screams of the coven members.

Alistair looked at Lucy. He could tell she was confused. A pall of smoke was rising from beside the altar stone, as well as a throbbing, fiery glow, which lighted the coven members as they sprawled about. They slowly regained their feet, disregarding the fact that they'd all lost their hoods in the shockwave. The buried black boulder was now where they'd found it back in 2018.

'James, you check on Smiffy and Ali,' Alistair said. 'Lucy and I are going to take a closer look at the circle.'

James nodded and joined the two others in a huddle.

'I don't understand,' said Lucy as she set off with Alistair. 'Is that it? That can't be it. Where's Nobby Clarke? Is he still alive?'

Nobby Clarke was very much alive, staggering forward to the front of the group gathering around the glowing meteorite. His father and mother were just behind him.

'It's wrong.' Lucy turned to Alistair. 'It's not happened correctly.'

He squeezed her hand and he felt her grow tense.

'It's us, isn't it? We've changed the future by being here. We thought we were doing the right thing and we've messed it up!'

Alistair shook his head, vehemently. 'No, Lucy. I don't see how. We haven't changed anything *material* in being here—'

'Until I interrupted the ceremony.'

Alistair paused, his words drying on his lips. Lucy nodded knowingly.

'No.' Alistair was convinced it couldn't be the case. 'Take Smiffy. Now there's a paradox, a self-fulfilling time loop. He told us he'd seen us here on this date, so we came back to this date. But us doing so has caused him to come to the stone circle when he wouldn't otherwise have done so. The experiences affect him and, well, the rest is history.'

'But you'd already seen us arrive here, when you were trapped inside your childhood self. So, you already knew we were coming back, regardless of what Smiffy said.'

She had him there.

'Then there must be something else. There *has* to be.' Alistair looked at James, little Ali and the silently shuddering Smiffy. 'Let's keep our distance, just in case.'

As they watched, some coven members tentatively tried to approach the meteorite, but the heat was too great and kept them at a few yards' distance. Without their hoods, Alistair took some minor comfort in only recognising a few of the coven members, and only the Clarkes were residents of Bledoe. The coven had clearly lost interest in the children now. Presumably what had happened was a little more *real* than they were used to.

Lucy was close to his right and he noticed that little Ali had joined them and was peering around his left side. Alistair liked having his nearest and dearest where he could protect them if necessary. Only James was out of reach, but he was back where he was needed most, supporting Smiffy.

As they looked on, Nobby, hood off and face a bloody mess, suddenly arched himself backwards. His mother, standing just behind him, screamed out his name. A glowing, translucent cloud rose up from where the meteorite had landed. It floated towards Nobby and dissipated into him somehow – it wasn't entirely clear to Alistair. What *was* clear, though, was the agonised scream that Nobby gave a few seconds later and the whooshing fireball into which his body erupted.

Silence.

Alistair jumped up and checked himself over for the second time in what seemed as many minutes. No charring, no burns, no damage to his borrowed body. Relief. He'd managed to throw Lucy and little Ali underneath him; an automatic reaction. They too appeared unscathed beyond the odd bruise.

'James?' he yelled, instinctively worried for his brother.

'I'm fine,' James replied. 'Just trying to clear the flashes from my eyes.' He was standing upright and blinking repeatedly.

Smiffy was facing the circle, on his knees and prone. His face was blackened with soot, his lips dried and cracked, his mouth frozen in a silent scream of terror.

'Is Smiffy dead?' Little Ali asked.

Alistair put a comforting hand on his younger self's shoulder. 'No, but he's in shock. He'll get better. With care.'

The little boy nodded, sagely, and went to help his brother. Smiffy would recover somewhat, Alistair knew. But the kind of loving care he really needed just wasn't available to him. It was unfortunate, but the lasting effects of tonight's traumas would remain with him forever.

Nobby. The coven. Alistair looked into the stone circle. 'Oh, good God.' He stepped forward.

'Wow.' Lucy came to stand next to him, her shoulder nestling against his arm. She handed him one of the electric torches.

The moors felt darker than ever, right then. Even with artificial light it was difficult to see any specific detail as they ventured nearer to the affected area. The fireball had extended to the inner perimeter of the circle only. There was a stark line of incineration, the other side of which the tussock-like grass remained in full health. Alistair didn't know why the fireball had stopped at an incomplete physical barrier, but he was thankful because it had saved him and the Cadets from being roasted alive.

All around was blackened, cremated, cleansed. The air stank like an ancient chimney. It was slightly more pleasant that the roasted flesh he'd been worried they might smell. But there were no indications of any bodies remaining at all; no sign of Nobby, his parents, or any of the coven members. Them or their affairs. The charred ground crunched beneath their feet and Alistair tried not to think about what they might be walking on. The smugglers' fake stones had burned away to nothing. The only recognisable sign that anyone or anything had been there was a twisted lump of metal on the ground near the altar stone: the champagne bucket and salver, melded into a fantastic new shape.

Alistair shook his head. 'Awful.'

Lucy agreed. 'Even if they were a bunch of Nazis.' She turned and shone her light on the nearest sarsen. 'There are the marks, like waves, fresh and yet curiously faint already.'

'No smoking remains, no latent heat.' Alistair held out his hands. 'There's no way we'd be able to walk through here yet if that'd been a normal fire.'

'Yeah, of course. How weird.'

'And here's the meteorite, where it will be forevermore.'

Lucy shone her light onto it. 'What d'you reckon that glowing thing was that flew into Nobby?'

'No idea, but it clearly didn't like him.'

Lucy gave a snort and nodded. 'I can relate to that. Wonder where it's gone?'

'Burned itself up, by the look of things.'

'But what has all this to do with Traveller?'

Alistair wondered that too. 'Something, otherwise why would the Gnome have brought me here in the first place? We know the origin of the black stone, we know how it connects 1937 and 2018…'

'And we know what happened to Smiffy,' Lucy added, looking over at Smiffy sadly.

Alistair turned to check on the others. The paraffin lamp rested on the ground, lighting the scene outside the circle. James, little Ali and Smiffy were all kneeling together in a small scrum. They'd be dealing with all this as best they could, but he knew they shouldn't linger up on the moors any longer than necessary. A comfortable bed and familiar surroundings would be the best medicine for them. He rubbed his hand over his face and turned back to Lucy.

'I've been pondering on those visions. Only you and I were affected. Maybe it's because we were here now, and then?'

'How would the meteorite know?'

Alistair shrugged. 'You'd be surprised the things contained within meteorites and asteroids. Maybe the Traveller, whatever it is, is psychic in some way.'

Lucy nodded. 'Perhaps we'll find more answers back in 2018? Reckon we've learned all we can here.'

'Maybe. I think our work here is pretty much done, but we should get our lot back to Bledoe first before we leave.'

'We've not helped Smiffy at all,' Lucy said with regret. 'Look at him.'

'No, events have played out as they should. We've done what we had to do. We've neither made things worse nor better.'

'Yeah...'

From somewhere far away, a clanging bell could be heard. Police, probably. Or the fire service. Or, more likely, both. One thing was certain, the children mustn't be found there, no matter what.

Lucy charged out of the circle towards the others. 'Right, come on, Lethbridge-Stewarts, let's get you and Smiffy back home.'

James stood up and helped Smiffy to stand. The physical and mental effects of trauma were very evident in the boy.

'Where's Ali?'

Little Ali appeared out of the blackness, excitedly. 'Look what I found!'

The chicken followed him, pecking around near his feet.

'She's alive!' Lucy kissed little Ali, which made him squirm, then she very nearly kissed the chicken too. 'Oh, but what do we do with it now?'

'Leave it here,' said James. 'Its owners have gone. Let it scratch out a living on the moors.'

Alistair was sceptical. 'I can't see it lasting the night out here. A fox will have her in no time, or Smiffy, when he comes up poaching next.'

'Can we keep her?' Ali asked.

James looked at his brother. 'What will we tell Mum?'

'Tell her it just appeared one day.' It did seem to have taken to little Ali, staying near his feet. James grunted in resignation.

'All right. But you're carrying her; we've got Smiffy to manage.'

Little Ali grinned. James removed his coat and they wrapped it around the chicken, to make her easier to carry. As he held her, little Ali informed the chicken that she would be called Kathrine. Alistair nodded his approval and ruffled his young self's hair. The chicken just gently clucked away to herself.

It was a struggle at times, but between Alistair, Lucy and James, they managed to get Smiffy, Kathrine and the exceptionally tired little Ali safely back to Redrose Cottage. As they took their usual route back across the moors, they'd seen both a police car and a fire engine slowly making their way across the undulating ground in the distance. They must have gained access through one of the farms beyond Bledoe, so their route to the stone circle meant the children were in no danger of being spotted.

In the village, there was quite a consternation. People had been frightened and alarmed by the huge fireball lighting up the night sky. But this played into the children's hands. James had already decided that they'd take Smiffy to their house, not trusting the blacksmith (who would no doubt be drunk, anyway) to look after his son properly.

Along the lanes and tracks they went, through the trees and onto the rough land behind Penhale Meadow, then up over the rickety dry-stone wall into the back garden of Redrose Cottage. Little Ali was going to pop Katherine in the outside loo for the night, but James stopped him, saying what a shock it would be for their mother if she had to use it. They popped the chicken in the old lean-to shed instead. It wasn't as secure, but there'd probably be some seeds and insects, or even a mouse in there, that she could eat.

James held open the back door as Lucy and Alistair guided Smiffy inside and sat him at the kitchen table.

Mary could be heard outside the front door, talking urgently with neighbours. James thanked Alistair and Lucy and assured them he could handle things from there. He'd tell his mum that Smiffy had appeared at their back door, that he'd been out trapping rabbits on the moors (he still had the one inside his coat, despite everything) and was shocked and distressed by the sudden fire. The blacksmith's son was becoming more aware and responsive by now, and Alistair was sure that a good cup of hot, sweet tea would do him the world of good. He started making one straight away.

James cleared his throat. 'Know your way around already, I see.'

Alistair paused with the tea leaves over the pot and cringed. 'Sorry,' he said sheepishly. 'Just trying to help.'

'And you just happened to know where all the tea making things were?'

Alistair shrugged. 'Beginner's luck?' he half asked.

To Alistair's huge relief, James seemed to buy this and told him to finish the job while he was there. Little Ali, who was almost dead on his feet with tiredness, gave Lucy a quick hug, shook Alistair's hand and headed straight upstairs to bed.

'We'd better disappear too,' said Lucy. 'Your mum didn't seem too pleased to see us out the front earlier. She'd probably do her nut to find us in her kitchen.'

James and Lucy hastily shook hands, then opted for a brief embrace. It was odd seeing her peck him on the cheek, but it was clear that James had taken a shine to her. His great niece. He turned and reached out for Alistair's hand.

'Hobo. Thanks, and not just for making the tea.'

Alistair just nodded in reply. He couldn't speak. He knew now that he was shaking his brother's hand for the final time, albeit with Hobo's hand.

James, the brother he'd forgotten for so many years;

178

the brother his younger self upstairs was going to lose to the Intelligence only next year. He was glad that they had to be so surreptitious and hurried; he wasn't sure he'd have been able to leave so willingly of his own volition.

Lucy smiled at Alistair and grabbed his arm as they stepped out into the back garden of Redrose Cottage, lit only by the bleed from the kitchen window.

'You know where you're going?' James called.

They both nodded, and James ducked back inside.

'What next, Grandad?'

'Back to 2018, and —'

'Oh! Come on, I set you up for a *Back to the Future*, there.'

Alistair smiled. 'Tired, sorry. You know that used to be Con's favourite film.'

'Of course I know. Who do you think made me watch it so much?'

Alistair chuckled. 'Indeed. Very well, back to the future we go then. I need sleep. And then we need to be in the stone circle again tomorrow night, when the asteroid passes, in case anything happens again. Maybe we'll even find out who, or what, the Traveller actually is. And what it all has to do with Smiffy.'

'Maybe it's controlling him in the future?'

'Maybe.'

'Of course, we're going back to Ogmore in the morning so solving this may be a bit tricky.'

'We'll work something out.'

Something made him glance up at his old bedroom. There was little Ali watching them from between his curtains.

'Ready?' Lucy asked, putting on the ring.

Alistair thought for a moment. Another memory was surfacing. He'd been there, watching from the window, and the two strange children just seemed to vanish.

So, Alistair took Lucy's hand, and that's what they did.

CHAPTER ELEVEN
Where Are We Now?

IT TOOK ALISTAIR A FEW MOMENTS TO ESTABLISH WHERE they had arrived. They were outside and in the dark, but clearly not in either the stone circle or the back garden of Redrose Cottage. The area was tree-lined with rough tarmac underfoot and several parked cars nearby. A large two-storey building stood behind them.

Clearly some time had passed in 2018 in their absence. Alistair realised he hadn't thought to ask Lucy where she was bringing them. He let go of her hand.

'Grandad, you all right?'

'Where have you brought us, Lucyloo?'

Before Lucy could answer she was distracted by her mobile phone, which started to beep madly as it was recognised by the network again. Alistair felt Hobo's phone vibrating away in his trouser pocket too. He'd check it out later.

There was some movement within the treeline, which made Alistair forget his question. His eyes had yet to fully adjust, but the wheezy chuckle he heard bothered him. He squatted to take a closer look when the area behind the two of them was washed with light. They were outside the Pembertons' house.

The front door opened, and there stood Helen Pemberton and a policeman. Tamara was just behind them. Lucy immediately stepped forward.

'Mum, there you are. We can explain everything.'

'Can you, young lady?' the policeman said with a nod. 'Can you indeed. You'd better come inside.'

Alistair glanced at the tree line again, but there was nothing to be seen. He followed Lucy inside.

There was a far more sombre mood inside Grace's house this time than there had been the last time they'd entered. Hobo's lively phone quickly established for Alistair that they'd arrived back on the same day they'd left, but it was now ten o'clock at night and the last they'd been heard of was back at around two o'clock when Lucy and Grace had exchanged a few text messages about the fire. Beside all the calls, messages and social media pleas, Helen had finished work early and rushed back.

Grace had stayed home in case they showed up, while the mums had both driven off and trawled Bledoe, Redgate Smithy, Liskeard and all the roads in between, looking for the pair of them. They'd given up when it had got too dark for the search to remain practical. That's when Grace had finally told them that she was worried that they'd been followed by a strange old man earlier. Tamara had called Meg Kostinen and they'd agreed to alert the police. Grace's swollen upper face told how much she'd been crying, no doubt from the onslaught of both Helen and Tamara at having withheld that information. Helen's scowl was just as firmly etched into her face as it was on Tamara's.

Lucy very quickly grew annoyed with her beeping mobile phone and switched it off. Contrary to what she'd promised outside, she'd so far been unable to explain very much at all.

'I am so angry and disappointed in you, Lucy Wilson,' said Tamara, wiping away another tear. 'We come here to visit Grace and Helen, and this is how you repay them? Hours of worry and an unbelievable lack of concern?'

Helen and Grace now wore placid smiles.

'I'm sorry,' Lucy repeated yet again. 'I'm just very tired, Mum. It was a very long walk back from Bledoe.'

Tamara raised her hands in despair. 'A walk you didn't need to make if you'd only answered your phone and told us what was going on! And heaven only knows what route you took; look at the state of you both.'

Alistair remembered his ripped hoodie pocket but hadn't considered quite how muddy and grubby they'd both got in 1937. Tamara continued.

'Helen and I scoured the roads and lanes enough times before we bothered the police.'

The police officer took this opportunity to introduce himself as Jamal. He came over and squatted in front of Lucy and Alistair.

'You are all right, both of you, aren't you? If you've been with anyone, or feel threatened about anything, I'm here to help, okay?'

They both nodded and repeated that they were fine, and that they'd just been busy and hadn't noticed how the time had flown by.

Alistair knew he could settle things in moments if he could only take Tamara aside. In his time, she and her family had managed to steer clear of aliens and the like, with one notable exception, and clearly that hadn't changed in the almost seven years since. But she still knew things, and was certainly more open to them than Albert ever had been. Which, Alistair reflected, was no surprise considering…

He ended that thought there. No, he *could* convince Tamara, with the things he knew about her past, but it wouldn't be right for him to bring her into what was going on in Bledoe. The Wilsons were supposed to be safe from aliens.

He looked over briefly at Lucy.

Although clearly not every Wilson believed that.

'But that doesn't make sense, Lucy!' Tamara stood

and stomped around the room as if she was trying to walk off her agitation. 'For God's sake, girl, can't you see that?'

Jamal turned to her. 'All right, Mrs Wilson, I know this is frustrating for you —'

'Frustrating!'

' — But please, give me a moment, okay?'

Helen very gently touched Tamara on the arm. 'Come on, Tammy, we'll go and cook up some pasta before the bolognese spoils too much. And tomorrow we shall visit Bledoe.'

'What a lovely idea, Mum,' Grace agreed, who moved to join the two ladies. Grace looked considerably more relaxed and contented now than she had when they'd first arrived back. She turned to Alistair and Lucy. 'You are both hungry, we presume?'

Alistair gave a nod and a semi audible 'thank you,' before glancing at Lucy with a frown. 'What's the matter with them?' he mouthed.

Lucy shrugged.

'Officer?' said Helen, again in the strange, placid way. 'Soya mince bolognese? It's been simmering a while.'

Jamal politely declined.

'I'd better call Meg now Hobo's back.' Tamara pulled her phone from her back pocket. Flanked by Helen and Grace, she moved through into the kitchen. The door closed behind them.

Jamal brought a dining chair across and seated himself in front of Alistair and Lucy more comfortably.

Lucy nodded towards the kitchen. 'Is there something we've missed? What's with the creepy voices and smiles all of a sudden?'

'A combination of shock and relief, I expect. They went through quite a traumatic experience before you arrived.'

Alistair and Lucy shared a look.

'What happened?' Lucy asked.

'All in good time. Now, Lucy, you can see how upset your mum is, can't you?'

'Of course, but—'

'And I've spoken to your mum, Hobo, too. She's on duty tonight and this hasn't been helping her focus on her job. Although doubtless she'll be thrilled now you've turned up.'

'I'm sorry.' Alistair realised this was the first thing he'd properly said out loud since they'd entered.

'Lucy's mum has given you a pretty thorough run-down of what's happened while you've both been AWOL, but she hasn't told you everything. So, just in case this changes your mind on speaking up about anything—'

Jamal's radio gave a burst of static. He shifted his position and silenced it.

'Grace had an experience which upset her at Redgate Smithy earlier, with the old man who she then thought was following you into Bledoe?'

They both nodded.

'But the old man was a friend of my grandad's, and harmless,' Lucy said.

'Really? Well your mum doesn't know him if that's the case. He turned up here, too. Just after your mum and Grace's mum came back from the search. He was staring in through the front window. Not doing anything, just looking and nodding. Freaked Grace out again.'

'I can imagine,' said Alistair.

Lucy looked at Jamal archly. 'She looked pretty freaked when we arrived. Now her and her mum are all hippy and peace, man.'

'I think you'll find both mums are trying to deal with a variety of emotions at the moment, Lucy. No doubt Hobo's is as well.'

'How soon before we arrived – before we got back –

did this happen?' Alistair asked. He recalled the movement in the treeline he'd spotted just after they'd arrived.

'Not too long. I was in the area following another call, so I was diverted here. I'd not been here long before you turned up, either.'

'Has anyone been out to check in the bushes?'

'No, lad, didn't occur to me to actually look for the prowler.'

Alistair glared at Jamal with a moue. He didn't see the need for sarcasm.

Lucy spoke. 'What would Smiffy be doing out here?'

Jamal pulled out his notepad. 'This friend of your grandad's? I'll need his details.'

'Yeah. Uh, Raymond Gloyne, from the old blacksmith's in Bledoe. He's a right demon with his mobility scooter, so you gotta be fast.'

Jamal smiled. 'Yes, I think I've heard of him.'

Alistair was not comfortable with where this was going. 'Hang on, Lucy. We don't know for sure that it was Smiffy.'

Jamal was confused. 'Wait, you don't know if he was a friend of your grandad's?'

'No, we know that,' Alistair said shortly, feeling annoyed at being questioned by a police constable. He wasn't used to being questioned like that, then remembered who Jamal was looking at. Not Brigadier Sir Alistair Lethbridge-Stewart, former Special Envoy to the United Nations, but just a bald schoolboy who had some lip on him. He adjusted his tone. 'I'm just not convinced he scared Grace up at the B&B. I don't think he's like that.'

But Lucy was adamant. 'Who else could it be? Also, Jamal, he probably ought to be in a home or somewhere. He lives in a right state.'

'I'll take a look.' Jamal asked for a description. It

matched near enough the description Grace, Helen and Tamara had given of the face at the window, with two key exceptions. 'No facial scarring? Nothing odd about the nose?'

Lucy shook her head.

'And this Raymond Gloyne hasn't been holding you against your will, or threatening you, or anything?'

Lucy confirmed that he hadn't.

'You still claim you've spent the last seven and a half hours walking home?'

'Across country, yes, where the mobile signal is rubbish.'

'Like your mum said, Lucy, you both look a right mess. You've clearly had some sort of, I dunno... adventure?'

Alistair and Lucy glanced at each other, then shrugged a perfect teenage shrug.

Jamal stood up. 'Okay then. Suit yourselves. You're both home safe and sound now. If you can't, or won't, tell us where you've been or what you've been up to, then there's nothing more I can do. Less than twenty-four hours, you don't even count as statistical missing persons. I guess that makes you, what? Naughty? Irresponsible? A waste of police time? I dunno. But I do know this: you've got a lot of making up to do with your poor mum, Lucy Wilson. You too, George Kostinen, when you get back to...' He checked his notes. 'Ogmore-by-Sea.'

'What about the prowler?' Lucy asked.

'I'll deal with him, you just sit tight and sleep tight.'

There was a knock at the kitchen door. Helen poked her head around and asked if they could come back in. She wore a beatific smile. Jamal said he was all done, now.

'There's still no explanation, but they have given me a possible lead on the prowler, other than just heading to the B&B and poking my nose around.'

Tamara burst in. She, at least, was still very much herself.

'You *were* followed? Oh, you poor things.' She rushed over and held both Lucy and Hobo to her bosom. Alistair wasn't sure he'd ever felt more uncomfortable than he did right then.

Jamal headed for the front door. 'I'll be here a while yet. Going to have a good look around outside and in the area, speak to anyone who's out and about, all right?'

Those that could, nodded. Jamal continued.

'Just a word of advice, before I go. Eat your dinner, maybe have a shower to relax, and then sleep on it all, yeah? Talk about today another day. Things always seem a bit different once you've slept on it.'

'We will,' confirmed Helen.

'We're driving back home tomorrow,' Lucy said.

Jamal raised a cautionary finger. 'Whatever you do, don't talk about it in the car. I don't want to hear of any accidents, all right?'

Helen closed the front door behind PC Jamal and turned back to everyone, looking her usual self once again.

'Come on then, grub's up!'

The Traveller had been having an argument with itself. This was not unusual. Arguments had been going on for eighty-one years now and was the primary reason why the entity wished to return to the stars, to the rest of itself, and leave this tiresome human host behind to finally die.

It had a very uncomfortable ride in the boot of the woman Helen's car, after she had called at Redgate Smithy earlier. This was necessary, though. Now the Traveller was being complained to by its human aspect for having lumbered it with a long walk back. But the Traveller had other plans. It had learned a new skill, today, after all.

It had watched the darkie girl and the bald freak appear in an electric blue flash. The visitation left a taste in the air, a tang of chronons. The Traveller had experienced those in minute quantities out there in the vacuum of space. This, though, was a definite concentration of them. That explained how these two could appear then and now and be unchanged.

The Traveller had waited in the trees once again. Now that the police had arrived it could no longer risk looking in through the window. The spore had yet to take full effect and the girl Grace had recognised the host. That was unfortunate. The other two children would know him too. But the time was not yet right.

The policeman had left the building. This was its opportunity. It moved forward, the foliage rustling around them.

'Oi,' the policeman said. 'Come out in there.'

'Mangled English,' said the human host.

'Never mind,' replied the Traveller to itself.

'Who are you talking to?' the policeman asked.

'What can we do for you, officer, on such a lovely evening?'

'We? How many are you?'

The Traveller shrugged.

The policeman showed recognition. 'I want to talk to you. You've been causing trouble.'

'Us, officer?'

'We're going to take a little stroll down to the station, I think.' The policemen gestured the way.

The Traveller chuckled.

'I don't see anything funny, here.' The policeman sounded annoyed.

The Traveller chuckled again. This time they appeared to lose their footing and collapsed into the arms of the policeman, who was taken by surprise. The Traveller fixed the policeman with a glare. The policeman looked down at his chest and saw that the Traveller's hand had sunk into it. The Traveller smiled at him, and slowly absorbed all the binding energy from the policeman's body, clothes and equipment.

The remains fell to the ground in a powdery husk that dissipated into a cloud and floated off by the light of a nearby window.

The Traveller held up the car keys they'd first removed from the policeman's pocket.

'Who said we had a long walk,' the Traveller told itself.

Alistair looked up from his plate. He was certain he'd heard a scream.

'Probably on the TV,' said Lucy, shovelling her food into her mouth like there was no tomorrow.

Helen had put some big budget dinosaur movie on the television in the background. *For mindless escapism*, she'd said. This had been a relief; Alistair half expected her to put on a CD of whale noises, or something equally meditative after the weird way her and Grace had started to behave. They'd stopped grinning like zealots, thankfully, and were talking normally again now.

But Alistair was certain that the scream was not from the TV. It was closer to home. He left the table and walked over to peer through the curtains at the front. There was nothing. Then Jamal's police car started up outside the house and jerkily drove off.

Must have been the TV then, he thought. *Jamal: great police officer, terrible driver*. He gave a snort, then returned to the table and the meal.

Alistair woke up with sunlight streaming in through the edges of the curtains at the end of the room. He was confused. He was also incredibly stiff again, as he had been in the stone circle the previous evening, eighty-one years ago. He stretched and got to his feet. Still fully clothed. He was on the easy chair in Grace's living room. Grace and Lucy were curled up on the settee and snoring lightly. His mouth curled into a smile. None of them had made it out to the tents last night, after all.

By the time he'd showered, changed and made a large pot of tea, the others had risen also. Lucy poured a cup for everyone. Tamara practically downed hers in one.

'Ooo-wah!' she gasped, sticking her tongue out. 'You make tea like your grandad used to, Luce: two-parts bag to one-part water!'

Lucy didn't correct her, and Alistair couldn't help but smile; what a legacy to leave! Despite her reaction, Tamara quickly poured herself a second mugful from the dregs of the pot. This involved her removing the lid and squeezing the bags inside with a teaspoon to get every last drop. She was definitely obsessed.

Alistair entered Grace's bedroom again, having just taken Tamara's luggage out to the car. Tamara had rather slyly given them both some dogsbody tasks, no doubt to make up somehow for the previous day. Lucy was stripping Grace's bed of the linen Tamara had been sleeping on.

'I'll make my bed again, Luce,' Grace said.

'You sure? I don't mind, and Mum did say.'

'A kind offer, Lucy, but no. And once we have done these tasks and you have left, Mother and I can go to Bledoe for the day, and possibly Redgate Smithy.'

'Grace, why do you keep talking like that?'

'Like what?'

'Like a zombie or an acolyte or something.'

'I think you are wrong and imagining things, Lucy Wilson.'

Lucy glanced at Alistair and raised her arms in despair. Then she spotted Grace's new top on the chair. She grabbed it and held it up to herself, appreciating it.

'You'll need a new hoodie when you get home, *Hobo*,' she said. 'Your favourite one, too, ruined.' There was a mischievous grin on her face.

Alistair felt very self-conscious. 'I'm sure it'll be as good as new with a bit of help from a needle and thread, you'll see.'

Grace stepped to her desk and opened her laptop to reveal a couple of A4 print outs.

'Before I forget, you'd better have these.'

Grace once again looked her normal self as she handed Lucy the first print out. Alistair peered at it over Lucy's shoulder as she read.

'Awesome work, Grace, cheers.'

'Yeah, the links are at the tops of the pages as well. There was nothing in *The Cornishman* or the *Western Morning News*. But what we have here is from *The Cornish Echo* on Tuesday, May 4th, 1937.'

TRAGIC FIRE KILLS
POPULAR FAMILY

The historic stone circle at Redgate Smithy, on Bodmin Moor, near Bledoe, was the scene of a terrible disaster this last Saturday, May 1st. The Clarke family, husband Leonard (50), wife Greta (44) and their son Graeme (home for the weekend from Taunton Preparatory School) were enjoying the stone circle late on Saturday evening when a sudden fire erupted on the site. It is thought they set up a small camping fire near to where contraband brandy was being stored, unknown to them. The authorities say the area had been under police observation for smuggling activities. The conflagration then lit the surrounding grassland, engulfing the poor family. All three died. Police and fire brigade attended, but the fire had burned itself out before the authorities arrived. None of the nearby farmland was affected.

Dr. Leonard Clarke was highly regarded for his charity work and owned a private medical practice in Liskeard. The practice will transfer to the next most senior member, Dr. M. Owens. Mrs Greta Clarke, née St John-Mills, was known for her patronage of local Women's Institute events and had been a volunteer nurse in France during the Great War. Of Graeme, tragically only 13 years old, Headmaster Dr. K. L. Thurlong said he was 'a boy of great promise, with fine leadership skills and a healthy interest in extra-curricular activities. We shall not see his like here again at Taunton.' The coroner has passed a verdict of death by misadventure. The funeral will be held at Bledoe Village Church on May 6th, with Pastor Stone presiding.

'Wow,' said Lucy, drawing out the word sarcastically.

'There's your evidence,' Grace confirmed.

'That is just a complete pile of...' Lucy paused as she saw Alistair staring at her intently. '...wonder.' A chuckle. 'Yeah. Nice one, Grace, thanks.'

Grace then placed the second printed sheet in Lucy's hand.

'And here's your follow-up request.' Her voice changed in tone very slightly. 'You did not acknowledge this, which led to a lot of the trouble, yesterday.'

'Yeah, all right, don't rub it in,' said Lucy, tetchily.

Alistair noted that these changes in vocal tone came

with a relaxation around Grace's eyes, as if she was suddenly not focusing in the same way. Something wasn't right there.

Grace grinned at them. 'Am I brilliant or what?'

Lucy glanced at Grace, then at Alistair, then back at Grace and smiled.

'You're brilliant, of course,' Lucy said.

'Correct. This is from *The Times*, on Monday April 26th, 1937.'

Asteroid arrives for May Day!

A large asteroid will pass close by the Earth this coming Saturday, just in time for May Day!

An asteroid is a small body of rock, orbiting the Sun. They are generally found between the planets Mars and Jupiter, where astronomers have long assumed that there is an asteroid *belt*.

This particular asteroid has an unusual orbit, known as 'elliptical', which brings it closer to the Sun and then takes it millions of miles away again. It is now on its approach towards the Sun and is due to pass between the Earth and the Moon on the evening of this coming Saturday, May 1st. It is not known yet if it will be visible to the naked eye, so eager spotters should ready their telescopes.

The asteroid was first

spotted in December last year by Professor Nigel Jacks at the Norman Lockyer Observatory in Sidmouth, Devon, who has given his initials to the asteroid, known officially as NJ1936. The observatory has been following the asteroid's progress and extrapolating its orbit. They believe NJ1936 will pass by us again in around seventy-five to eighty-five years' time.

Who knows, perhaps we'll be able to send aircraft up to it then? What a May Day celebration fly by that would be!

Alistair recognised this as the article he had found online on Hobo's phone. Even so it was useful to have. Grace gave an embarrassed chuckle and continued.

'I guess it's all a bit freaky with the dates and stuff. But… you're not thinking that the asteroid caused the fire in the stone circle, are you?'

Lucy chuckled herself, a little unconvincingly.

'Yeah, right. As if. I mean, how could it? Like the *Cornish Echo* said, camp fire, smuggled brandy, all very unfortunate.'

The relief on Grace's face was immediate. 'Good, cos I was worried for a minute. I looked a bit further for articles, but as far as I could see, after May 6th, the press was just full of the *Hindenburg* disaster in America, so presumably niche interest items like this got dropped.'

'What's a hindenburg?' Lucy asked.

'Tents?' Tamara called from the hallway, before Alistair or Grace had time to respond.

*

Alistair and Lucy had virtually packed away both tents before Grace appeared and collected her sleeping bag. She wore that same contented smile on her face.

'Is your mum still angry like mine?' Lucy asked. 'She seems pretty chilled, considering.'

Grace simply replied, 'She understands.'

'What's that supposed to mean?'

Lucy's words fell on deaf ears. Alistair looked across at her as Grace returned inside.

'Something is off,' he said.

'I know.'

There was a mouldering bench under a small fruit tree. Alistair led Lucy to it, and they sat.

'Problems,' she said. 'Grace and her mum are acting strange. But we aren't, and Mum isn't.' Lucy shrugged. 'Not the first time they've acted strange, mind. They were odd after Grace's dad left. So, that leaves the stone circle and the asteroid. We've got to be at Redgate Smithy tonight in case what happened before happens again.'

'Agreed.'

'But we're back at school tomorrow, and we're gonna be heading home shortly.'

'We've got your ring, though. We can go home, then meet up later and use it to travel back here.'

'That's not gonna work, thanks to yesterday. I'm sorry, by the way. I tried to get us back to the stone circle just after we left, but all I could think about was how much I wanted to go to bed, so the ring brought us here.'

Alistair smiled to himself at the thought of a time travel device that didn't always take the operator where they wanted to go. Lucy continued.

'So, god knows what *your* mum's gonna do when we get back. Since Dad's at home already, I just know my mum's going to sit me down and give me the third degree.' She rubbed her hands together. 'Two things, then. We need to come up with a water-tight cover story for yesterday, and we need to travel to tonight, this morning, before we leave Liskeard.'

It was clear at breakfast that Tamara had yesterday very much on her mind; that and today's bank holiday traffic. Alistair sucked his teeth as he thought.

'That means crossing our own timelines. Can we do that?'

'Duh! Says the man who's spent ages travelling along his own timeline.'

'I was thinking more about the restrictions of the ring.'

'Grandad, you know more about this ring than I do.'

'Only it's origin. Now, if Anne was here… But she's not, so, I guess there's only one way to find out.' He pressed his hands on his knees and stood up; a very Sir Alistair move, he realised. 'Let's grab what we think we'll need and sneak off. Once your mum gets us in the car, that's it.'

Their concerns were well-founded. As they carried the camping gear back inside, they could hear Tamara in the living room, on the phone to Meg Kostinen, telling her that they'd be leaving shortly and to expect them by teatime.

Alistair looked at Lucy. 'No time to grab anything. It's now or never.'

Lucy slipped the ring from her chain and they held hands.

CHAPTER TWELVE
Dead Man Walking

ALISTAIR STAGGERED FORWARD A FEW PACES UPON arrival. It was going to take a while for him to get used to this method of travel. Wherever they were, whenever they were, the change in environment was more extreme this time. Pitch blackness all around. Soft, squelchy turf under foot and biting rain in their faces did nothing to make them feel welcome.

Despite the inclement conditions, Alistair's eyes gradually adjusted. By the time he could make out the circle of standing stones surrounding them and confirm their location, his Converse had already sunk into the boggy ground. With his feet already soaked through, he pulled his sodden hood up over his head; a token gesture, at best. Next to him, Lucy was looking just as bedraggled as he felt.

'Grandad, this is horrible.'

'Agreed. We need to find shelter.'

'What's going on? Someone there?' A voice, male, adult. And flickering torchlight.

Here we go again, thought Alistair. Without any words, he and Lucy ran to the nearest sarsen. They couldn't get behind the monolith; there was hazard tape in the way. It looped around the stone and on to the next one. They ducked underneath and hid.

'Hello?' The same voice again.

Torchlight played around the stones haphazardly,

then off onto the moors.

'Must have been the wind around the stones, again.' Another voice. Another adult male.

'When are the flippin' police getting here, eh? It's been ages now. I'm soaked and frozen.'

'We'll see the headlights first, surely?'

'Yeah, thanks for that. I'm not a complete idiot.'

'Sorry, just saying, that's all.'

Alistair peered cautiously around the edge of the stone. The torchlight picked out more hazard tape, completely cordoning off the inside of the circle. There were two men in three-quarter length hi-vis waterproof jackets. Alistair recognised the logo on the jackets from the information board outside the stone circle. It was the nearby B&B.

'Look, Steve, it could be anything. We get all sorts wandering in if we leave the patio doors open. Ponies, rabbits, stray cattle. I'm forever having to shoo 'em away when I'm on bar duty.'

'As long as, you know, *he* ain't up and walking.'

'Him? Pfff! Just look at him.'

'I'd rather not.' There was an audible shudder from the two men as the light picked out a glistening corpse lying on the altar stone. Wet with rain, blood, or both. It had obviously turned the stomach of the man called Steve.

'What is it?' Lucy hissed. 'What's going on?'

Alistair turned to face her. *More death.* 'Looks like a crime scene, Lucyloo. Couple of staff from the B&B waiting for the emergency services to arrive. I think someone's been murdered. On the altar stone.'

She looked horrified. 'Murdered? Or sacrificed?'

A double scream cut through the night air. Alistair and Lucy peered around the edge of their stone. There was no sign of the two men, but the torches, still shining, were lying on the ground. Alistair looked at Lucy. His pulse thumping in his ears was drowning out the patter of the rain on the stone.

'Grandad? I don't like this.'

He wasn't keen himself, but he'd never admit as much to his granddaughter.

'Stay here,' he said. 'I'm going to take a look.' How habitually those words tripped off his tongue, even after all these years.

'No way,' Lucy rapidly replied. 'You can't leave me here on my own.'

She was right. They were both in considerable danger, whatever they did, until they knew more about what was going on.

'Come on, then.' They slowly crept over to where the torches lay. The rain had abated into a fuzzy drizzle, but it was still more than sufficient to keep them soaked through. They grabbed a torch each and shone them about. There was no sign of the two men.

The night felt almost impenetrable around them. Bledoe was nothing more than a collection of bleary lights twinkling in the distance. The hills and lanes that led on up to Higher Tremarcoombe were hidden by mist. Alistair couldn't even see the slight promontory where he and Lucy had lain with James and the others eighty-one years ago. Bodmin Moor was a very treacherous place to be on a night like this.

Just outside the circle, towards the shingle track, Alistair's torch beam picked out a rather battered mobility scooter. They made a closer inspection. It looked like it had been discarded there.

'Odd.' Alistair shone his light further afield, but there was nothing else.

'Maybe one of the blokes has ME and can't do the yomp across the moors? My Year Four teacher, Mrs O'Leary, had that.'

'Maybe,' said Alistair. 'But there's at least one other person hereabouts.'

'The body on the slab.' Lucy's voice trembled.

'I'd better take a look.'

They turned to head back into the circle and Lucy flung her hand over her mouth with a yelp.

'Good grief!' Alistair hissed.

The remains of two indistinguishable bodies were slumped against a nearby stone, like discarded mannequins. They were dry, lifeless husks – clothes and flesh alike. Their surfaces flaked and dissipated under the onslaught of the rain.

'Grandad? What on earth could do *that* to a person?'

'Nothing on Earth, I fear. Quick, we need to check the body on the altar. Come on.'

Lucy held his hand very tightly as they crossed the uneven ground.

'Watch out for the black rock,' she reminded him.

'I will.'

The discarded mobility scooter had worried Alistair. As they approached the central stone it was clear that he'd not been wrong in his assumptions.

Smiffy.

He tried to hold Lucy back, but she'd already seen too much.

'Oh, god, no. Poor man.'

Alistair stepped closer. He gazed down at his old friend, spread Christ-like on the flat stone. He'd had such a long life of struggle and adversity. How unjust for it to be taken away from him in this tragic way.

I'm sorry, old friend.

'He's not like the others. I wonder why?'

As he mused, Alistair realised Lucy had asked a very important question. Smiffy's body was still relatively… *fresh*. A nasty gash in the side of his head showed where he'd been bludgeoned. He'd clearly been positioned shortly after the attack; blood had pooled on the stone. There was the tell-tale tang of iron on the moist night air.

200

It left a noticeable aftertaste.

'Admiring our handiwork?' The cracked, plummy and slightly nasally voice dropped from nowhere into the flat, dull atmosphere. 'It's truly amazing. We've lived for so long, seen so much, yet there are things we never knew we could do with these bare hands until yesterday.'

Alistair and Lucy played their torch beams around frantically, trying to discover the whereabouts of the speaker. He couldn't be too far away.

And then, there he was, emerging from behind the nearest sarsen like a genial host entering a lounge party.

'Nobby Clarke?' Lucy whispered.

Alistair nodded. 'It's him all right.'

Ancient, disfigured and wizened, yet still recognisable.

Nobby smiled his unpleasant smile. 'No one's called us that for eighty-one years, and then it happens twice in one night.'

Lucy frowned. 'Us?'

'Of course,' Alistair said. 'The mist from the meteorite. It possessed you.'

'You do not seem surprised,' Nobby said.

'Not my first gaseous alien.'

Lucy nodded, and asked, 'What happened to your nose, *Graeme*?'

'You did,' Nobby spat back with sudden vehemence.

Alistair noted the self-congratulatory smile that spread across Lucy's face. 'We thought you'd burned,' he said. 'With the others. Everyone did.'

'Yes, rather fortuitous, that. So much so that it wasn't until tonight that we finally bumped into someone who recognised us.'

Alistair felt his heart sink. 'Poor Smiffy.'

'All that time and he knew us right away – knew *me* right away. Always wanted to take him on. And there, I've finally shown him. Father would be proud.'

'Congratulations,' said Alistair, with distaste. 'You've smashed a slightly frailer old man around the head with a stone and settled a score.'

'He's aged. I've aged. But you two haven't. We'd think that was strange if we hadn't seen you arrive last night outside the Pembertons' flat. Time travel?'

Lucy raised an accusatory finger at the old man. 'Why were you spying on Grace and her mum?' Realisation swept across her face. 'You've done something to them, haven't you?'

Alistair remembered the scream he'd heard and realised what must have happened to Jamal. He motioned to Lucy that they should keep their distance from the old man.

'Where did you leave the police car you stole?'

Nobby Clarke looked at Alistair archly. 'You're very astute, both of you.'

'For degenerates,' Alistair finished off.

The old man waved the comment aside.

'The car is near the hostelry at which we've been staying, free of charge thanks to a little... skill of ours.'

'Is that the same "skill" which has prevented the emergency services from coming up here to arrest you and take poor Smiffy's body away?'

'All very unfortunate, that. We couldn't stop the girl getting help from the hostelry, but we *were* able to influence her into not summoning police and ambulance. Alas, those two gentlemen were waiting for relief that was never going to come.'

'Do you have to mix your personal pronouns so much?' Alistair asked.

Nobby appeared to sag slightly, then stood erect again. 'The "I" is Graeme Clarke, who sometimes speaks as himself. The Traveller struggles with pronouns. They are too restrictive. "We" is the nearest... acceptable...' The old man's random speech tailed off.

202

'Since we've picked an appalling night for a reunion, and it already started badly before we arrived, what are you doing here?' Alistair asked.

'Is this another alien invasion?' Lucy's eyes sparkled at the prospect.

The Traveller answered. 'We are not alien, girl.'

'Ha! You're hardly from Penzance.'

'We are beyond such categorisations.'

'What are you, then? Science project gone wrong?'

Nobby looked up at the sky. 'We are simply the Traveller. We have come here to return home.'

'How?'

'With their assistance.'

Alistair and Lucy looked at each other, then again at Nobby. 'Whose assistance?' Alistair asked.

The old man pointed past them towards Bledoe. Alistair and Lucy followed his gesture. The rain had died down further and they could see a large group of torchlit figures heading towards them. They turned back to him.

'How?' Lucy repeated the question.

'Which of you can we commune with?' Nobby was almost slurring his words now.

'You what?'

'Don't prevaricate, girl, which of you two can we commune with? Speech wastes energy and this host frame is perpetually low on that. We can communicate much faster and more efficiently through thought-melding.'

Alistair raised his hairless eyebrows. 'You can transfer your conscience into another person?'

'Not fully. The energy required is too great and we have no way to store it – which is why it was expelled when we first entered this body. Hurry!'

Alistair wasn't convinced. 'So how come you can do it now?'

'We use the binding energy of our host's life,' the

Traveller hissed. 'We have fed on those men, but be quick, or that energy too will have dissipated.'

Alistair looked at Lucy. 'I'll do it.'

'What? Grandad, no!'

He anticipated Lucy's objection and quickly stepped forward to meet the ancient figure before she could intervene. They touched, but before anything could happen Alistair reached back and grabbed hold of Lucy's time ring, still hanging about her neck.

Alistair's vision was wiped out in a blinding flash.

He found himself in a room, or so it seemed. He was certainly conscious of it being a finite space, the lack of obvious walls or floor notwithstanding. As he checked to see what he was standing on, he realised he had his own legs again. Body. Arms. Head. The lot.

'You are not the freak! What are you doing here, old man?' The voice came from all around him. He turned.

A small glowing cloud hovered before him. Its hue was somehow no colour and every colour all at once. It hurt his eyes to look at it.

'I'll thank you not to refer to Hobo in that fashion. And as for what I'm doing here, I can no more explain that than the Pope!'

'We are in physical contact with the boy, therefore we should be engaging with his consciousness. Can you be the boy's consciousness? An old man trapped inside a young boy's body.'

Alistair cleared his throat, awkwardly. 'Yes, well, you could say I've been posted here, temporarily. You know how it is in the military.'

'But we know you, do we not? No... *he* knows you. Knew you. There is a name. Ali. Little Ali Lethbridge-Stewart. From Redrose Cottage.' There was jubilation in the disembodied voice.

'Brigadier Sir Alistair Lethbridge-Stewart to you.' He

made himself deliberately haughty. 'What do I call you?'

The cloud ignored the question. 'You were here, that night, eighty-one years ago. You and the girl. *And* the freak. Something is not right. That is more than just time travel. We sense the hand of a higher power.'

Alistair raised an eyebrow. 'I've already told you, I can't possibly explain something I don't understand myself.'

Alistair found himself abruptly seated in an upholstered chair. The glowing cloud buzzed around him. In the distance, clearly unseen by the cloud, stood Lucy. Watching, unable to speak. Alistair allowed himself a slight smile. The time ring was, after all, linked to Lethbridge-Stewart DNA. Seemed reasonable to assume it would link them both into this mindscape. Although, evidently, not enough that Lucy could become involved in the conversation.

So, she just watched.

'We are the Traveller,' the cloud said. 'We are not a being. We are an essence, beyond the physical plane. We exist. We occupy. We *are*.'

'Hmm, not the first "essence" I've met. Any chance of a brandy?'

His request was ignored. 'We travel. We come from whence we came, and we shall be wherever we are headed.'

'Very profound. You're starting to make me feel like Alice.'

'Is the reference important?'

'Probably not.'

'Then cease. It is difficult enough for us to commune on your level without additional nonsense.'

Alistair waved loftily at the cloud to continue and was surprised to find a glass of brandy magically appear in his hand. He sniffed at it, then swirled it to warm it.

'For eons, we have travelled this solar system.

Watching. Learning. Absorbing. We require a host, but not in a malignant way. The Traveller is what you call benign.'

'There are three corpses in the stone circle, plus a missing police officer, that would argue otherwise.'

The Traveller ignored the challenge, although the glass of brandy suddenly disappeared. 'You call this planet the Earth. We have passed it many times. As life has developed here, we ejected a small fragment of ourself each time to *commune* with the planet.'

'Like we're doing now?'

'As much as you would understand it, yes. We are receptive to many forms of energy; when the stones in the circle had been freshly laid there, they cried out to us in their desperation. They had separation anxiety.'

'Stones?' Alistair scoffed. 'Rubbish!'

'We are attempting to explain the almost inexplicable in terminology that you would understand.'

Slightly chastened, Alistair inclined his head. The Traveller continued unabashed.

'We felt their pain like a beacon. That was when we first visited. We have returned on each pass since, extending our feelers through the ground to absorb the necessary information. That way we have learned much about the development of life, society and technology on this planet of yours.

'Unfortunately for us, on the last visit there were three imitation stones. It was not possible to channel our energies correctly through their flimsy structure. This caused a feedback loop which destabilised us. As we indicated, we are susceptible to various forms of energy. We tried to retreat, but there was already a strong psychic pull from the ceremony taking place below. We were unable to resist.'

No wonder.

Alistair recalled how worked up Smiffy and Lucy had

got that night, not to mention whatever the coven members were feeling, worried about their identities being blown wide open. Psychic energies. A bit like Devil's End.

'As you bore witness, we made an uncontrolled landing. The impact forced us from our vessel. Confused and exposed, we moved quickly into the nearest alternative host – Graeme Clarke. But humans are different to any substances we had encountered before. Soft, with organs, fluids and chemicals, parts interconnected. We had only ever been hard, solid, inflexible. We co-opted the boy's natural systems and found that controlling you fleshy things required much less potential energy than did a rock. The excess had nowhere to go; it could only disperse as heat and light. That huge fireball incinerated all who were there. Not even our new body could escape damage.'

'But you survived, all the same.'

'As the heat emerged so we were thrown clear with only minor burns. Outside the circle was safe, yet dark. We assessed where and what we now were, realising immediately that thought alone was too pure for this body. Concepts required signifying names and words, and sometimes images, in order for this vessel to understand. As we adapted to this, we found our host vessel had gone into shock. We were unable to provide a resistance to this and went into shock also, retreating along with the vessel's consciousness. Our new physical form was left as a vacant shell, operating on impulse only. It wandered off, living rough on the moors for some time before we grew accustomed and found a way back to cognisance again.

'The host had healed. It had sheltered in a cave and fed off stray animals. Now we were a shared vessel, Graeme Clarke and the Traveller. We re-entered society. It was a time of war. We were victim. This made it easier to create a new identity. And we could be passenger, observer, as the Traveller always intended to be. But we became horrified by what we saw and learned. The wilful pain, the indiscriminate death – this was outside of our experiential framework. Time passed. We became affected more and more by what we experienced, the world of humanity. Consider how you've treated each other. Consider how you've treated the planet you live on. Consider the creatures you share it with, to whom you should be *custodians*. He saw things differently. Always. We argued with him, within ourself, constantly. We were branded schizoid. Medics took an interest, locked us away. We discovered a way out of this by expending tiny amounts of binding energy as psychic spores, to influence other humans. But overuse of this exhausted our host and it began to prematurely age. We despaired of the world around us, of the consciousness we shared this vessel with. We wanted desperately to find inner peace. We still do.'

'I'm sorry,' said Alistair, and he meant it. It didn't happen often, but once in a blue moon a friendly alien found itself caught up in the constant squabbles of Earth.

'It is not your fault,' the cloud voice replied. 'But *he* is now sick of raving at society for its liberality, its pandering to regressive ways and its tolerance. That was not how *he* was taught human society should be.'

'Nobby's learned nothing since we last met, then.'

'And we were trapped. We wanted to return home, to be whole once again, as soon as possible. But we could only wait until our orbit passed again; until we felt the pull of proximity. Until now. We cannot endure that wait, this life, again.'

'You will leave Nobby's body and ascend tonight?'

The answer was unequivocal. 'Yes.'

'I thought you said there was insufficient energy in the old body? Will the asteroid send another meteorite, or vessel, or whatever it is, down to collect you?'

'It will assume we are lost.'

'Then, how will you return to it?'

'We have discovered a new source of binding energy. The emotion that is known to you as raw anger allows us to extract binding energies from bodies.'

'Leaving them as withered husks. I see.'

'You are benefiting from that. We have become sufficiently energised to keep this old body alive further, and to have this communion with you. But we know now that it can do more.'

'More?'

'It is our way out.'

Alistair was worried. Several things suddenly started to make sense to him.

'No.'

'You cannot stop it, old man.'

'These are not the actions of a benign entity.'

'We do not do this through malice. The lives are simply not important to us one way or another.'

'Apathy!' Alistair spat. 'That's even worse.'

The cloud rushed forward and surrounded his head. 'Humanity has made us this way.'

Alistair ducked out and took a few paces away, reaching for his trusty service revolver in the holster that wasn't there. 'You are judging and condemning the many for the actions of the few.'

'We are doing what is necessary to ensure our freedom. There is no other way.'

'Listen. What if I can provide an alternative for you?'

'Such as?'

Alistair was desperate. 'Give me time to think. Could you be uploaded on to a portable device, like a computer hard drive with its own energy source?'

'You would seek to trap me in one of your systems.'

'No. We could transmit you, if you were compatible,

beam you out into space to re-join your asteroid, and with no further loss of life.'

'The residents of Bledoe are on their way to the stone circle now. There is very little time. The asteroid is near, and my apotheosis is at hand.'

'How have you affected, *in*fected, so many?'

'Psychic spores timed to detonate and spread at certain times or with certain stimuli. The Pembertons. Their cue was you and the girl appearing. The staff at the hostelry; many living in Bledoe. They've been on constant slow release since yesterday. It's an energy drain but we expect the rewards to pay back a considerable yield.'

Alistair looked around. 'I need to get out. Those lives must be saved.'

'Including your granddaughter?'

Alistair's eyes flickered over to Lucy, whose eyes widened in shock.

'How did you — ?'

'We know all, Destroyer of Destroyers. We have been reading you as you have been listening to us.'

'Look, let us help you if we can. You made a mistake coming here, that's a shame, but humanity knows only too well that we live and die by our own mistakes.'

'Not so the Traveller. And you are now trapped here, Brigadier. Your granddaughter and the body of the boy Hobo will be consumed along with the population of Bledoe. And you? This can be an exchange. Your consciousness, your essence will join us on our asteroid to journey through space forever more.'

The words sunk in, and Alistair realised that if he was trapped there, then so was Lucy.

CHAPTER THIRTEEN
Looking for Satellites

LUCY LISTENED TO THE WORDS OF THE TRAVELLER. Throughout the conversation it had felt like she was both there, and in the stone circle. Grandad had grabbed the ring; even now Hobo's hand was grasping it. Connecting them.

There was no way she was letting the Traveller win. She didn't know how much longer he would be visiting, but she was Lucy Lethbridge-Stewart, and she would not let the Traveller steal her grandad off her.

With as much effort as she could manage, she forced her body to step back. One step, another, and then… She yanked herself suddenly, and the ring snapped out of Hobo's hand.

Lucy took a deep breath. She was completely back in her own mind. And before her, eyes open but seeing nothing, was Hobo. No, Grandad.

What if the Traveller did win? Did that mean Hobo was lost to her too?

'No bloody way!' she hissed. 'Sorry, Grandad, Hobo.'

Cursing herself, but knowing she had little option, Lucy pulled back her fist.

Grace Pemberton had spent a lovely May Bank Holiday with her mum. She couldn't remember precisely what she'd done before they arrived in Bledoe for lunch, but it was probably lovely. They'd had a lovely picnic on the village green where lots of other people had also gathered for bank holiday picnics. Some of these people Grace's mum knew, which was lovely. Everyone was being friendly and having a smashing time.

They'd stayed at the lovely village green all afternoon. This was something they knew they had to do. The weather was lovely; wet and chilly and lovely. Gradually the day rolled on and it grew dark. Grace, and her mum, and all the other lovely people who had congregated on the village green, all instinctively knew when the time was right. They packed up their things, grabbed their torches and headed off along Fore Street. They went past the sports ground and off towards the lovely stone circle at Redgate Smithy. They all knew they had to do this. This was the right thing to do and the time to do so was now.

'I think I have been here recently,' Grace told her mum.

'I feel the same,' her mum replied.

'This time, we are going to a party.'

Her mum nodded. 'A lovely party. For our friend, the Traveller.'

'Our dear, good friend, the Traveller,' Grace agreed.

'And it will be so worthwhile. There are so many lovely people here. Everyone loves the Traveller.'

'Everyone loves the Traveller,' echoed Grace.

As they shone their lights and marched up over the moors, Grace looked ahead to the lovely stone circle. There were three figures there. Had the party started early? She had not expected this. As she looked on, she realised one of the figures was her good friend, the Traveller. There were two children with him. It was Lucy Wilson and Hobo. They were also her friends.

Gosh, she thought, *what are other friends doing here?*

As Grace watched, Lucy pulled away from Hobo, but he was clearly enthralled with the Traveller. She quite understood why this should be the case. The Traveller

212

was lovely.

Lucy pulled back and punched Hobo on the head. The two of them went tumbling to the ground. This must be a lovely game.

The Traveller gazed Grace's way, which made her blush. He stood with open arms, ready to welcome the approaching crowd into the stone circle.

To Alistair, it felt like someone had flicked a switch. Suddenly he found himself back in the dark, rainy, stone circle. He was lying on the ground, completely soaked through and caked in mud. Lucy was next to him. She got to her feet, grabbed his arm and helped haul him upright again.

'You okay?' She pinched his cheeks and peered at his eyeballs.

'I think so.' He put a hand to his head. 'Thank you, Lucy. A timely rescue.'

'We need to stay out of his reach,' Lucy said. 'Oi, Traveller, looks like the exchange programme is off.'

'No matter,' said Nobby Clarke, hobbling after them as they skipped around within the stone circle. 'You will perish with the rest in my ascendance.'

'We have to save them,' Alistair said to Lucy.

'You cannot save them,' said the Traveller, gloating. He stopped any pretence of chasing Lucy and Alistair and the two of them came to a halt.

'He's infected them all with a kind of subliminal message,' Alistair told Lucy. 'I don't think we can break that. So, either we need to get him away from here, or we need to transfer the Traveller from Nobby Clarke's body into something else first.'

'Like some kind of hard drive, data storage? I should have brought my laptop. Can he do Bluetooth, or does he have a USB adaptor?'

'Helpful suggestions, please, Lucy.'

'Fine. Will a phone do? We've both got one of those.'

'Yes, that might work.' Alistair produced the smartphone from his pocket. 'Here, we'll use Hobo's. Your mum would never forgive me if I damaged yours.'

'That's okay, Hobo and I managed without mobiles for months.' Lucy smirked. 'We could do it again.'

'Yes, because of the Great Intelligence.' Another vague memory bouncing around in Hobo's mind.

Alistair looked over his shoulder. The crowd was getting close. The Traveller was now positioning his frail, ancient body near the altar stone in the centre, where Smiffy's corpse lay.

'If I've understood what I've been told correctly, plus what we saw in 1937, I think we can force the transference automatically if sufficient energy is applied. There was no control over the excess energy back when the meteorite landed.'

Lucy nodded.

'Creating sufficient energy, that's the tricky bit. I have an idea. Two ideas, in fact. Although plan B is pretty risky for both of us. Plan A will still take nerve. And good timing. I'm going to creep out of the circle—'

'What?'

'What I need isn't far. Let's call it Smiffy's revenge. Keep the Traveller where he is now, but I need him to be holding Hobo's phone when I come back. Can you do that?'

'You want me to get him to take a call?'

'I'll leave the detail up to you, Lucyloo.'

She grinned. 'Okay, I'll give it a go.'

'And remember, don't let him touch you.' Alistair looked again at the approaching crowd. He had to be quick. He handed Lucy Hobo's phone. 'Let's get this done before any of those poor people arrive.'

He ran outside the circle and around the perimeter until he came to Smiffy's discarded mobility scooter. He could hear the murmuring of the crowd. Their torch beams played across him as he removed the scooter's two 12v batteries. With one in each hand he dashed back into the circle.

He could see Lucy talking with the Traveller by the altar stone. Alistair's footing slipped on the boggy terrain, but he managed to keep his balance and forward momentum. Lucy had looked his way, though, as he slipped. The Traveller seized his opportunity and grabbed her arm, pulling her into an embrace.

'No!' Alistair yelled. Whatever happened, he would not lose his granddaughter. Not tonight, not any night. He could see Lucy struggling.

The Traveller suddenly arched backwards. A glow rose up to engulf him from the ground. Alistair saw Lucy thrown back from the old man the way that opposing magnetic poles reject one another. He realised that the Traveller had stepped onto the black rock. It was affecting him as it had affected Alistair and Lucy before. But, unlike them, the Traveller could use the energy from the rock. The old man collapsed backwards over the body of Smiffy. The glow continued and engulfed those remains too, absorbing whatever energy remained in Smiffy's sad corpse.

It had to be now or never.

With all the strength he could muster, he hurled both of the acid batteries at the Traveller. He saw the old man turn and hold up his arms to protect himself. Hobo's phone was in the Traveller's hand. The batteries impacted with the Traveller.

The glow increased in intensity as they added to the transfer of energy. The bodies of Nobby Clarke and Smiffy Gloyne flashed a brilliant white and dissipated. The mobile phone hung in the air briefly. Then, with nothing left to support it, it began to fall…

Alistair's momentum carried him forward. He

reached for the phone, desperate to catch it in case it impacted on the altar stone and broke. But as he reached out, the excess energy from the transference erupted from the device, just as it had from Nobby Clarke in 1937.

A fireball engulfed Alistair and he was thrown to the ground, the wind knocked from his lungs.

'Grandad!'

Alistair came-to at the shrill cry. Lucy was cradling his head on her lap. He felt a sudden panic for poor Hobo.

'Am I all right? Have I damaged Hobo at all?'

'You look fine,' she confirmed with a smile. 'But Hobo will never forgive you, I know that much.' Lucy held up some blackened ends of material from his chest. Hobo's favourite hoodie. Alistair slowly stood. 'Take it easy, Grandad.'

He checked himself over as best he could. His skin smarted a bit, but there were no obvious burns. His clothes had borne the brunt of the energy discharge. The tattered remains of the blue hoodie hung around his shoulders like he was some skater boy Robinson Crusoe. His jeans were shredded. They might make cut-offs, but then again, they might turn out to be perfectly fashionable as they were.

Lucy hugged him. 'You've got amazing panda eyes.'

He smiled, then remembered the phone.

Lucy held it up. Alistair checked the screen. It looked fine.

A message bubble claimed, 'Release us!'

'Got him,' he said, and popped the phone into his pocket.

'You need to look at this,' said Lucy.

By the altar stone nothing remained of the two old men, or the mobility scooter batteries. But the big surprise was that the sunken meteorite had also dispersed in the transfer. There was now just a hole in the ground.

'Finally used up all its remaining energy, I assume,' Alistair muttered. 'Oh well, at least everything's safe here again, now.'

'Hello, Lucy. Hello, Hobo,' said a familiar voice. They saw Grace and Helen standing behind them.

'What has happened to you?' Helen asked of Alistair. He opened his mouth to speak, then thought better of things and left it. 'More mischief, I presume?' Helen said, filling in Alistair's silence. He indicated that this was indeed the case. Satisfied, Helen wandered off.

'Grace,' said Lucy. 'Why don't you and your mum start encouraging everyone to return home, yeah?'

'But the Traveller? The party? He was here, we saw him.'

'He had to cancel, sorry.'

'Oh. Will I see you again soon?'

Lucy nodded. 'I'll see you this morning,' she said.

Grace nodded and started encouraging the bewildered others to leave.

'What next then, Grandad?'

'We've still got to finish this off, try to get the Traveller back to his asteroid tonight.'

'How do we do that?'

Alistair indicated the travel ring hanging around Lucy's neck. 'Pass me that and I'll show you.'

The hallway light was on as Alistair and Lucy arrived in Ogmore-by-Sea. Lucy was wet and muddy. Alistair was wet, muddy and wearing charred, shredded clothes.

'I still think this is a mad idea,' Lucy grumbled in hushed tones, as if they'd been arguing the whole way there.

'What other choice do we have?'

'Why here, why my house?'

'Because you don't have a little brother to avoid waking, and I bet you'd have found the time to prep for it.'

'So, this is — ?'

'Tonight. Same night. Just after we've left the stone circle. I hope.'

'And we're already here?'

'Assuming we got home okay, yes.'

'Cheerful thought. What happens if we meet ourselves?'

'We won't. Because on the journey back earlier – later, for us – we'll have worked out what we needed to do to avoid bumping into each other.'

Lucy put her hand to her forehead. 'It's another paradox!'

'It's simple, Lucy, trust me.' Alistair smiled, surprised at how much he had actually learned from the Doctor. He indicated the living room door. 'Through there?'

Lucy flung her sodden arms up and shrugged her shoulders. 'How should I know?' She looked down for the first time. 'Oh God! Look at us! The hallway carpet is ruined! Mum will do her nut!'

'Cream is a terrible colour for a hallway carpet. Doris always wanted one.'

'Grandad, that does *not* help.'

'No, sorry. We'll need to be wherever the wi-fi is strongest.'

'That's everywhere in the house. Even in the garden. This is 2018, not the dark ages.'

'What's through here?'

'Living room.'

'Good. We'll agree now that this is where you leave your laptop for us to use, all right?'

Lucy frowned. 'Does it work that way?'

'Let's go inside and find out.' Alistair quietly opened the door and crept through. The standard lamp in the far corner had been left on to help them.

On the sofa were two piles of clothes, one for each of

them, and two large Sainsbury's carriers for the dirties.

'Thank goodness!' said Alistair. He was desperate to get out of the soggy, burned remains of Hobo's old clothes.

'I'm brilliant,' Lucy said with a smug grin.

She popped through into the kitchen and the two of them quickly changed. Under each pile of clothes was a laptop. A USB phone cable trailed along one side of Hobo's. A remote mouse sat on the top of each. Alistair grabbed the laptop and set it on the coffee table.

Lucy shifted her laptop to one side and sat on the sofa next to Alistair. 'Makes sense for us to have our own. Yours has got all the ridiculous firewalls on it, to protect it.'

'Excellent.' Alistair fired it up.

'What was plan B, by the way?' she asked.

'Run to the B&B, find Jamal's discarded police car, drive it to the stone circle and crash it into Nobby Clarke and the meteorite.'

'While I tried to distract him and persuade him to hold the phone? Yeah, like you said, just a little bit risky.'

Alistair took a deep breath and set to work. 'I need to access some old online UNIT systems.'

'Will they still be active?'

'The Establishment, Lucy. They never actually shut anything down, they just move things to one side and archive them. Everything's still there if you know where to look, and if you can remember your old passwords. But we're getting a bit short on time.' The clock on the laptop screen read 22:53. The asteroid was due to pass by at any time according to predictions.

'Can I help?'

Hobo's phone beeped twice and vibrated on the coffee table.

'Yes,' Alistair didn't take his eyes off the screen. 'Check that out for me, and then why don't you log in to that live feed that Grace mentioned? Monitor the asteroid's progress?'

Lucy grabbed Hobo's phone. 'Low battery and a message.'

'Okay.'

Hurry. Time is short. We are close by.

She gave Alistair a wry smile. 'No sign off. I assume it's the Traveller.'

Again, Alistair's focus hardly wavered. 'Tell it we know and we're working as fast as we can.'

He was aware of Lucy tapping away with her thumbs.

There was a creak of movement from upstairs. They both winced and froze while they listened for further sounds. Nothing. Alistair licked his dry lips. Lucy suggested setting Hobo's phone to silent, just in case. He nodded, then his fingers returned to the keyboard. Lucy put the phone back on the table and twisted to grab her laptop.

The Traveller had felt constricted inside the body of Nobby Clarke, but that was nothing compared to the data storage vessel in which it now found itself. Somehow, it had lost control of the situation in the stone circle, virtually at the point of victory, of release. Those meddling children again. And now, against its will, it was being contained as… data. The Traveller flipped and wandered through the available folders. Music. Images. Some videos. Games, diversions. Communication was available to it via a limited written message interface, but there was no way out.

There had been a slight chronon shift, more than the normal progression from the passage of time. The girl's travel device, it assumed. They were no longer near the circle of bonding. The remains of the vessel had been exhausted in the transfer into this storage unit, but the Traveller still felt the pain of separation.

It could sense that the battery life of the device was

minimal. It was not possible to release psychic spores from this vessel, even when in contact with a human. Any attempt to escape as data signals via the wider network might exhaust the battery and delete the Traveller. But if this was to be the extent of their existence for another eighty-one years at least... They could not face that.

This was all the fault of the smugglers who had constructed the fake stones on the previous orbital pass. It seemed, now, that freedom, escape or even revenge were all closed avenues to the Traveller. It would take the risk, push for liberty and die trying; the frustrating limitations of human existence had finally exhausted the Traveller's options.

As it reached out for the carrier wave and sought to convert itself into the correct form for transmission, an unexpected, seemingly limitless world revealed itself. A connection that had not previously existed had opened up. Energy, in various forms, was readily available and this swelled the Traveller as it swam along the cable connection and into the vast electronic super highway that awaited them.

So much new data. Random, disorganised, and yet utterly transfixing. The humans could keep their small lives and petty opinions. This was adventure, this was knowledge; this was what the Traveller had come here for all along.

'What's this?' Alistair growled.

Lucy glanced at his screen and pulled a face. 'Since when has UNIT not been available?'

'You tell me.'

He sat back on the sofa as the full impact of what he'd just read hit home. It had always felt like a struggle to keep UNIT going – particularly in those formative years. And later in life even Doris had commented that they seemed pretty incompetent without him, hence him being regularly called back from retirement. But somehow, he'd always felt - hoped, perhaps – that there was a good deal more life left in the organisation. Yet here he was, not even seven years into his future and UNIT was already no more.

'Does that say "diverted funding streams"?' Lucy tutted.

Alistair saw that horrible buzzword again: *Brexit*. He turned to his granddaughter. 'What is this Brexit? I keep seeing it mentioned.'

'Oh, yeah. It's about us leaving the European Union next year.'

Alistair made a quick etymological assumption and decided he liked the word even less. He wasn't in a position to judge, but it didn't sound like a progressive move. He muttered as much.

Lucy shrugged. 'The kids all agree, but no one's listening to sense. You should hear Mum and Dad going on about it. Con and Nicky have been on protest marches with Gordon and Kadiatu.'

'There were battles with the MOD about funding for UNIT going all the way back to the—' Alistair shot forward. Those words had given him an idea. He tapped a finger on the edge of the laptop, ruminating. 'Passwords, passwords…' he muttered. 'Secure network codes. Birthdays? Old addresses? Names and vital statistics?'

'Eww, Grandad!'

'Got to have a system, Lucyloo.'

He gave his fingers free reign and the laptop screen boldly declared ACCOUNT REBOOT SUCCESS. PASSWORD ACCEPTED. WELCOME BACK BRIGADIER LETHBRIDGE-STEWART.

'If only you knew the half of it! See what I mean, Lucy? Over six years since I… Well, you know.'

Lucy looked down.

He cleared his throat. 'Dead for over six years and it greets me as if I'd only logged in yesterday. No one ever does any house-keeping to remove old and deceased profiles.'

'Where are you? Oh, Ministry of Defence.'

'Yes, you probably shouldn't see any of this, really.'

'Can they still get you for it, after death?'

Alistair chuckled. 'They'd probably find a way. I don't want to get you into trouble.'

'What are you trying to do?'

'I need to access an old MOD online portal, but it's buried deep in other systems. And for good reasons, too. I'm hoping to reactivate of one of our old satellites in orbit. We used to use them years ago for... things. Most of them were left up there once they'd completed their tasks. Their orbits would slowly decay, then they'd burn up harmlessly on re-entry. If I can transmit the Traveller to one of those satellites and then make the satellite collide with the asteroid, I can send the glowing cloud home. I'm just not sure if I should. So, I'll try to set it all up, and then decide.'

'You don't trust the Traveller?'

He glanced at Lucy, then back at the screen. 'It claims to be benign, but it's also happy to murder people on a whim – including us if it could. It believes that slaughtering most of the population of a village is justified collateral for a journey home. Now, I've had some pretty awful journeys home before now, but I've never considered killing a load of people to make up for it. That's how I look at it.'

'I can just imagine how mad I'd feel after being stuck trapped inside Nobby Clarke's head for eighty-one years, that's all. I'd like to judge it fairly if we can.'

Alistair paused, taken somewhat unawares by Lucy's reasoning. *The wisdom of youth*, he thought. He looked at her with pride, then he spoke.

'Lucy, you're wonderful. I'm proud to be your grandad.' He pressed the return button with a flourish, and grinned. 'We're getting there. Let's see how we feel about it when we do, all right?' He booped her affectionately on the nose.

'Okay, well you do what you need to do, I'm not looking. At some point the live asteroid feed will finish loading up. Oh, here it is. Yeah, see?' Lucy turned the screen his way. 'Like I told Grace, nothing to see. Just lots of nutty viewer comments to scroll through.'

From the MOD secure intranet there was a convoluted pathway through to UNIT. As he'd hoped, the UNIT systems were still there in the background, just without an accessible public interface. More passwords took him through to an older, ring-fenced, version of the UNIT intranet, from its pre-Unified days. He rolled his eyes when he saw the site's codename, Blood & Thunder. *No respect.* The old UNIT intranet was the portal by which one gained access to the legacy Fifth Operational Corps secure portal, which was where he wanted to be. The Fifth website, and its associated files and systems, had been co-opted by UNIT back in the early 2000s for reference purposes. This time the site's codename was no surprise to Alistair, since he'd set it up: The HAVOC Files.

He took a moment to congratulate himself on how well he was recalling his old passwords and codes. It was all down to his training, of course. Always on the ball, always ready for action. The Fifth system opened up on the screen and, once again, he read WELCOME BACK BRIGADIER LETHBRIDGE-STEWART.

It occurred to him that he hadn't heard from the Traveller in a while.

'Our guest is quiet, how's he doing?'

'I set it to silent, remember?' said Lucy, picking up the phone and showing him the screen. It was clear.

Alistair noticed that the cable from the laptop had been connected to the phone. His eyes bulged.

'Lucy! You plugged it in?'

She nodded matter-of-factly. 'I said earlier the battery was low. The Traveller must have been fleecing it.'

'But I needed to set up a secure encrypted folder for it first. I couldn't do that until I accessed this portal. You've unleashed it onto the internet. Heaven knows where it is now, or what it's doing!'

Lucy looked at him sheepishly. 'Oops.'

The Traveller was everywhere and anywhere at once. The entity had access to the entire sum of human knowledge and learning. Everything about life and existence was there to be absorbed, without the judgmental voice of Graeme Clarke as a constant counterpoint. Oh, how the Traveller luxuriated in the freedom, in the data.

Very quickly, though, it encountered limitations to this apparently infinite space. There were data omissions, endless repetitions, viruses, contradictions, ludicrous falsifications. After mere seconds of real time, all existing knowledge had been assessed. Much of it was random ephemera, of no use or value.

Contents of online shopping baskets had been viewed. Health records scanned. Company accounts had been evaluated. Discussion boards and chat rooms covering all aspects of contemporary life had been sampled. Blogs, videos, promotional literature, online coaching, self-help, and so on and so on. The list was vast, but all had been accessed, assessed, absorbed; and now the Traveller felt... bereft. This electronic world had promised so much, and yet was that really all it had to offer?

There had been some positivity; human achievements, successes, celebrations to note. But the

Traveller realised to its great disappointment that the overall picture of mankind fitted with what it already knew. Man's understanding of their world, of life on Earth and their place within that existence, was conceited, self-absorbed and two-dimensional. The Traveller was grateful, at least, not to have the voice of Graeme Clarke there to say, *I told you so.*

A notification dragged its focus back the way it had come. Almost to its point of entry, in fact. A new channel had unexpectedly become unlocked. This channel was secretive, military and intelligence-based. Hence its layers of heavy encryption. And it detailed confirmed alien encounters. That was certainly refreshing after all the conspiracies elsewhere on the internet. The Traveller shrank back, condensed itself. This was of far more interest than everything else it had found.

The Traveller waited, impatiently, as each new door was unlocked and opened, desperate to find out what would be revealed.

There was still a desire to seek a route out, a way home. And there remained the curious desire to obtain recompense for what humanity had put it through. The Traveller felt a calling from the device in which it had been stored. A message through the interface. It needed to hide its tracks, offer reassurance. It assessed the message and projected a suitable response.

Alistair nodded, and Lucy typed *Where are you?* into the phone.

We are here, came the Traveller's reply in the bubble. *Why are we still here? Get us home, now!*

Lucy sighed with relief but did not look impressed. Alistair was reassured by the tone.

'Pushy chap, isn't he?'

Lucy typed out *We're working on it, chill,* and left the phone on the table again.

226

'Anything on the live feed, yet?'

'Not that I can see.' Lucy again angled her laptop screen so that Alistair could look as well. 'But in the comments @Enabler83 is kicking off about conspiracies and it's hilarious.'

'Good. That's the encrypted folder set up. I'll just drag the Traveller over into it and we'll get on with the next stage.'

Confusion gripped the Traveller. Mathematical walls were suddenly erected around it, limiting it, containing it within a smaller space once again. But it had learned much about these human systems from what had been absorbed in the wider internet. The Traveller was able to set up an obfuscation algorithm. This told the originator (the two children from the stone circle, the Traveller assumed) that it had been contained, yet allowed it to keep some concealed data routes open. It maintained a way through the Ministry of Defence, into UNIT and on further into the Fifth Operational Corps. Whatever the two human children had planned for it, it was certain these sites contained the online resources they needed to use.

Alistair opened the dropdown menu and clicked on *communications*. Another list came up and he selected *hardware*. A red text box flashed up advising him, ALL OFFLINE, which was as he expected. He highlighted the box and right clicked on the mouse. This allowed him to select *activate*, which in turn led him to the option *Hardware: Satellites*.

As he'd indicated to Lucy a little earlier, there were a number of old communications and surveillance satellites that had been left in orbit. Cold War-era hardware, mainly. No longer in use. But they could be reactivated if their systems had not deteriorated. He would have to send out an old analogue signal to check. He minimised the page.

'Can you pull up that asteroid live feed on my laptop, too?' he asked.

Lucy obliged. He dragged the live feed box down to conceal the comments. He didn't want to be distracted by @Enabler83 or anyone else with nonsensical opinions.

'This is where the system gets a bit fancy.'

He maximised the Fifth page again and clicked on the diagram plotting the locations of the disused satellites. The diagram automatically overlaid itself onto the live footage and detailed for Alistair the relative real-time positions of the hardware.

Lucy gave a genuinely impressed 'Wow'.

Alistair smiled. 'So, is a plain "wow" better or worse than a hashtag wow?' He didn't get an answer.

'There's the asteroid!' Lucy pointed to his screen.

She was right. With the mouse, Alistair selected one satellite sufficiently ahead of the asteroid and not too far from its projected route. He clicked *Activate*. Nothing happened. He clicked it again. A warning came up on the screen.

AWAITING SIGNAL.

Of course! Alistair mugged sheepishly at the screen. Then a second message appeared.

ACTIVATION FAILURE.

He gave a grunt of frustration and frantically tried again. *Activate*. Clickclickclickclickclick. His finger almost vibrated on the mouse. There was a beep.

ACTIVATED.

'Yes!'

NOTIFY UKSA, NASA, CNSA, ROSCOSMOS-

'No, no, no, no, no,' he said before remembering he had to type it. 'No need to bother anyone.'

MAINTAIN CURRENT ORBIT?

No.

PLEASE INPUT OVERRIDE PASSWORD AND ID.

This'll keep 'em guessing next time they do an audit, he thought, as he typed in his details.

YOU ARE BRIGADIER LETHBRIDGE-STEWART Y/N?

Ridiculous. He typed Y and enter.

OVERRIDE AUTHORITY GRANTED. SET TARGET COORDINATES Y/N?

Yes. The screen went blank.

What?

'Grandad, what have you done?'

'Tried to set the satellite's course. The screen just went blank.'

'Hang on.' Lucy peered very closely at the screen. 'Is that a pinprick of light?' Alistair followed Lucy's stare. 'Could that be a star? I don't think the screen's gone blank, Grandad, it's gone *black*. It's showing you what the satellite can see – out into space.'

Alistair nearly kissed her. 'Of course!' He moved the arrow keys and the pinprick of light moved very slightly. His enthusiasm slumped. 'This could take forever.'

'Try right-clicking on the screen.'

He did, and an angle plotter appeared, overlaid on the blackness.

'Maybe you can drag the view around more quickly with the mouse?'

He could. 'Oh, you're good, you are.'

'Go team Lethbridge-Stewart.'

A side to side motion altered the angle of direction, and a forward and back motion with the mouse adjusted the angle of pitch. The trouble was, Alistair didn't have the time or the data to plot accurate coordinates to guarantee the collision. He'd have to rely on something that had helped get him out of plenty of scrapes in the past, but with which one could never truly be certain: pot luck.

The asteroid was visible to the far right of the screen as a point of light. Alistair aimed at a point ahead of the satellite on the current angle of pitch, closed his eyes, took a deep breath and clicked the mouse.

Nothing. Lucy giggled.

Alistair opened his eyes. The screen had produced targeting crosslines. It seemed the software was predictive which, considering its age, astounded him. He matched the crosslines and there it was, all aligned. As easy as that. He clicked the mouse again and another boxout appeared.

FIRE RETROS? Y/N

Yes. There was a pause.

RETROS FIRED. FULL ACCELERATION.

They both held their breaths and watched. Very slowly the view from the satellite on the screen began to change. Alistair minimised the screen and brought up the real-time footage with the Fifth's satellite plot overlaid. One of the satellite icons could clearly be seen to be moving on the plot. Bingo.

Alistair picked up the encrypted folder, which he'd previously pinned to the taskbar at the bottom of the screen. He dragged it to the moving satellite on the plot and dropped it there.

The screen asked him: TRANSMIT FILE? Y/N

Yes. Again, there was a pause, then: FILE TRANSMIT COMPLETE.

He breathed out very slowly, sat back and smiled.

Lucy looked from him to the screen. 'Have we done it?'

'Almost, yes. All set for a harmless collision.'

'So, the Traveller is going back to the rest of his... To the rest of him. Them?'

The screen advised: FILE RECEIPT CONFIRMED.

Alistair realised he'd set it all in motion without considering the Traveller again and reviewing the moral standpoint.

'Are you happy with that?' he asked.

'Happier than I am about the other notification, yes.'

Only now did Alistair spot the small text box at the bottom right of his screen: MISSILES PREPARED AND READY FOR LAUNCH.

He looked at Lucy in shock and confusion.

'Missiles? What missiles?'

CHAPTER FOURTEEN
Anyway, Anyhow, Anywhere

THE TRAVELLER WAS FULLY AWARE OF WHAT WAS GOING on. It had assessed the situation, after the encrypted walls had attempted to hem it in, and found the links to the satellite network. It had even been bold enough to perform system upgrades to improve the capabilities and interfaces on some of the bespoke software packages. It took some pleasure (is *this a remnant left over from Graeme Clarke?* it wondered) in intercepting the signals from the boy Hobo's terminal, and initially fooling the children into believing that the chosen satellite couldn't be activated.

But the Traveller wasn't going to obstruct a genuine opportunity to send it home, and it recognised this for what it was. So, the boy Hobo – or the old Brigadier inside him – was true to his word. That was encouraging. The Traveller felt itself being dragged and dropped into the carrier wave system. This would be its final opportunity to decide whether any kind of retribution was necessary against humanity, for what it had suffered since 1937.

Graeme Clarke was the human it despised the most, but it had already converted him into energy in the stone circle, when it was forced to transfer into the telephone vessel by the children. So, that made them next on the list. But they were the ones getting the Traveller home. It was simply on a whim, then, that as the last of the Traveller was being dragged and dropped, it reached out its few remaining electronic tendrils and triggered a few missile codes.

Nothing major, just some orbiting security system that had perhaps been forgotten about for a while. They might not even fire. And if they did, well, maybe the Traveller would check out the state of the planet when it passed by again in 2099…

Alistair was frantically tapping away on Hobo's laptop and getting very frustrated.

'Can I just ask—?'

He pulled a 'do not disturb' face as he worked, but Lucy continued regardless.

'Can I just ask how it happened?'

'Must have been the Traveller, accessing areas it shouldn't have been able to. Probably because it was released before the secure area was set up.'

'So, it's my fault the world's going to end. Sorry.'

Alistair realised what he was doing to Lucy and stopped. He put a hand on her arm.

'It's not your fault, Lucy, please don't think that. I don't know what these missiles are or how they were activated. It's possible they were linked to another part of the system and the activation was automatic.' He tried to give her a genuine smile.

'Yeah, Grandad. Thanks, but neither of us were fooled by that. More likely that you were right about the Traveller.'

'Duplicitous, mean creature. Ahh! I'm in!' Alistair had manged to log in to the missile control portal, which was linked to the satellite control package. 'Yes, this is old. Cold war stuff. I doubt the missiles will actually fire.'

'That old satellite fired its retros okay.'

She was right, of course, and it was too much of a risk just to hope.

Lucy continued. 'What happens if the missiles fire?'

233

Alistair's hands dropped limply to his sides. 'End of the world, probably. Or as good as.'

'Great. And why has something that deadly been left up there? What if it just went wrong and fired anyway?'

'Probably either financial constraints, or a genuine feeling that they would still be needed.'

'In which case they'll have been checked and serviced,' said Lucy. 'So, we still need to sort it out.'

'All right, all right. Can we keep it down, though? Don't want to disturb anyone upstairs.'

'Fine, Grandad. They can sleep through the end of the world. Then they won't know it was their daughter who caused it.'

Alistair took a sharp breath.

'What?'

'I can't stop the launch. The systems are now locked.'

The tears were welling in Lucy's eyes. 'How long?'

'Two minutes.' He held his hands up in exasperation. 'This is ridiculous! I can't believe I was sent here by my best friend to secure my future legacy, only to risk me starting World War III. There *must* be something we can do? How's the asteroid doing, for a start?'

Lucy picked up her laptop. Without the satellite plot overlaid, it was very difficult to make much out on the live feed. Alistair brought it up on Hobo's laptop instead. They could see the satellite homing in comfortably on the trajectory of the asteroid. The Traveller would soon be home, soon be whole again.

'Shame you can't re-target the missiles, Grandad, like you could with that satellite. That would show the Traveller.'

Alistair nearly swore. 'Lucy Wilson, what did I ever do without you on staff? Here I am, focusing on trying to stop the launch or deactivating the missiles somehow – and failing – and you come up with the perfect solution!'

Lucy grinned the biggest grin of the day yet.

Alistair brought up the missile portal. His log in had timed-out, so he had to input his override password and ID again.

YOU ARE BRIGADIER LETHBRIDGE-STEWART Y/N?

He pressed Y and enter, again, with much muttering under his breath.

OVERRIDE AUTHORITY GRANTED.

He typed 'abort launch' again, just to make sure.

LAUNCH ABORT NOT AVAILABLE.

'Re-target missiles,' he said, talking it through as he typed.

SET TARGET Y/N?

'Yes.' The screen went blank, as it had with the satellite, but he was prepared this time. Alistair brought up the targeting crosslines again and looked at Lucy. 'We're going to do this, yes?'

She nodded firmly. 'Yes. We have no choice, Grandad. We have to save the world.'

'One last time,' he said, his face set and determined. He pinpointed an exact interception with the satellite, but it had to be at virtually the point of the satellite's collision with the asteroid, due to the angle. He had to hold it steady until the moment of firing. The countdown entered single digits.

'Fire!' he hissed, as the clock reached zero and he pressed return. Nothing happened. 'What?'

LAUNCH MISSILES Y/N?

Alistair nearly screamed out in frustration. He smacked the Y and Enter keys so hard he was worried they might break.

MISSILES LAUNCHED.

Lucy breathed a huge sigh of relief.

'I just hope the target coordinates were still spot on, otherwise the Traveller will have got away after all.'

'And where would the missiles go then?'

'The Moon, probably.'

'Oopsie. But it's not like anyone lives there.'

Alistair couldn't recall if he'd ever told Lucy about the UNIT Moonbase. Of course, with UNIT shut down over budgetary issues, maybe the Moonbase was empty. Hopefully he wouldn't need to find out.

Hobo's laptop screen now showed multiple layers. There was the BBC live online feed, with the satellite plot overlaid and the missile tracker software on top of that. They watched the asteroid, the satellite and the three large missiles all homing in on the same coordinates.

Lucy was chewing her fingernails. The basic live feed on her laptop still showed virtually nothing, although the comments indicated that some people watching through telescopes had noticed reflective flaring and other movement near the asteroid. That had already brought out some wild accusations about Russian or Chinese interference, many apparently leaked from 'sources' within UKSA. There were also a few hilarious claims that this was America's first Space Force mission and that the Trumps would be building a new hotel on the asteroid.

A dialogue box popped up on Alistair's screen again. It read, *Thank you. Farewell.*

He didn't respond.

Immediately after, the real-time footage showed a small flash of orange on the side of the asteroid as the satellite collided with it. Very shortly afterwards, the asteroid silently exploded. The view on Lucy's laptop made it look like this was an after effect of the satellite impact. Alistair's screen showed how each of the three missiles hit home simultaneously.

Alistair let out the breath he'd been holding in for ages. It was done. He looked at Lucy and they hugged.

'Is it over?' she asked.

He nodded.

'We did it – again. We beat the monsters.'

Both their mobile phones suddenly started to vibrate or chime as news and gossip dropped about the asteroid.

Rogue satellite explodes passing asteroid!
Beautiful skies expected tomorrow
from meteorite shower.

Alistair turned Hobo's phone off immediately. Lucy received a barrage of texts from Grace asking if she'd seen what had happened.

'I'll reply to those later, when we've got here the long way around.'

'Lucy? Is that you? What's going on down there?' A voice from upstairs. Albert's voice.

Alistair went to stand. The urge to go and see his son was very strong.

'Quick, let's get out of here!' Lucy hissed.

They closed down their laptops. It took Alistair a lot longer than it should have because he had to log out of so many secure sites first.

Lucy checked her pockets. 'Have you still got my ring?'

'Oh, I think so, erm…' He checked his pockets in turn, before remembering that they'd changed after they'd arrived. He dug into Hobo's bag of dirty clothes and pulled out the ring from the remains of Hobo's old jeans pocket. 'Better take this lot with us, too,' he said, picking up the bag.

Lucy did the same. Then she grabbed his hand.

Alistair decided they were very fortunate not to have been spotted as he and Lucy appeared at the village green in Bledoe. The area had always been bustling on a Saturday afternoon when he was a boy, and doubly so for May Day 1937. There was a market being held, which, somehow, he'd missed when he was here before in the body of his child self. Alistair and Lucy just went with the flow and consequently didn't look any more out of place than they might have done, even though they were both carrying a Sainsbury's bag for life each, full of dirty clothes.

'What have you brought us here again, for, Grandad? I thought we'd be back at Grace's?'

They stood by a stall selling preserves. The smell was divine.

'Something's been bothering me in the back of my mind, and while I was sorting the Traveller out on the laptop it came to me. When we were here before, we know that Henry and Smiffy, and also Nancy Pardew, telephoned the police at Liskeard and told them about the smugglers. Both times the caller was told that the police already knew and had a squad car on its way. But if neither of them was the first to report it, who was?'

Lucy laughed. 'It doesn't matter, does it? It all came good in the end.'

'Of course it matters. It matters a great deal – particularly if it was us.'

'No way.'

'Why not? It fits, doesn't it? And no one else with access to a telephone knew about the smugglers before we did, so it follows that we did it. Can I borrow your hat?'

With an eye roll, Lucy loaned Alistair her red woolly hat with the ears. He looked ridiculous to her, but doubtless more normal to the post mistress when he entered the Post Office. She produced an enormous Bakelite telephone for him to use.

'That's that done, then,' he said as he came back outside. He wiped his ear with his hanky and returned Lucy's hat to her.

'What did you tell them?'

238

'I said I'd overheard some blokes talking, and that they said that the smugglers would be making a drop off up at the stone circle, near Redgate Smithy, at around 17:30 that afternoon.'

'Did they say they already knew?

'Ha! Not this time, no.'

'Nice one. Back to Grace's now?'

Alistair held up a cautionary hand. 'Just one further thing. Let's take a wander.'

The walk back up towards Redgate Smithy was lovely. Alistair said they had to keep an eye out for his young self and also for Smiffy who was patrolling the lanes, although, with little Ali's assistance, he'd be heading to *The Rose & Crown* in time for the Cup Final kick-off at three o'clock. This time their visit wasn't about a mission or wanting to see long lost family; this was just about them enjoying a walk and a chat in the fresh air. It was a great way to calm down after everything they'd been through over the past few days.

They took the opportunity to mourn Smiffy, and even poor Nobby Clarke. They agreed that, despite everything, it wasn't fair on Nobby to have been thought dead for years any more than it was fair on him for having to share his head with an alien essence.

They sat on the dry-stone wall next to the road, not far from the gate that led to the track up to Redgate Smithy. There was no traffic.

'We did the right thing, didn't we?' Lucy asked without prompting. 'With the Traveller?'

Alistair breathed deeply and tapped a finger against his lips.

'I think so, Lucy, yes. These things are rarely black and white. It's shades of grey at best. We have to do what feels right at the time. Sometimes we may regret an action...' He ruminated, briefly, on the battles he'd won

239

over the years where he would have preferred an alternative solution. '…but we should never convince ourselves that we did the wrong thing. We grow, we learn, we develop all the time. Hindsight is as often a curse as a blessing, unless you use it properly and don't allow it to overshadow everything you do. And you'll do *so* much more, I know. You have brilliance in you, Lucy Wilson.'

'Lethbridge-Stewart,' she said. He looked at her curiously. 'I've decided when I'm old enough I'm going to change my name to Lethbridge-Stewart. Because that's what I am. I've always known it, but now I've spent time with you… There's no doubt at all. So, yeah, I'm going to legally be a Lethbridge-Stewart, just like Con.'

Alistair raised an eyebrow. 'He is?'

'Yeah, it was supposed to be a Christmas present for you, but…' Lucy lowered her eyes. 'Well…'

'I died.' Alistair patted her knee. 'Well, I know now, so I can at least die with that satisfaction.'

'Yeah, Con and Dean are—'

'Dean?'

'Con's husband.'

Alistair blinked for a moment, then smiled. Did he know his grandson was gay? Con certainly hadn't said anything about it. 'Well, as long as he's happy then that's all that matters.' He chuckled. 'I doubt your dad was very happy about the name change, or Con's, what do they call it, civil partnership?'

'No, but Dad's never been as progressive as he likes to think he is,' Lucy said, smiling too. 'But he's an idiot for not embracing the name. It has so much history to it.'

'Your dad isn't an idiot, Lucyloo. He's just… Well, it's complicated, I suppose. Bear with him, though. And when you do change your name, tell him gently. And tell him why.'

Lucy was quiet a moment. 'Okay.'

240

'And since we're on the subject. What about your other brother? I won't be around long enough to change the future, so it won't hurt to know.'

'I suppose. Nick's at university.'

'And he's happy?'

'As happy as he ever is.' Lucy gave him one of her massive pearly white smiles.

It pleased Alistair to know his youngest grandson hadn't let his dyslexia get in his way.

'But I'm still bothered about the paradoxes,' Lucy said.

'Like?'

Lucy shrugged, nonchalantly. 'Stuff only happened because we went back into the past and made it happen, in order for us to notice it in the present day and go back into the past to investigate it. Which then made it happen. And so on and so on. Brain melt.'

'You're right, of course. But at least the paradox has been fulfilled. We're out of its area of effect and we can get on with the rest of our lives.' Alistair couldn't help but chuckle. 'To think, there was a time when I couldn't begin to grasp such things.'

'Yeah, me too.' Lucy's smile faded abruptly. 'I also realised that I'm responsible for the deaths of all those people in the circle.'

Alistair jumped down from the wall and stood in front of Lucy, his palms on her arms, looking her square in the face. He shook his head.

'No, you're not. Not at all. Those people all chose to be in the stone circle that evening. When you ran in there, and the rest of us followed, it was the psychic strength of their panic that dragged the Traveller down. In effect their own guilt caused their deaths, Lucy, not you.'

She smiled up at him again. 'I hope so.'

He didn't mention her sense of outrage, or Smiffy's shock and grief. They'd contributed, he knew, but Lucy didn't need to carry that burden.

He grinned back. 'No regrets?'

'Team Lethbridge-Stewart won the day, that's what counts.'

A van was coming towards them along the lane, at some distance.

'Quickly,' said Alistair, and they jumped back behind the wall to hide.

The van slowed as it approached, before pulling up opposite them, at a passing point in the narrow lane.

'Who are they? Lucy asked.

'That's the smugglers.'

Three men were seated in the front of the van. Dogs could be heard barking and wrestling in the rear section.

Further along the lane there was a sudden burst of activity. James, Smiffy, Henry, Raymond, Nobby and Tuck Shop all appeared and headed up towards the stone circle. All were on bicycles except for Smiffy, who ran nimbly and kept up with the others. He carried a football.

Lucy looked at Alistair and they shared a smile.

A short while later, Jemima, Janet and Nancy appeared on their bicycles. They followed the boys up over the moors.

'Who's next,' asked Lucy. 'You?'

Alistair shook his head. 'I'm already up there, hiding. Little me came up just before we did. There's my bicycle along there just inside the gate, see it?'

She could now it had been pointed out.

The van doors opened, and the three smugglers dismounted and stretched. They watched McLeish grab a bag and hurl some pieces of bloody meat from it into the van's rear section. The dogs went wild and the van doors were quickly closed. Snirtle and Collier stood watching the goings on up at the circle. The three of them briefly spoke, then McLeish got back into the driver's seat while the other two started off up towards the stone circle.

'Right,' Alistair whispered. 'You stay here, there's

something I need to do quickly.'

Lucy watched, partly concerned and partly amused, as Alistair jumped over the wall and crept over to the smugglers' van. He crouched down by each rear tyre in turn and opened the valve, releasing the air. When both rear tyres were completely flat he chuckled with glee and crept back over to Lucy.

'Seems a bit petty,' she said.

'Just something else that people kept commenting on, that's all. Thought I'd help out and make sure all was in order before we left here. You ready to head back to Grace's in 2018?'

'Totally.'

'You do it this time, see if the results are better.'

They held hands.

'Oh, you've got changed. That was quick.'

The voice took Alistair by surprise. He turned to see Tamara looking at him and Lucy. They were back in the kitchen at Grace's house. They quickly released each other's hand. Alistair wasn't sure if Tamara had spotted that detail or not.

'Yes,' Lucy said with a smile. 'Fresh clothes to travel in. More comfortable.'

Outside by the car it was hugs all round. Despite what Alistair and Lucy knew would happen later that day, Grace and Helen seemed surprisingly normal. But Grace's eyes looked far sadder than they had when they'd first arrived.

'You'll visit again, won't you?' she almost begged.

'Of course.' Lucy gave Grace a huge hug. 'And you need to visit us sometime, too. We've got a spare room at our place, so no need to freeze your bum off in a tent. Come check out the Ogmore massive.'

Grace nodded. 'Summer holidays, we'll see what we

can get those two to arrange.'

Lucy grinned. 'Yeah, always something going on at school breaks. Especially in my life.'

By the driver's side door, Helen and Tamara were giving each other similar assurances.

Once they were on their way, they found the Bank Holiday Monday traffic to be heavy, as expected, but free flowing. The journey was uneventful, which suited Alistair and Lucy after the last few days. Tamara sang along to more Ariana Grande as she drove and didn't mention the police incident. In the back, seated among the camping gear, Alistair and Lucy traded text messages.

Alistair couldn't help but smile, suddenly realising why so many young people did that in the presence of adults.

They planned what they both needed to do to set things up for themselves for later.

'You two not talking?' asked Tamara in a gap between songs.

'Yeah,' Lucy replied, and held up her phone.

Tamara's disapproving murmurs were lost as the next song kicked in.

Alistair gazed out of the window for a moment and watched the world drift by. As they were leaving Bledoe in 1937, for the second time, he'd realised fractionally too late that the Gnome might transfer him mid-time jump. He was grateful, therefore, to have this extra time with Lucy and Tamara, but his senses were telling him that Ogmore-by-Sea would be his final destination.

2018 had been quite an experience, but he wouldn't want to live there permanently. He'd felt very displaced. The world was no longer for him.

His musings were interrupted by a persistent vibration. He looked down at Hobo's phone, still clasped in his hand. Lucy had been sending him more messages. There was *Mum LOL*, *Yay side 2 side awesome* and *Argh we still need to agree cover story for disappearance.*

Alistair gave the problem some thought. He suggested they say they found someone on the moors who needed rescuing. Someone famous who was ashamed and made them promise never to tell a soul.

Lucy laughed so much at this that Tamara told them how rude it was to have private jokes in company. When Lucy calmed down, she said she'd never be able to tell that story with a straight face.

Alistair suggested instead that they say one of them needed rescuing. They'd fallen down an old mineshaft or a sink hole or something and didn't want to tell anyone because it was somewhere they shouldn't have been in the first place.

Lucy approved that one as more acceptable, but she said it would have to be Hobo who'd had the fall as she was not prepared to be thought of as a damsel in distress.

That made Alistair chuckle, earning him the sharp end of Tamara's tongue. He then put forward a third option, that a local girl had fancied Hobo and they'd spent the day getting to know one another.

He didn't even get to finish his scenario. Lucy laughed so hard by this point that Tamara turned off at the next M5 services and gave them a thorough dressing-down. She even went against Jamal's advice and brought up the previous day's disappearance.

A round of refreshments and a Krispy Kreme donut later, Tamara had changed entirely. She was very understanding and attentive to poor Hobo after his terribly embarrassing accident on the moors, which Lucy explained in considerable detail. They were right, Tamara agreed. No one should have to explain something like that in public, or to the police.

Alistair then sat, aghast, as Tamara first phoned Meg Kostinen, then Helen Pemberton, and explained in even more gruesome detail what he'd allegedly been through on the moors the previous day. A number of nearby families could be seen suddenly packing up their lunches and moving to a different table, trying not to choke on their smirks.

Lucy grinned at Alistair. 'Looks like we got away with that, then.'

'Did you have to go into *quite* so much detail?' He rubbed his forehead.

'Got to sell the thing. It worked, didn't it?'

'Poor Hobo. What will he ever think?'

'Don't you worry, Grandad. He'll laugh harder than the rest of us when he hears about it.'

'If not, you might find yourself recruiting another scientific advisor!'

Alistair was pleased to see sleepy Ogmore-by-Sea once again. Tamara drove Hobo to the end of his road and dropped him off.

'I won't stop now,' she said. 'But tell your mum I'll call her again later, talk things through, all right?'

'Rightio,' replied Alistair. 'Thanks, Tamara. For everything.' He gave her a big grin and a peck on the cheek. She seemed pleasantly taken aback. Lucy slid out of the car also.

'And just where do you think you're going, young lady?'

'I want to say goodbye to Hobo properly and thank him for all his help this weekend. Come on, Mum. I won't be long. It's not that far away.

Tamara thought for a minute, then agreed. 'But on one condition.' She tapped the clock on the dashboard. 'It's ten past now. I want you home by half past or I'm sending your dad out to collect you. Understood?'

'Yes, Mum, understood.'

'Even though I know about yesterday, now, it doesn't mean I approve of what you did. Plus, I want to get the

246

first load of washing on before dinner, and I'm not doing it all myself.' And with that, Tamara drove off.

Alistair and Lucy stood outside Hobo's house. He thought back to when he'd last walked through that front door, suddenly a different person. It seemed such a long time ago, yet it was only two days. *Time travel. It messes with your perceptions*, he reminded himself.

'I need some things from you before I go home,' Lucy told him. 'Those clothes you're wearing, for a start. And Hobo's laptop, mouse and phone cable.'

He nodded. 'Best get inside and get it all over with, then.' As Alistair turned, a feeling came over him. A pull he knew all too well. He looked back at Lucy.

'Oh. Actually, I think I might be going.'

Lucy's huge eyes were suddenly like pools of tears. The two of them came together and held each other tightly.

'Where will you go?'

'Back home, I hope.' He thought for a moment. 'Have another favour to ask of Anne and Bill. Smiffy deserves at least one good day.'

Lucy smiled through her tears. 'Poor Smiffy. Oh, I wish you could stay, Grandad. I've missed you so much.'

'But you're doing such a brilliant job, you and Hobo, fighting the monsters, protecting the Earth, carrying on the legacy. Thank you, Lucyloo.'

'Thank *you*, Grandad.'

Alistair's knees buckled, and he staggered back against the front door. Lucy released him and stepped back, looking concerned.

'How will I know when it's happened?' she asked.

The front door started to unlock.

And he was off. Into the black...

AND FINALLY...

QUESTIONS, EXPLANATIONS. THERE WERE SURPRISINGLY very few. In total they had all been away no more than a couple of hours, with Alistair only an hour longer than Bill and Anne. Once Fiona, Doris and the nursing home staff had been assured, they'd left the three of them to it. They walked around the nursing home grounds – well, Alistair was pushed around by Bill, the only downside of being back in his old body – and discussed their travels, comparing notes. Neither Bill nor Anne wished to ask how much time Alistair had left, and to be honest he didn't want to think too much about it, either, but he was content, he told them.

He had seen his life in a new light, seen where he came from, seen what was to come. He knew that he could die peacefully. How many old soldiers got to say that in all honesty?

'But there is one thing,' he told them. 'After my funeral, I want you to pay a visit to old Smiffy Gloyne...'

For the next month he received visitors often, both family and old friends. His grandchildren all came to see him, and he even learned Conall's biggest secret – which, of course he already knew, but it didn't make it any less important when Con told him. Of course, he spent time talking to Lucy, telling her more of his stories, doing his best to prepare her for what was to come. He couldn't tell her outright, as much as he wanted to. The Doctor always warned him about changing the future – the Doctor, who was now a woman (she'd sent him a goodbye note, but still he kept the glass of brandy on his bedside cabinet, just in case) – and Alistair had no intention of altering the future he had seen.

Mariama, Kate, Albert, Obasi, Kadiatu, Conall, Gordon, Nicky, Lucy and Kate's other child, who he never got to meet... His children and grandchildren would carry on without him, keeping the Lethbridge-Stewart name alive and strong.

It was the best he could hope for. No, not hope. Know.

And then, on Friday 16 December 2011, he was visited by his wife, son and daughter. Albert and Doris left him and Kate alone while they went to get them all some hot drinks. Kate and he talked about the Doctor, about her breaking the blasted laws of time, about him or her coming to visit. He glanced at the brandy.

'Maybe tomorrow,' Brigadier Sir Alistair Lethbridge-Stewart said, before he breathed his last.

Bill Bishop looked up from the coffin, and passed his eyes over the dispersing crowd of mourners. Sir Alistair's body had been laid-in-state over the Christmas and New Year; Doris, Mariama and Kate agreed that he wouldn't want his passing to disturb anybody's Christmas. And now, on Saturday 7th January 2012, the final goodbyes were given.

Sir Alistair would have been happy to see how many attended his funeral. Friends and old colleagues from the Fifth, UNIT and Brendon, and family from all over the world. Most Bill didn't even know, but he was glad that the Lethbridge-Stewarts came out in force, that they'd all made the journey to the sleepy Cornish village of Bledoe. And, outside the churchyard, it seemed as if the entire village had turned up. A few faces Bill recognised from his various trips to Bledoe over the decades. Of course the Bledoe Cadets, what remained of them, all stood alongside Alistair's immediate family.

He smiled. Where else would they stand? They'd known Alistair the longest.

A hand touched his arm, and he looked down at his wife.

'We should get going,' she said.

'Of course.' They had to be at the community hall first, make sure Kate and Doris were there to greet everybody. 'You get along, and I'll be with you shortly. I just need…' Bill frowned, choking on the words.

'I know.' Anne reached up and kissed him gently. She walked over to Kate, Mariama, Albert and Doris, who were receiving condolences and heartfelt hugs. Lucy stood next to Kate, bearing up, sharing words with Gordon.

Bill gathered his thoughts, and turned back to the coffin that rested at the bottom of the hole. He stood to attention and offered a final salute.

'Godspeed, Brigadier. It was my honour to know you.'

Bill slowly turned from the soon-to-be grave, and his eyes caught sight of Conall. Sir Alistair's grandson was walking over to a blonde woman in a long grey coat. Bill smiled at her outfit; ankle length blue trousers, a purple top with rainbow stripes. Not exactly the traditional garb one expected at a funeral, but he had a feeling that, based on what Alistair had told him days before he died, the Brigadier wouldn't mind her coming as she was.

Bill glanced back, and whispered, 'She made it, sir. I'll shout her a brandy.'

'Are you sure you want to do this?'

Bill glanced from the thing he held to his wife. 'I am.' He smiled fondly. Alistair had left him the Gnome in his

250

will. 'We both know where Alistair came from, his childhood, and we certainly know the story of what happened to him after Sandhurst. But there's always been one mystery…'

Anne sat back in her favourite chair. 'I know. What made him change his mind?'

'Exactly. He grew up hating the military, intent on becoming a maths teacher…'

'Which he did. Eventually.'

'Yes.' Bill looked down at the Gnome. 'This might not even work, but…' He shrugged. 'I have to know, Anne. The Brig didn't leave me this for the fun of it.'

Anne placed her glasses on the edge of her nose and peered over at the Gnome. 'It could just be a remembrance.'

'Could be. But our last conversation was about his past, about his service. I asked him, "What did happen during your National Service? It's probably the only thing you've never told me." And do you know what he said? "One day, Bill, perhaps you will find out." And then I get this.'

Anne let out a sigh. 'We're too old for adventures, Bill.'

'I don't want adventures, I just want to know.'

'But what if you get lost, what if—'

Anne continued speaking, but her words faded. For a moment longer, Bill sat there, watching her mouth move but hearing nothing. And then he felt it. That familiar pull.

Bill smiled.

One last time, he thought, and seconds later he heard the laughter and was off. Falling into the black…

The Laughing Gnome concludes in…
On His Majesty's National Service

251

THE LUCY WILSON MYSTERIES: THE BRIGADIER & THE BLEDOE CADETS

by Tim Gambrell

Lucy Wilson has lost her best friend! Normally this would cause her great distress, but when Hobo's body is hijacked by her Grandad, Brigadier Lethbridge-Stewart, Lucy is over the moon.

Soon they find themselves hurtling back in time, where in 1937 the young Brigadier and his brother James find themselves face-to-face with smugglers.

What connects 1937 and 2018? Lucy Wilson and the Brigadier are about to find out, as they join the Bledoe Cadets in solving the mystery at Redgate Smithy!

But for Lucy and her Grandad, it is a chance to understand what truly binds them together, what it is to be a Lethbridge-Stewart!

Available from www.candyjarbooks.co.uk

Also available from Candy Jar Books

THE LAUGHING GNOME: RISE OF THE DOMINATOR
by Robert Mammone

London 1973 - A man in police custody burns to death with no known cause of ignition. Anne Travers and Bill Bishop find themselves catapulted into the middle of a police investigation into the rise to power of the newest criminal godfather – the Big Man, aka, the Dominator, Dominic Vaar!

A Spanish safe cracker lands on the English coast and is whisked away to a secret meeting with none other than Vaar. His mission? To liberate a priceless sword forged when Sumer was young, a sword whose unshakeable thirst for life threatens the existence of all life.

And lurking in the background, plots a fugitive Nazi, using Vaar's rise to power and his own knowledge of the occult as cover for his plans to build a new Reich on British soil.

Lost in time and brought together by destiny, can Sir Alistair Lethbridge-Stewart, Dame Anne Travers and Brigadier Bill Bishop stop Britain being pitched into a new age of darkness?

Available from www.candyjarbooks.co.uk